Sirius

a fantasy of Love and discord

Sirius

A fantasy of love and discord

olaf stapledon

VICTOR GOLLANCZ

LONDON

The right of Olaf Stapledon to be identified as the author
of this work has been asserted by him in accordance with
the Copyright, Designs and Patents Act 1988.

This edition published in Great Britain in 2000 by
Victor Gollancz
An imprint of Orion Books Ltd
Orion House, 5 Upper St Martin's Lane,
London, WC2H 9EA

To receive information on the Millennium list, e-mail us at:
smy@orionbooks.co.uk

A CIP catalogue record for this book is available
from the British Library.

ISBN 0 57507 057 9

Printed in Great Britain by
The Guernsey Press Co. Ltd, Guernsey, C.I.

CONTENTS

I should like to acknowledge my debt to Mr. J. Herries McCulloch's delightful study, *Sheep Dogs and Their Masters*. He must not, however, be held in any way responsible for my sheer fantasies.

Sirius

A Fantasy of
Love and Discord

CHAPTER I

FIRST MEETING

PLAXY and I had been lovers; rather uneasy lovers, for she would never speak freely about her past, and sometimes she withdrew into a cloud of reserve and despond. But often we were very happy together, and I believed that our happiness was striking deeper roots.

Then came her mother's last illness, and Plaxy vanished. Once or twice I received a letter from her, giving no address, but suggesting that I might reply to her "care of the Post Office" in a village in North Wales, sometimes one, sometimes another. In temper these letters ranged from a perfunctory amiability to genuine longing to have me again. They contained mysterious references to "a strange duty," which, she said, was connected with her father's work. The great physiologist, I knew, had been engaged on very sensational experiments on the brains of the higher mammals. He had produced some marvellously intelligent sheep-dogs, and at the time of his death it was said that he was concerned with even more ambitious research. One of the colder of Plaxy's letters spoke of an "unexpectedly sweet reward" in connection with her new duty, but in a more passionate one she cried out against "this exacting, fascinating, dehumanizing life." Sometimes she seemed to be in a state of conflict and torture about something which she must not explain. One of these letters was so distraught that I feared for her sanity. I determined therefore to devote my approaching leave to walking in North Wales in the hope of finding her.

I spent ten days wandering from pub to pub in the region indicated by the addresses, asking everywhere if a Miss Trelone was known in the neighbourhood. At last, in Llan Ffestiniog, I heard of her. There was a young lady of that name living in a shepherd's cottage on the fringe of the moor somewhere above Trawsfynydd. The local shopkeeper who gave me this information said with an air of mystery, "She is a strange young lady, indeed. She has friends, and I am one of them; but she has enemies."

Following his directions, I walked for some miles along the winding Trawsfynydd road and then turned to the left up a lane. After another mile or so, right on the edge of the open moor, I came upon a minute cottage built of rough slabs of shale, and surrounded by a little garden and stunted trees. The door was shut, but smoke rose from a chimney. I knocked. The door remained shut. Peering through a window, I saw a typical cottage kitchen, but on the table was a pile of books. I sat down on a rickety seat in the garden and noted the neat rows of cabbages and peas. Away to my right, across the deep Cynfal gorge, was Ffestiniog, a pack of slate-grey elephants following their leader, the unsteepled church, down a spur of hill towards the valley. Behind and above stood the Moelwyn range.

I was smoking my second cigarette when I heard Plaxy's voice in the distance. It was her voice that had first attracted me to her. Sitting in a café I had been enthralled by that sensitive human sound coming from some unknown person behind me. And now once more I heard but did not see her. For a moment I listened with delight to her speech, which, as I had often said, was like the cool sparkling talk of small waves on the pebbly shore of a tarn on a hot day.

I rose to meet her, but something strange arrested me. Interspersed with Plaxy's remarks was no other human voice but a quite different sound, articulate but inhuman. Just before she came round the corner of the house she said, "But, my dear, don't *dwell* on your handlessness so! You have triumphed over it superbly." There followed a strange trickle of speech from her companion; then through the gate into the garden came Plaxy and a large dog.

She halted, her eyes wide with surprise, and (I hoped) with joy; but her brows soon puckered. Laying a hand on the dog's head, she stood silent for a moment. I had time to observe that a change had come over her. She was wearing rather muddy corduroy trousers and a blue shirt. The same grey eyes, the same ample but decisive mouth, which had recently seemed to me to belie her character, the same shock of auburn, faintly carroty hair. But instead of a rather pale face, a ruddy brown one, and a complete absence of make-up. No lip-stick, even. The appearance of rude health was oddly contradicted by a darkness under the eyes and a tautness round the mouth. Strange how much one can notice in a couple of seconds, when one is in love!

Her hand deserted the dog's head, and was stretched out to me in welcome. "Oh well," she said smiling, "since you have nosed us out, we had better take you into our confidence." There was some embarrassment in her tone, but also perhaps a ring of relief. "Hadn't we, Sirius," she added, looking down at the great dog.

Then for the first time I took note of this remarkable creature. He was certainly no ordinary dog. In the main he was an Alsatian, perhaps with a dash of Great Dane or Mastiff, for he was a huge beast. His general build was wolf-like, but he was slimmer than a wolf, because of his height. His coat, though the hair was short, was superbly thick and silky, particularly round the neck, where it was a close turbulent ruff. Its silkiness missed effeminacy by a hint of stubborn harshness. Silk wire, Plaxy once called it. On back and crown it was black, but on flanks and legs and the under surface of his body it paled to an austere greyish fawn. There were also two large patches of fawn above the eyes, giving his face a strangely mask-like look, or the appearance of a Greek statue with blank-eyed helmet pushed back from the face. What distinguished Sirius from all other dogs was his huge cranium. It was not, as a matter of fact, quite as large as one would have expected in a creature of human intelligence, since, as I shall explain later, Trelone's technique not only increased the brain's bulk but also produced a refinement of the nerve fibres themselves. Nevertheless, Sirius's head was far loftier than any normal dog's. His high brow combined with the silkiness of his coat to give him a look of the famous Border Collie, the outstanding type of sheep-dog. I learned later that this brilliant race had, indeed, contributed to his make-up. But his cranium was far bigger than the Border Collie's. The dome reached almost up to the tips of his large, pointed Alsatian ears. To hold up this weight of head, the muscles of his neck and shoulders were strongly developed. At the moment of our encounter he was positively leonine, because the hair was bristling along his spine. Suspicion of me had brushed it up the wrong way. His grey eyes might have been wolf's eyes, had not the pupils been round like any dog's, not slits like the wolf's. Altogether he was certainly a formidable beast, lean and sinewy as a creature of the jungle.

Without taking his gaze off me, he opened his mouth, displaying sierras of ivory, and made a queer noise, ending with an upward inflection like a question. Plaxy replied, "Yes, it's Robert. He's true as steel, remember." She smiled at me deprecatingly, and added, "And he may be useful."

Sirius politely waved his amply feathered tail, but kept his cold eyes fixed on mine.

Another awkward pause settled upon us, till Plaxy said, "We have been working on the sheep out on the moor all day. We missed our dinner and I'm hungry as hell. Come in and I'll make tea for us all." She added as we entered the little flagged kitchen, "Sirius will understand everything you say. You won't be able to understand him at first, but I shall, and I'll interpret."

While Plaxy prepared a meal, passing in and out of the little larder, I sat talking to her. Sirius squatted opposite me, eyeing me with obvious anxiety. Seeing him, she said with a certain sharpness fading into gentleness, "Sirius! I tell you he's all right. Don't be so suspicious!" The dog rose, saying something in his strange lingo, and went out into the garden. "He's gone to fetch some firewood," she said; then in a lowered voice, "Oh, Robert, it's good to see you, though I didn't want you to find me." I rose to take her in my arms, but she whispered emphatically, "No, no, not now." Sirius returned with a log between his jaws. With a sidelong glance at the two of us, and a perceptible drooping of the tail, he put the log on the fire and went out again. "Why not now?" I cried, and she whispered, "Because of Sirius. Oh, you'll understand soon." After a pause she added, "Robert, you mustn't expect me to be wholly yours ever, not fully and single-heartedly yours. I'm too much involved in—in this work of my father's." I expostulated, and seized her. "Nice human Robert," she sighed, putting her head on my shoulder. But immediately she broke away, and said with emphasis, "No, *I* didn't say that. It was just the female human animal that said it. What *I* say is, I can't play the game you want me to play, not whole-heartedly."

Then she called through the open door, "Sirius, tea!" He replied with a bark, then strode in, carefully not looking at me.

She put a bowl of tea for him on a little table-cloth on the floor, remarking, "He has two meals generally, dinner at noon and supper in the evening. But to-day is different." Then she put down a large crust of bread, a hunk of cheese, and a saucer with a little lump of jam. "Will that keep you going?" she asked. A grunt signified approval.

Plaxy and I sat at the table to eat our bread and rationed butter and war-time cake. She set about telling me the history of Sirius. Sometimes I put in an occasional question, or Sirius interrupted with his queer speech of whimper and growl.

The matter of this and many other conversations about the past I shall set down in the following chapters. Meanwhile I must say this. Without the actual presence of Sirius I should not have believed the story; but his interruptions, though canine and unintelligible, expressed human intelligence by their modulation, and stimulated intelligible answers from Plaxy. Obviously he was following the conversation, commenting and watching my reaction. And so it was not with incredulity, though of course with amazement, that I learned of the origin and career of Sirius. I listened at first with grave anxiety, so deeply involved was Plaxy. I began to understand why it was that our love had always been uneasy, and why when her mother died she did not come back to me. I began to debate with myself the best way of freeing her from this "inhuman bondage". But as the conversation proceeded I could not but recognize that this strange relationship of girl and dog was fundamentally beautiul, in a way sacred. (That was the word I used to myself.) Thus my problem became far more difficult.

At one point, when Plaxy had been saying that she often longed to see me again, Sirius made a more sustained little speech. And in the middle of it he went over to her, put his fore-paws on the arm of her chair, and with great gentleness and delicacy kissed her cheek. She took the caress demurely, not shrinking away, as human beings generally do when dogs try to kiss them. But the healthy glow of her face deepened, and there was moisture in her eyes as she stroked the shaggy softness under his neck, and said to me, while still looking at him, "I am to tell you, Robert, that Sirius and Plaxy grew up together like the thumb and forefinger of a hand, that he loves me in the way that only dogs can love, and much more now that I have come to him, but that I must not feel bound to stay with him, because by now he can fend for himself. Whatever happens to him ever, I—how did you say it, Sirius, you foolish dear?" He put in a quick sentence, and she continued, "Oh, yes, I am the scent that he will follow always, hunting for God."

She turned her face towards me with a smile that I shall not forget. Nor shall I forget the bewildering effect of the dog's earnest and almost formal little declaration. Later I was to realize that a rather stilted diction was very characteristic of him, in moments of deep feeling.

Then Sirius made another remark with a sly look and a tremor of the tail. She turned back to him laughing, and softly smacked his face. "Beast," she said, "I shall not tell Robert that."

When Sirius kissed her I was startled into a sudden spasm of jealousy. (A man jealous of a dog!) But Plaxy's translation of his little speech roused more generous feelings. I now began to make plans by which Plaxy and I together might give Sirius a permanent home and help him to fulfil his destiny, whatever that might be. But, as I shall tell, a different fate lay in store for us.

During that strange meal Plaxy told me that, as I had guessed, Sirius was her father's crowning achievement, that he had been brought up as a member of the Trelone family, that he was now helping to run a sheep farm, that she herself was keeping house for him, and also working on the farm, compensating for his lack of hands.

After tea I helped her to wash up, while Sirius hovered about, jealous, I think, of my handiness. When we had finished, she said they must go over to the farm to complete a job of work before dark. I decided to walk back to Ffestiniog, collect my baggage and return by the evening train to Trawsfynedd, where I could find accommodation in the local pub. I noticed Sirius's tail droop as I said this. It drooped still further when I announced that I proposed to spend a week in the neighbourhood in the hope of seeing more of Plaxy. She said, "I shall be busy, but there are the evenings."

Before I left she handed over a collection of documents for me to take away and read at leisure. There were scientific papers by her father, including his journal of Sirius's growth and education. These documents, together with a diary of her own and brief fragmentary records by Sirius himself, all of which I was given at a much later date, form the main "sources" of the following narrative; these, and many long talks with Plaxy, and with Sirius when I had learnt to understand his speech.

I propose to use my imagination freely to fill out with detail many incidents about which my sources afford only the barest outline. After all, though a civil servant (until the Air Force absorbed me) I am also a novelist; and I am convinced that with imagination and self-criticism one can often penetrate into the essential spirit of events even when the data are superficial. I shall, therefore, tell the amazing story of Sirius in my own way.

CHAPTER II

THE MAKING OF SIRIUS

PLAXY'S father, Thomas Trelone, was too great a scientist to escape all publicity, but his work on the stimulation of cortical growth in the brains of mammals was begun while he was merely a brilliant young research worker, and it was subsequently carried on in strict secrecy. He had an exaggerated, a morbid loathing of limelight. This obsession he justified by explaining that he dreaded the exploitation of his technique by quacks and profit-mongers. Thus it was that for many years his experiments were known only to a few of his most intimate professional colleagues in Cambridge, and to his wife, who had a part to play in them.

Though I have seen his records and read his papers, I can give only a layman's account of his work, for I am without scientific training. By introducing a certain hormone into the blood-stream of the mother he could affect the growth of the brain in the unborn young. The hormone apparently had a double effect. It increased the actual bulk of the cerebral cortices, and also it made the nerve-fibres themselves much finer than they normally are, so that a far greater number of them, and a far greater number of connections between them, occurred in any given volume of brain. Somewhat similar experiments, I believe, were carried out in America by Zamenhof; but there was an important difference between the two techniques. Zamenhof simply fed the young animal with his hormone; Trelone, as I have said, introduced his hormone into the foetus through the mother's blood-stream. This in itself was a notable achievement, because the circulatory systems of mother and foetus are fairly well insulated from each other by a filtering membrane. One of Trelone's difficulties was that the hormone caused growth in the maternal as well as the foetal brain, and since the mother's skull was adult and rigid there must inevitably be very serious congestion, which would lead to death unless some means were found to insulate her brain from the stimulating drug. This difficulty was eventually overcome. At last it became possible to assure the unborn animal a healthy maternal environment. After its birth Trelone periodically added doses of the hormone to its food, gradually reducing the dose as the growing brain approached what he considered a safe maximum size. He had also devised a technique for delaying the closing of the sutures between the bones of the skull, so that the skull might continue to expand as required.

A large population of rats and mice was sacrificed in the attempt to perfect Trelone's technique. At last he was able to produce a number of remarkable creatures. His big-headed rats, mice, guinea-pigs, rabbits, though their health was generally bad, and their lives were nearly always cut short by disease of one kind or another, were certainly geniuses of their humble order. They were remarkably quick at finding their way through mazes, and so on. In fact they far excelled their species in all the common tests of animal intelligence, and had the mentality rather of dogs and apes than of rodents.

But this was for Trelone only the beginning. While he was improving his technique so that he could ensure a rather more healthy animal, he at the same time undertook research into methods of altering the tempo of its life so that it should mature very slowly and live much longer than was normal to its kind. Obviously this was very important. A bigger brain needs a longer life-time to fulfil its greater potentiality for amassing and assimilating experience. Not until he had made satisfactory progress in both these enterprises did he begin to experiment on animals of greater size and higher type. This was a much more formidable undertaking, and promised no quick results. After a few years he had produced a number of clever but seedy cats, a bright monkey that died during its protracted adolescence, and a dog with so big a brain that its crushed and useless eyes were pushed forward along its nose. This creature suffered so much that its producer reluctantly destroyed it in infancy.

Not till several more years had elapsed, had Trelone perfected his technique to such an extent that he was able to pay less attention to the physiological and more to the psychological aspect of his problem. Contrary to his original plan, he worked henceforth mainly on dogs rather than apes. Of course apes offered the hope of more spectacular success. They were by nature better equipped than dogs. Their brains were bigger, their sight was more developed, and they had hands. Nevertheless from Trelone's point of view dogs had one overwhelming advantage. They were capable of a much greater freedom of movement in our society. Trelone confessed that he would have preferred to work on cats, because of their more independent mentality; but their small size made them unsuitable. A certain absolute bulk of brain was necessary, no matter what the size of the animal, so as to afford a wealth of associative neural paths. Of course a small animal did not need as large a brain as a large animal of the same mental rank. A large body needed a correspondingly large brain merely to work its machinery. A lion's brain had to be bigger than a cat's. An elephant's brain was even larger than a much more intelligent but smaller man's. On the other hand, each rank of intelligence, no matter what the size of the animal, required a certain degree of complexity of neural organization, and so of brain bulk. In proportion to the size of the human body a man's brain was far *bigger* than an elephant's. Some animals were large enough to accommodate the absolute bulk of brain needed for the human order of intelligence; some were not. A large dog could easily do so, but a cat's organization would be very gravely upset by so great an addition. For a mouse anything of the sort would be impossible.

Not that Trelone had at this stage any expectation of raising any animal so far in mental stature that it would approach human mentality. His aim was merely to produce, as he put it, "a rather super-sub-human intelligence, a missing-link mind. For this purpose the dog was admirably suited. Human society afforded for dogs many vocations requiring intelligence at the upper limit of the sub-human range. Trelone chose as the best vocation of all for his purpose that of the sheep-dog. His acknowledged ambition was to produce a "super-sheep-dog."

One other consideration inclined him to choose the dog; and the fact that he took this point into account at all in the early stage of his work shows that he was even then toying with the idea of producing something more than a missing-link mind. He regarded the dog's temperament as on the whole more capable of development to the human level. If cats excelled in independence, dogs excelled in social awareness; and Trelone argued that only the social animal could make full use of its intelligence. The independence of the cat was not, after all, the independence of the socially aware creature asserting its individuality; it was merely the blind individualism that resulted from social obtuseness. On the other hand he admitted that the dog's sociality involved it, in relation to man, in abject servility. But he hoped that with increased intelligence it might gain a measure of self-respect, and of critical detachment from humanity.

In due course Trelone succeeded in producing a litter of big-brained puppies. Most of them died before reaching maturity, but two survived, and became exceptionally bright dogs. This result was on the whole less gratifying than disappointing to Trelone. He carried out further experiments, and at last, from an Old English Sheep-dog bitch, produced a big-brained family, three of which survived, and reached a definitely super-canine level of mentality.

The research continued for some years. Trelone found it necessary to take more trouble about the "raw material" to which his technique was to be applied. He could not afford to neglect the fact that the most capable of all the canine races is the Border Collie, bred through a couple of centuries for intelligence and responsibility. All modern champions are of this breed, and all are descendants of a certain brilliant animal, named Old Hemp, who was born in Northumberland in 1893. The Border Collie of to-day is hardy, but rather small. Trelone, therefore, decided that the best raw material would be a cross between some outstanding champion of the International Sheep-Dog Trials and another intelligent but much heavier animal. The Alsatian was the obvious choice. After a good deal of negotiation with owners of champion sheep-dogs and enthusiasts for Alsatians, he produced several strains, which blended the two types in various proportions. He then applied his improved technique to various expectant mothers of these types, and in due season he was able to provide several of his friends with animals of "almost missing-link intelligence" as house-dogs. But there was nothing spectacular about these creatures; and unfortunately all were delicate, and all died before their somewhat protracted adolescence was completed.

But at last further improvements in his technique brought him real success. He achieved several very bright animals with normally strong constitutions, predominantly Alsatian in appearance.

He had persuaded his wife Elizabeth that, if ever he succeeded to this extent, they should take a house in a sheep district in Wales. There she and the three children and the forthcoming baby would live, and he himself would spend the vacations and week-ends. After much exploration they found a suitable old farm-house not far from Trawsfynedd. Its name was "Garth." A good deal of work had to be done to turn it into a comfortable family home. Water-closets and a bathroom had to be installed. Some of the windows were enlarged. Electricity was laid on from the village. An out-house was converted into a palatial kennel.

Some time after the fourth baby had been born, the family moved. They were accompanied by Kate, the long-established servant, who had somehow become practically a member of the family. A village girl was engaged as her assistant. There was also a nursemaid, Mildred; and, of course, the children, Thomasina, Maurice, Giles, and the baby Plaxy. Thomas took with him two canine families. One consisted of a bitch and four hardy little animals that he intended to train as "super-sheep-dogs." The other family of four were orphans, the mother having died in giving birth to them. They had there-fore to be hand-nursed. The brains of these animals were very much bigger than the brains of the other family, but unfortunately three of them were much less healthy. Two died shortly after the removal to Wales. Another was subject to such violent fits that it had to be destroyed. The fourth, Sirius, was a healthy and cheerful little creature that remained a helpless infant long after the other litter were active adoles-cents. For months it could not even stand. It merely lay on its stomach with its bulgy head on the ground, squeaking for sheer joy of life; for its tail was constantly wagging.

Even the other litter matured very slowly for dogs, though far more rapidly than human children. When they were nearly adult all but one of them were disposed of to neigh-bouring farms. The one was kept as the family dog. Most of the local farmers had proved very reluctant to take on these big-headed animals even as gifts. But a neighbour, Mr. Llewelyn Pugh of Caer Blai, had entered into the spirit of the venture, and he subsequently bought a second pup as a colleague for the first.

The production of these super-sheep-dogs and others which followed formed a camouflage for Thomas's more exciting venture, of which Sirius was at present the only outcome.

The public would be led to believe that super-sheep-dogs and other animals of missing-link mentality were his whole concern. If the little Alsatian really developed to human mental stature, few people would suspect it. Thomas was always morbidly anxious that it should not be exploited. It must grow up in decent obscurity, and mature as naturally as possible.

The super-sheep-dogs, on the other hand, were allowed to gain notoriety. The farmers who had accepted them mostly with great reluctance soon found that fate had given them pearls of great price. The animals learned their technique surprisingly quickly, and carried out their orders with unfailing precision. Commands had seldom to be repeated. Sheep were never hustled, and yet never allowed to break away. Not only so, but Trelone's dogs had an uncanny way of understanding instructions and carrying them out with no human supervision. They attached the right meanings to the names of particular pastures, hill-sides, valleys, moors. Told to "fetch sheep from Cefn" or from Moel Fach or what not, they succeeded in doing so while their master awaited them at home. They could also be sent on errands to neighbouring farms or villages. They would take a basket and a note to a particular shop and bring back the required meat or haberdashery.

All this was very useful to the farmers, and extremely interesting to Trelone, who was of course allowed every chance of studying the animals. He found in them a startlingly high degree of practical inventiveness, and a rudimentary but remarkable understanding of language. Being after all subhuman, they could not understand speech as we do, but they were incomparably more sensitive than ordinary dogs to familiar words and phrases. "Fetch wood from shed," "Take basket to butcher and baker," and all such simple familiar orders could be distinguished and obeyed, as a rule without distraction. Thomas wrote a monograph on his super-sheep-dogs, and consequently scientists from all over the world used to turn up at Garth to be shown the animals at work. Throughout the district their fame was fully established among farmers, and there were many demands for puppies. Very few could

be supplied. Some farmers refused to believe that the offspring
of these bright animals would not inherit their parents'
powers. Naturally, all attempts to breed super-sheep-dogs
from super-sheep-dogs without the introduction of the hormone into the mother were a complete failure.

But it is time to return to the little Alsatian, in fact, to Sirius.
Trelone was from the first very excited about this animal.
The longer it remained a helpless infant, the more excited he
became. He saw in it the possibility of the fulfilment of his
almost wildest hopes. Discussing it with Elizabeth, he fired
her imagination with the prospects of this canine infant, and
unfolded his plan before her. This animal must have as far as
possible the same kind of psychological environment as their
own baby. He told her of an American animal-psychologist
and his wife who had brought up a baby chimpanzee in precisely the same conditions as their own little girl. It was fed,
clothed, cared for, exactly as the child; and with very interesting
results. This, Thomas said, was not quite what he wanted
for little Sirius, because one could not treat a puppy precisely
as a baby without violating its nature. Its bodily organization
was too different from the baby's. But what he did want was
that Sirius should be brought up to feel himself the social equal
of little Plaxy. Differences of treatment must never suggest
differences of biological or social rank. Elizabeth had already,
he said, proved herself an ideal mother, giving the children
that precious feeling of being devotedly loved by a divinely
wise and generous being, yet fostering their independence and
making no greedy emotional claims on them. This was the
atmosphere that Thomas demanded for Sirius; this and the
family environment. And their family, he told her, had taught
him a very important truth. Unfortunate experiences in his
own childhood had led him to regard family as a hopelessly
bad institution, and one which ought to be abolished. She
would remember his wild ideas of experimenting with their
own children. She had tactfully and triumphantly resisted
every attempt to remove her own first two children from her;
and before the third was born Thomas was already convinced
that a really good family environment was the right influence
for a growing child. No doubt she had made mistakes.

Certainly he had made many. No doubt they had to some extent unwittingly damaged their children. There was Tamsy's occasional mulishness and Maurice's diffidence. But on the whole—well it would be false modesty and unfair to the children not to recognize that they were all three fine specimens, friendly, responsible, yet independent and critical. This was the ideal social tradition in which to perform the great experiment with baby Sirius. Dogs, Thomas reminded Elizabeth, were prone to servility; but this vice was probably not due to something servile in their nature; it sprang from the fact that their great social sensitivity was forced to take a servile turn by the tyranny of the more developed species which controlled them. A dog with human intelligence, brought up to respect itself, would probably not be servile at all, and might quite well develop a superhuman gift for true social relationship.

Elizabeth took some time to consider her husband's suggestion, for the responsibility would be mainly hers. Moreover, she was naturally anxious about the effects of the experiment on her own baby. Would her little Plaxy suffer in any way? Thomas persuaded her that no harm would be done, and indeed that the companionship of child and super-canine dog must be beneficial to both. With fervour he insisted that the most valuable social relationships were those between minds as different from one another as possible yet capable of mutual sympathy. It is perhaps remarkable that Thomas, who was not himself gifted with outstanding personal insight or sympathy, should have seen intellectually the essential nature of community. It would be very interesting, he said, to watch the growth of this difficult but pregnant companionship. Of course it might never develop. There might be mere antagonism. Certainly Elizabeth would have to exercise great tact to prevent the child from overpowering the dog with its many human advantages. In particular the little girl's hands and more subtle eyesight would be assets which the puppy could never attain. And the whole human environment, which was inevitably alien and awkward for the dog, might well breed neurosis in a mind that was not human but humanly sensitive. Everything possible must be done to prevent Sirius from becoming either unduly submissive or defiantly arrogant in the manner so familiar in human beings suffering from a sense of inferiority.

One other principle Thomas wanted Elizabeth to bear in mind. It was, of course, impossible to know beforehand how the dog's nature would develop. Sirius might, after all, never reach anything like human mental stature. But everything must be done on the assumption that he would do so. Hence it was very important to bring him up not as a pet but as a person, as an individual who would in due season live an active and independent life. This being so, his special powers must be fostered. While he was still, as Thomas put it, a "schoolboy," his interests would, of course, be "schoolboy" interests, physical, primitive, barbarian; but being a dog, his expression of them would necessarily be very different from a real schoolboy's. He would have to exercise them in normal canine occupations, such as desultory roaming and hunting and fighting. But later, as his intelligence opened up the human world to him, he would want some kind of persistent "human" activity; and obviously sheep could provide him with a career, even if he far excelled the typical super-sheep-dog mentality. With this in view, and whatever his destiny, he must be brought up "as hard as nails and fit as hell." This had always been Elizabeth's policy with her own children; but Sirius would some time need to face up to conditions far more Spartan than those of the most Spartan human family. It would not do simply to force him into such conditions. Somehow she must wile him into wanting them, for sheer pride in his own nature, and later for the sake of his work. This, of course, would not apply to his childhood, but in adolescence he must begin of his own free will to seek hardness. Later still, when his mind was no longer juvenile, he would perhaps drop the sheep-dog career entirely and give his mind to more adult pursuits. Even so, the hard practical life of his youth would not have been in vain. It would endow him with permanent grit and self-reliance.

Elizabeth was a good deal more sceptical than her husband about the future of Sirius. She expressed a fear, which did not trouble Thomas, that such a disunited being as Sirius might be doomed to a life of mental torture. Nevertheless, she finally made up her mind to enter into the spirit of the experiment, and she planned accordingly.

CHAPTER III

INFANCY

WHILE he was still unable to walk, Sirius showed the same sort of brightness as Plaxy in her cot. But even at this early stage his lack of hands was a grave disadvantage. While Plaxy was playing with her rattle, he too played with his; but his baby jaws could not compete with Plaxy's baby hands in dexterity. His interest even in his earliest toys was much more like a child's than like the ordinary puppy's monomania for destruction. Worrying his rattle, he was attentive to the sound that it made, alternately shaking it and holding it still to relish the contrast between sound and silence. At about the time when Plaxy began to crawl, Sirius achieved a staggering walk. His pride in this new art and his joy in the increased scope that it gave him were obvious. He now had the advantage over Plaxy, for his method of locomotion was far better suited to his quadruped structure than her crawl to her biped form. Before she had begun to walk he was already lurching erratically over the whole ground floor and garden. When at last she did achieve the upright gait, he was greatly impressed, and insisted on being helped to imitate her. He soon discovered that this was no game for him.

Plaxy and Sirius were already forming that companionship which was to have so great an effect on both their minds throughout their lives. They played together, fed together, were washed together, and were generally good or naughty together. When one was sick, the other was bored and abject. When one was hurt, the other howled with sympathy. Whatever one of them did, the other had to attempt. When Plaxy learned to tie a knot, Sirius was very distressed at his inability to do likewise. When Sirius acquired by observation of the family's super-sheep-dog, Gelert, the habit of lifting a leg at

gate-posts to leave his visiting card, Plaxy found it hard to
agree that this custom, though suitable for dogs, was not at all
appropriate to little girls. She was deterred only by the
difficulty of the operation. Similarly, though she was soon
convinced that to go smelling at gate-posts was futile because
her nose was not as clever as Sirius's, she did not see why the
practice should outrage the family's notions of propriety.
Plaxy's inability to share in Sirius's developing experience of
social smelling, if I may so name it, was balanced by his
clumsiness in construction. Plaxy was the first to discover
the joy of building with bricks; but there soon came a day
when Sirius, after watching her intently, himself brought a
brick and set it clumsily on the top of the rough wall that
Plaxy was building. His effort wrecked the wall. This was not
Sirius's first achievement in construction, for he had once been
seen to lay three sticks together to form a triangle, an achievement which caused him great satisfaction. He had to learn to
"handle" bricks and dolls in such a way that neither his
saliva nor his pin-point teeth would harm them. He was
already enviously impressed by Plaxy's hands and their
versatility. The normal puppy shows considerable inquisitive-
ness, but no impulse to construct; Sirius was more persistently
inquisitive and at times passionately constructive. His
behaviour was in many ways more simian than canine. The
lack of hands was a handicap against which he reacted with a
dogged will to triumph over disability.

Thomas judged that his weakness in construction was due
not only to handlessness but to a crudity of vision which is
normal in dogs. Long after infancy he was unable to distinguish between visual forms which Plaxy would never confuse.
For instance, it took him far longer than Plaxy to distinguish
between string neatly tied up in little bundles and the obscure
tangle which, at Garth as in so many homes, composed the
general content of the string-bag. Again, for Sirius, rather fat
ovals were no different from circles, podgy oblongs were the
same as squares, pentagons were mistaken for hexagons,
angles of sixty degrees were much the same as right angles.
Consequently in building with toy bricks he was apt to make
mistakes which called forth derision from Plaxy. Later in life

he corrected this disability to some extent by careful training, but his perception of form remained to the end very sketchy.

In early days he did not suspect his inferiority in vision. All his failures in construction were put down to lack of hands. There was indeed a grave danger that his handlessness would so obsess him that his mind would be warped, particularly during a phase when the infant Plaxy was apt to laugh at his helplessness. A little later she was brought to realize that poor Sirius should not be ragged for his misfortune, but helped whenever possible. Then began a remarkable relationship in which Plaxy's hands were held almost as common property, like the toys. Sirius was always running to ask Plaxy to do things he could not manage himself, such as opening boxes and winding up clock-work toys. Sirius himself began to develop a surprising "manual" dexterity, combining the use of fore-paws and teeth; but many operations were for ever beyond him. Throughout his life he was unable to tie a knot in a piece of cotton, though there came a time when he could manage to do so in a rope or stout cord.

Plaxy was the first to show signs of understanding speech, but Sirius was not far behind. When she began to talk, he often made peculiar little noises which, it seemed, were meant to be imitations of human words. His failure to make himself understood often caused him bitter distress. He would stand with his tail between his legs miserably whining. Plaxy was the first to interpret his desperate efforts at communication, but Elizabeth in time found herself understanding; and little by little she grew able to equate each of the puppy's grunts and whines with some particular elementary sound of human speech. Like Plaxy, Sirius began with a very simple baby-language of monosyllables. Little by little this grew into a canine, or super-canine, equivalent of educated English. So alien were his vocal organs to speech, that even when he had perfected the art no outsider would suspect his strange noises of being any human language at all. Yet he had his own equivalent of every vocal sound. Some of his consonants were difficult to distinguish from one another, but Elizabeth and Plaxy and the rest of the family came to understand him as easily as they understood each other. I described his speech

as composed of whimpers and grunts and growls. This perhaps
maligns it, though essentially true. He spoke with a notable
gentleness and precision, and there was a fluid, musical quality
in his voice.

Thomas was, of course, immensely elated by the dog's
development of true speech, for this was a sure sign of the fully
human degree of intelligence. The baby chimpanzee that was
brought up with a human baby kept level with its foster-sister
until the little girl began to talk, but then dropped behind;
for the ape never showed any sign of using words.

Thomas determined to have a permanent record of the dog's
speech. He bought the necessary apparatus for making
gramophone discs, and reproduced conversations between
Sirius and Plaxy. He allowed no one to hear these records
except the family and his two most intimate colleagues,
Professor McAlister and Dr. Billing, who were influential in
procuring funds for the research, and knew that Thomas's
secret ambition soared far above the production of super-
sheep-dogs. On several occasions Thomas brought the
distinguished biologists to see Sirius.

There was a time when it seemed that these gramophone
records would be the sole lasting and tangible evidence of
Thomas's triumph. In spite of inoculation, Sirius developed
distemper and almost succumbed. Day after day, night after
night, Elizabeth nursed the wretched little animal through this
peculiarly noisome disease, leaving her own child mainly to
Mildred, the nursemaid. Had it not been for Elizabeth's skill
and devotion, Sirius would not have come through with his
powers unimpaired. Probably he would have died. This
incident had two important results. It created in Sirius a
passionate and exacting affection for his foster-mother, so
that for weeks he would scarcely let her out of his sight without
making an uproar; and it bred in Plaxy a dreadful sense that
her mother's love was being given wholly to Sirius. In fact
Plaxy became lonely and jealous. This trouble was soon put
right when Sirius had recovered, and Elizabeth was able to
give more attention to her child; but then it was the dog's
turn to be jealous. The climax came when Sirius, seeing
Elizabeth comforting Plaxy after a tumble, rushed savagely at

her and actually nipped her little bare leg. There was then a terrible scene. Plaxy screamed and screamed. Elizabeth was for once really angry. Sirius howled with remorse for what he had done; and actually, out of a sense that retribution was needed, made a half-hearted attempt to bite his own leg. Then matters were made much worse by the family's super-sheep-dog, Gelert, who rushed to the scene of uproar. Seeing Plaxy's bleeding leg, and Elizabeth being very angry with the puppy, Gelert assumed that this was a case for severe punishment, and set upon the abject culprit. Sirius was bowled over and none too gently mauled by the furiously growling Gelert. The puppy's remorse gave place to fright, and his whimpers to screams of terror, to which the weeping Plaxy added screams of fear for her beloved friend. The other children rushed upon the scene, followed by Kate and Mildred with brooms and a rolling pin. Even the infant Plaxy seized Gelert by the tail and tried to drag him off. But it was Elizabeth herself who snatched Sirius from the jaws of death (as it seemed to him) and roundly cursed the officious Gelert.

This incident seems to have had several important results. It made both Sirius and Plaxy realize how much, after all, they cared for one another. It persuaded Plaxy that her mother had not discarded her for Sirius. And it proved to Sirius that Elizabeth loved him even when he had been very wicked. The unfortunate Gelert alone gained no comfort.

The only further punishment inflicted on Sirius was deep disgrace. Elizabeth withdrew her kindness. Plaxy, in spite of her secret knowledge that Sirius was very dear, was filled with self-pity once more when he had been rescued, and treated him with cold self-righteousness. To punish Sirius, Plaxy showed a violent affection for the kitten, Tommy, who had recently been imported from a neighbouring farm. Sirius, of course, was tortured with jealousy, and was afforded good practice in self-control. He succeeded all the better because on the one occasion when he did attack Tommy, he discovered that the kitten had claws. Sirius was very sensitive to neglect and censure. When his human friends were displeased with him he lost interest in everything but his misery. He would not play, he would not eat. On this occasion he set himself to win

Plaxy over by many little attentions. He brought her a beautiful feather, then a lovely white pebble, and each time he timidly kissed her hand. Suddenly she gave him a hearty hug, and both broke into a romp. Towards Elizabeth, Sirius was less bold. He merely eyed her askance, his tail timorously vibrating when he caught her glance. So comic was this spectacle that she could not help laughing. Sirius was forgiven.

At a stage in his puppyhood shortly after this incident Sirius conceived a respectful admiration for Gelert. The slightly older and biologically quite adult super-sub-human animal treated him with careless contempt. Sirius followed Gelert about and mimicked all his actions. One day Gelert by great good fortune caught a rabbit and devoured it, growling savagely when Sirius approached. The puppy watched him with mingled admiration and horror. The spectacle of that swift pursuit and capture roused in him the hunting impulses of the normal dog. The scream of the rabbit, its struggle, sudden limpness and hideous dismemberment, shocked him deeply; for he had a sympathetic and imaginative nature, and Elizabeth had brought up her family in a tradition of tenderness towards all living things. But now a conflict arose which was to distress him throughout his life, the conflict between what he later called his "wolf-nature" and his compassionate civilized mentality.

The immediate result was a strong and guilty lust for the chase and an intensified, awed passion for Gelert. He became obsessed by the rabbit-warren. He was for ever sniffing at the entrances to the burrows, whimpering with excitement. For a while Plaxy was almost forgotten. Vainly she tried to win him back into partnership in her games. Vainly she hung about the burrows with him, bored and cross. In her presence he once caught a frog and disgustingly mangled it in an attempt to eat it. She burst into tears. His hunting impulse was suddenly quenched, and horror supervened. He rushed whimpering to his darling and covered her face with bloody kisses.

Many times henceforth he was to suffer the torturing conflict between his normal canine impulses and his more developed nature.

His admiration of Gelert was gradually damped down by

the discovery that the older dog had no interest in anything but hunting and eating. Once more there was a conflict. Hunting now gripped Sirius as the main joy of life; but it was a guilty joy. He felt its call almost as a religious claim upon him, the claim of the dark blood-god for sacrifice; but he was also disgusted with the sacrifice, and deeply disturbed by Plaxy's horror. Moreover, after his first obsession he began to recover interest in the many activities which he shared with Plaxy. These were of no interest to Gelert.

The final disillusionment came when Sirius began to realize that Gelert not merely would not but could not talk. This suspicion had long haunted Sirius, but he had believed that Gelert's unresponsiveness was merely due to his haughty disposition. There came a day, however, when this theory ceased to be possible. Young Sirius, whose four-foot locomotion was far more developed than Plaxy's running, had been trying to keep up with Gelert at the outset of a hunting expedition. They came upon a sheep with a broken leg. Though Gelert was not in the sheep-tending profession, he knew very well that sheep were things to be cherished. He knew also that Mr. Pugh of Caer Blai was in this case the responsible man. He therefore hurried off to Caer Blai, far outstripping the loose-limbed puppy. When at last Sirius arrived in the farm-yard, he found Gelert making an inarticulate fuss around Pugh, vainly trying to persuade him to come up the hill. Sirius knew that he himself could not make Pugh understand, but he knew also that he could explain to any member of his own family. He therefore set off to find one of them and encountered Giles on his way home from school. He pantingly told Giles the story, and the two hurried to Caer Blai. Giles momentarily forgot the great family taboo about "not telling people about Sirius," and said to Pugh, "Sirius says there's a sheep with a broken leg in Nant Twll-y-cwm, and it may get drowned." Pugh looked at him with incredulity, but was impressed by the boy's earnestness and the antics of the dogs. He accompanied them up the valley, and there was the sheep. After this incident Sirius regarded Gelert as a nit-wit, and the farmer suspected Sirius of being an altogether "super" super-sheep-dog.

The discovery that Gelert could not speak, and was in other respects also a half-wit, was a shock to Sirius. Gelert excelled him in all those ways in which he outshone his human friends, in speed, in endurance, in scent and in hearing. For some time he had taken Gelert as his model. Mimicking Gelert's taciturnity, he had even tried not to talk. So successful had he been that Elizabeth in one of her letters to Thomas said that Sirius's human mentality seemed to be waning. The realization that the older dog simply could not talk changed the puppy's attitude. Suddenly he became garrulous, and showed an increased desire to keep pace with Plaxy in acquiring all sorts of human skills. Also he devised an amusing way of ridiculing Gelert. He would hold imaginary conversations with the super-sheep-dog, pretending that Gelert's silence was due to deliberate taciturnity. The older animal would at first ignore the garrulous puppy; but presently, particularly if the spectators laughed, his super-canine though sub-human mind would begin to suspect that Sirius was making a fool of him. He would look very self-conscious and perplexed, and sooner or later drive the insolent youngster away, or seize him and chastise him.

Plaxy was by now being taught to read and write. Her mother devoted an hour a day to this task. Sirius had at first shown a mild curiosity about the queer business, but under the influence of Gelert he had thrown it over for the sake of hunting. Elizabeth made no effort to compel him to carry on his studies. Either his distaste was a passing phase, soon to be outgrown, or his mind was after all not sufficiently super-canine to persist in this alien occupation, in which case compulsion would be disastrous. However, when his idol had fallen, he reverted to the game of reading and writing. He had missed a good deal, so Elizabeth undertook to coach him up to Plaxy's standard. Of course his handlessness made it impossible for him ever to write save with some special apparatus. It was also discovered that, apart from his obvious disability for writing, his reading also was doomed to be very seriously hampered, so crude was his perception of visual form. Plaxy used to spell out simple words with her box of letters, but Sirius found it very difficult to distinguish between C, G, D, O and Q, and also between B, P, R, and K. He was also greatly confused by E and F, by S and Z, by A and H, by H and K. At a later stage, when Plaxy was mastering the lower-case letters, and these in small type, Sirius was still more handicapped. Sometimes it almost seemed that his intelligence was after all sub-human. Elizabeth, who, in spite of her triumphant impartiality towards her child and her foster-child, had always a secret desire for Plaxy to excel, now wrote to Thomas that after all Sirius was not much better than a moron. But Thomas, whose secret desire was the reverse of his wife's, replied with a dissertation on the poor vision of dogs, and urged her to encourage Sirius by telling him of this canine disability, to praise his enterprise in learning to read and write at all, and to remind him that he had great advantages over human beings in other spheres. Encouragement tapped a surprising fund of doggedness in Sirius, for he spent hours every day by himself practising reading. Great progress was made, but after a week or so Elizabeth felt bound to intervene because of symptoms of mental breakdown. She praised him and petted him, and persuaded him that he would learn more quickly and permanently if he tried a bit less hard.

Sirius recognized, of course, that in writing he could not possibly reach Plaxy's standard, but he was determined not to be entirely without this valuable art. It was he himself that invented a way out of his disability. He persuaded Elizabeth to make him a tight leather mitten for his right paw. On the back of the mitten was a socket into which a pen or pencil could be inserted. When this article was completed, he made his first experiment in writing. He was very excited. Lying in the "couchant" position with his left foreleg on the paper to hold it in place, he kept his right elbow on the ground, and was able to scrawl out DOG, CAT, PLAXY, SIRIUS, and so on. The neural organization of his leg and the motor-centres of his brain were probably not at all well adapted to this activity; but once more his doggedness triumphed. Long practice brought him after some years the skill to write a letter in large, irregular but legible characters. In later life, as I shall tell, he even ventured on the task of writing books.

Thomas was more impressed than Elizabeth by Sirius's

achievement, because he probably appreciated more fully the difficulties that the puppy had overcome.

So far as possible, Sirius took part in all the simple lessons that Elizabeth gave to Plaxy. He was never very good at arithmetic, perhaps because of his poor visual powers; but he managed to avoid being outclassed by Plaxy, who was none too good herself. His spelling, too, was very bad, probably for the same reason. But at an early age he showed a great interest in language and the art of precise expression. Poetry had sometimes a deep effect on him. In spite of his visual weakness he read a good deal, and he often begged members of the family to read aloud to him. This they did very frequently, knowing how great a boon it was for him.

But to return to his puppyhood. There came a time when it seemed desirable for Plaxy to attend the village school. Sirius, of course, could not do so. It was sometimes with thankfulness for his freedom, but sometimes with envy, that he watched his little foster-sister set off with her books in the morning. He was now of an age to do a great deal of free roaming, and the passion for the scents and adventures of the countryside was now strong in him. But the thought that Plaxy was outstripping him in knowledge of the great world of men worried him sorely. In the afternoons, when she returned from school, she often assured him that lessons were a bore; but he could tell from her tone that she felt important and proud, and that a good deal that happened at school was great fun. He made a habit of gleaning from her the most useful bits of information that she had acquired during the day. It became a regular custom with her to do her homework with him, to the profit of them both. Meanwhile Elizabeth continued Sirius's education in a desultory but stimulating way. Often he was able to pay his debt to Plaxy by passing on to her the fruits of his own lessons, though she generally adopted a superior attitude to his tit-bits. Sometimes he told her about conversations with Thomas, who had made a habit of taking Sirius for walks on the hills and telling him all sorts of significant scraps of science or world-history. Plaxy herself, of course, was sometimes present on these walks. But generally Thomas needed vigorous exercise at the week-ends, and his little daughter could not keep up with him as well as Sirius. During his puppyhood Sirius often came home tired after long expeditions with Thomas, but when he reached mid-adolescence he used to look forward with pleasure to the almost weekly trek over Arenig, the Rhinogs or Moelwyn, listening to the far-ranging flow of Thomas's thought, or probing him with questions. These the great physiologist answered with all the patience and care which he was accustomed to give to his students. This was Sirius's main intellectual education, this frequent contact with a mature and brilliant mind. Often the two would discuss Sirius's future, Thomas encouraging him to believe that a great work lay before him. But of this later. I have let myself pass beyond the dog's puppyhood, and now I must return to it.

Not only in reading and writing but in another way also Sirius was inevitably inferior to Plaxy, and indeed to nearly all human beings. He was entirely colour-blind. I understand that there is still doubt about colour-sensitivity in dogs. Dissection, I believe, has revealed that they have approximately the same equipment of "rods and cones" in their retinae as that of human beings. But psychological experiments have not yet proved that dogs are in fact sensitive to colour. Possibly the truth is that, though some dogs are aware of colour, the incidence of colour-blindness in the canine species is much greater than in man. However that may be, it is certain that Sirius was completely colour-blind. Until quite late in his puppyhood, long after he had learned to talk, he himself had no suspicion that his seeing lacked any qualities possessed by Plaxy's. Thomas had told Elizabeth that dogs were almost certainly colour-blind, but she refused to believe it of Sirius, insisting that he could distinguish between her differently coloured dresses. "No," said Thomas, "he probably does it by scent or the touch of his sensitive tongue. Besides, haven't you noticed that he goes badly adrift in his use of the names of colours? Anyhow, let's test him." For this purpose Thomas bought a child's box of wooden picture-blocks, and covered the faces of the cubes with paper of different colours very carefully selected so that their tone values and tactual and olfactory qualities should be identical. Any differences of odour that might be due to differences of pigment he blotted out by drenching the blocks in eau-de-Cologne. He then presented the "box of bricks" to Plaxy and Sirius. Plaxy at once produced a chequer of pink and blue squares. Sirius was obviously uninterested in the blocks, but he was persuaded to copy Plaxy's chequer. He put the pieces together quite at random. It was soon obvious even to Sirius himself that Plaxy saw something which he missed. He at once set about the same kind of self-education which he had undertaken in order to read. With Plaxy's aid he must discover the thing that had escaped him in the bricks, and then strengthen his powers of seeing it. Plaxy displayed coloured objects to him one after another, naming their colours. She showed him a coloured print and a monochrome photograph. Giles produced a flash-light with red and green glasses. But all was in vain. Sirius was quite unable to discover what colour was.

He was at first greatly distressed, but Thomas comforted him by assuring him that all dogs were colour-blind, and probably all mammals but apes and men. And he reminded Sirius that dogs were at any rate far superior in hearing and smelling. Sirius had long known that human noses were very poor instruments. He had often been contemptuous because Plaxy could not smell out her mother's track in the garden, or tell with her nose whether a certain footprint was Gelert's or another dog's. Moreover at an early age he was surprised and disappointed at her obtuseness to all the mysterious and exciting smells of the countryside after rain. While she mildly enjoyed an indiscriminate freshness and fragrance, he would analyse the messages of the breeze with quivering nostrils, gasping out words between the sniffs. "Horse," he would say; then after another sniff, "And not a horse I have smelt before." Or, "Postman! Must be coming up the lane." Or perhaps, "Sea-smell to-day," though the sea was several miles away behind the Rhinogs. A slight veering of the wind might bring him whiffs of a distant waterfall, or more fragrant odours of the moor, or peat or heather or bracken. Sometimes, gripped by some strange enticing scent, he would rush off to trace it. Once he came trotting back after a few minutes of exploration and said, "Strange bird, but I couldn't see him properly."

On another occasion he suddenly rushed out of the house, sniffed the breeze, raced off up the moor, cast about till he picked up a trail, and then streamed along it round the hill shoulder. After an hour or so he returned in great excitement, made Plaxy fetch out the animal book and turn the pages till she came to The Fox. "That's him!" he cried, "Gosh, what a smell!" Once in the middle of a romping game in the garden he came to a sudden halt, sniffing. His hair bristled, his tail curled under his belly. "Let's go inside," he said, "there's some dreadful thing up wind." Plaxy laughed, but he seemed so disturbed that she consented. Twenty minutes later Giles arrived from school, full of the news that he had seen a menagerie pass along the road to Ffestiniog.

Giles was so tickled by Sirius's reaction that he clamoured for Sirius to be taken to see the wild beasts with the rest of the family, arguing that the little coward had better learn that bad smells were not really dangerous. After much persuasion Sirius consented to go. The experience had a lasting effect on him. As he entered the enclosure the appalling confusion of odours, some enticing, some formidable, tore his nerves as though (as he said long afterwards) all the instruments of an orchestra were tuning up together at full blast. With tucked-in tail and scared eyes he kept close to Elizabeth as the party moved from cage to cage. Many of the animals roused his hunting impulse; but the great carnivora, the abject and mangy lion, tiger, and bear, forlornly pacing their narrow cages, tortured him, partly by their terrifying natural smell, partly by their acquired odour of ill-health and misery. The slit-eyed wolf, too, greatly affected him with its similarity to himself. While he was gazing with fascination at this distant cousin, the lion suddenly roared, and Sirius, shivering with fright, shrank up against Elizabeth's legs. Stimulated by the lion, the rest of the animals started to give tongue. When the elephant rent the air with a blast of his trumpet, Sirius took to his heels and vanished.

The world of odour was one in which Plaxy had only slight experience. In the world of sound she was not so completely outclassed, but she was far behind Sirius. He could hear approaching footsteps long before Plaxy or any other human being could detect them, and he could unfailingly tell who it was that was coming. The cry of a bat, entirely beyond the range of most human ears, was described by Sirius as a sharp needle of sound. Both Elizabeth and Plaxy soon discovered that he was incredibly sensitive to their tone of voice. He could distinguish unerringly between spontaneous praise and mere kindly encouragement, between real condemnation and censure with an undertone of amusement or approval. Not only so, but he seemed able to detect changes of temper in them before they themselves had noticed them. "Elizabeth," he would suddenly ask, "why are you sad?" She would reply, laughing, "But I'm *not!* I'm rather pleased because the bread has risen nicely." "Oh, but you *are* sad, underneath," he would answer. "I can hear it quite well. You are only pleased on top." And after a pause she would have to say, "Oh, well, perhaps I am. I wonder why."

His nose, too, gave him a lot of information about people's emotional states. He sometimes spoke of a "cross smell," a "friendly smell," a "frightened smell," a "tired smell."

So sensitive was he to odour and to sound, that he found human speech quite inadequate to express the richness of these two universes. He once said of a certain odour in the house, "It's rather like the trail of a hare where a spaniel has followed it, and some time ago a donkey crossed it too." Both scent and sound had for him rich emotional meaning, innate and acquired. It was obvious that many odours that he encountered for the first time roused a strong impulse of pursuit, while others he sought to avoid. It was obvious, too, that many odours acquired an added emotional meaning through their associations. One day when he was out on the moor by himself one of his paws was badly cut on a broken bottle. It happened that while he limped home there was a terrifying thunderstorm. When at last he staggered in at the front door, Elizabeth mothered him and cleaned up his foot with a certain well-known disinfectant. The smell of it was repugnant to him, but it now acquired a flavour of security and kindliness which was to last him all his life.

Many sounds stirred him violently. Thunder and other great noises terrified him. The tearing of calico made him leap with a purely physiological fright, and set him barking in merry protest. Human laughter he found very infectious. It roused in him a queer yelping laughter which was all his own. The tones of the human voice not only told him of the emotional state of the speaker but also stimulated strong emotional responses in himself. The odours of emotion had a similar effect.

Like many dogs, young Sirius found human music quite excruciating. An isolated vocal or instrumental theme was torture enough to him; but when several voices or instruments combined, he seemed to lose control of himself completely. His fine auditory discrimination made even well-executed solos seem to him badly out of tune. Harmony and the combination of several themes resulted for him in hideous cacophany. Elizabeth and the children would sometimes sing rounds, for instance when they were coming down the moor after a picnic. Sirius invariably had to give up his usual far-ranging course and draw into the party to howl. The indignant children would chase him away, but as soon as the singing began again he would return and once more give tongue. On one occasion Tamsy, who was the most seriously musical member of the family, cried imploringly, "Sirius, *do* either keep quiet or keep *away*! Why can't you let us enjoy ourselves?" He replied, "But how can you *like* such a horrible jarring muddle of sweet noises? I have to come to you because they're so sweet, and I have to howl because it's a mess, and because—oh because it *might* be so lovely." Once he said, "If I were to paint a picture could you just keep away? Wouldn't you go crazy because of the all-wrongness of the colour? Well, sounds are far more exciting to me than your queer colour is to you."

The family refused to admit that their singing was a mess. Instead, they determined to "teach Sirius music." He accepted his fate with doglike docility and fortitude. After all, painful as the process must be, it would help him to find out more about human beings; and even at a very early age he had begun to be curious about the difference between himself and his friends.

The whole family gathered in the sitting-room to "teach Sirius music." Elizabeth produced her cherished but now

neglected violin. On the few earlier occasions when she had
played on it within earshot of Sirius, he always came hurrying
to her, howling. If the door was shut, he gave tongue outside.
Otherwise he rushed into the room and leapt up at her till she
had to stop. On this occasion he at first made some effort
to keep a hold on himself during the painful operation that
his family were determined to perform on him. But excitement
soon overcame him. Tamsy was at the piano. Maurice and
Giles were ready, if wanted, with their recorders. Plaxy sat on
the floor with her arms around the resigned but rather mischievous Sirius, "to keep him from going mad on us." For
it was clear that Sirius was going to be difficult. When Plaxy
let him escape, he bounded from instrument to instrument,
making mock attacks on each. His tail thrashed from side to
side in a conflict of agony and delight, knocking the bow from
Elizabeth's hand, and sending a recorder flying across the room.
Even when Plaxy held him, he turned the experiment to chaos
by giving tongue with such vigour and virtuosity that the simple
tones of the instrument were drowned. When at last he was
persuaded to co-operate seriously, it was soon found that he
had at any rate a far better ear for pitch than any of the
family. When Elizabeth moved her finger so slightly on the
string that none of the children could hear any difference,
Sirius detected a change. Elizabeth was amazed to find that
he could also sing accurately in tune. Once when she played
a single tone and he could not restrain himself from giving
tongue, the main element in his wail was obviously in tune
with the violin. With a little encouragement he produced the
pure note without any trimmings. When Maurice played a
scale on his recorder, Sirius sang in unison with it, keeping
perfectly in tune even with the inaccurate tones produced by
the young musician on an imperfect instrument.

   With his usual doggedness Sirius set about conquering htis
excruciating thing, music. He showed surprising aptitude for
singing, soon outstripping Plaxy in reproducing the family
songs. Sometimes he sang without words; sometimes he used
his own canine equivalent of the English words of the song.
(His lingo, being simply mispronounced English, rhymed and
scanned appropriately.)

With practice he became less tortured by human music. In fact he actually came to like it, so long as it was not too badly out of tune. He would often join in singing the rounds that had formerly tormented him. Sometimes when Elizabeth played her violin he would come to listen. In certain moods he would retire to a favourite point of vantage on the moor and spend hours singing to himself. He would go over and over the songs that Elizabeth had so often sung about the house.

It was a tune-loving family. Under Elizabeth's influence it had developed an amusing system of musical calls which served the function of bugle-calls. A certain little tune meant "Time to get up," another "Breakfast is ready," another "All is now prepared for starting on the expedition," and so on. Plaxy and Sirius, the two youngest members of the family, invented a number of private calls of their own. One of these, for instance, meant "Come and help me!" Another said, "Something interesting here. Come and investigate;" another "Come and play with me!" One little trickle of sound meant, "I am going to pee." To this there were two possible musical answers. One said, "Right oh! So am I," and the other "Nothing doing by me." It was curious, by the way, that if one of them made water the other had always to follow suit on the same spot, in the approved canine manner. Always? No! Plaxy soon found that she could not keep pace with Sirius in this etiquette of leaving tokens.

When Thomas heard of Sirius's habit of retiring on to the moor to practise singing, he feared lest his precious animal should become notorious as "the singing dog," and be exploited. It was indeed startling for the natives to hear the sweet, accurate, but inarticulate and inhuman voice, and to come upon a large dog squatting on his haunches melodiously giving tongue. Thomas, it was rumoured, had sinister powers. He could put demons into dogs. Fortunately the farther these rumours spread, the less they were believed. No craze equivalent to the case of the talking mongoose or the Loch Ness monster developed over the singing dog.

In his puppyhood Sirius sang only human music. Throughout his life he was deeply interested in the great classical achievements of man's musical genius, but as he had always found the fundamental structure of human music crude, and inadequate to his interest in sound-form and the emotions which sought musical expression, he began to experiment with new scales, intervals, and rhythms, suited to his more sensitive hearing. He made use of the quarter-tone and even the eighth-of-a-tone. Sometimes, in his purely canine mood, his melodies divided the octave in quite a different manner from any human musical mode. Thus to the human listener his most distinctive music became less recognizably musical and more like the baying of a dog, though a strangely varied and disturbing baying.

A supple and mellow voice was Sirius's only medium of expression. He often longed to play some instrument, so as to be able to introduce harmony into his experiments, but his tragic lack of hands prevented him. Sometimes he sat at the piano trying to finger out a two-note accompaniment to his singing, but his paws were far too clumsy to do even this properly. For long spells he would give up music entirely because his handlessness prevented him from doing what he wanted with it. At these times he would wander about with tail and head low, refusing comfort. The mingled sense of helplessness and talent tormented him. But presently his buoyant spirits would revive, and he would resolve that, if instrumental music must remain for ever impossible to him, he would do new and marvellous things with his voice. Throughout his life Sirius alternated between self pity on account of his disabilities and a surprisingly detached and humorous acceptance of his nature and his environment, issuing in a zestful will to triumph in spite of everything.

CHAPTER IV

YOUTH

IN the foregoing chapter I should have written only about Sirius as a puppy, but in dealing with his disabilities and powers I was inevitably led on to speak of his later life. His

serious musical adventures, for instance, did not begin till
puppyhood was well over. I must now concentrate more
definitely on his adolescence and early maturity, preparing the
way for an account of that part of his life with which my own
life became for a while closely entangled.

Already in adolescence Sirius was larger than most sheep-
dogs. But though tall, he was at this time very slight and
lanky, and it was often said that he had "overgrown his
strength." He was also far from courageous. His caution in
his encounters with other dogs was increased by his discovery
in sundry minor brawls that his large cranium made his head
unwieldy and his seizing of his opponent rather less slick than
it might have been. This weakness was largely overcome when
he reached full maturity, for constant exercise developed the
muscles of his neck sufficiently to cope with his extra weight
of head. In youth, however, he was no match for the smaller
but more experienced collies that tended the sheep. One of
these, unfortunately a near neighbour, formed a habit of
persecuting Sirius whenever possible. There came a day when
he was ignominiously chased home by this animal, who bore
the appropriate name Diawl Du, black devil. It was the schoolgirl Plaxy who seized the yard broom and drove off the black
devil with blows and shrill curses. Later Sirius heard Plaxy
telling her mother about the incident. She ended the story with,
"I'm afraid poor Sirius hasn't much spunk." Sirius did not
know the word "spunk," but he detected in Plaxy's voice,
which she intended to be merely amused, a note of deep
mortification. He sneaked off to find a dictionary. With
some trouble and much use of his wet tongue for turning the
"India paper" pages he found the word; and he didn't like
the idea that Plaxy thought him lacking in spunk. For "spunk"
according to the Oxford Concise Dictionary meant "courage,
mettle, spirit, anger," and was connected with "spark."
Somehow he must regain Plaxy's respect, but how?

That same day Plaxy seemed to turn her attention away
from Sirius towards the young cat, Trix, successor to Tommy.
This impulse to make much of cats was a common reaction
with her when she was at all alienated from Sirius. She would
cuddle Trix in front of him and remark on her lovely tortoise-

shell coat or her dainty nose. Also, Sirius noted, she would become strangely catlike herself, sitting about in lofty silence and indolence, "hugging herself," as he sometimes put it.

Shortly after his defeat by Diawl Du, Sirius got himself into serious disgrace over Trix. The cat was contemplating a leap into Plaxy's lap when Sirius lost control of himself and attacked his minute rival with noisy rage. She arched her back and stood firm, slashing Sirius's face, so that he retreated, yelping. Plaxy's scream turned into a laugh. Reviling Sirius for a bully and a coward, she snatched up Trix and lavished endearments on her. Sirius slunk away in shame and misery.

A fortnight later it was remarked in the family that Sirius had developed an unexpected craze for worrying an old spade-handle which had been lying in the outhouse. Whenever possible he would persuade some sturdy human being, preferably Maurice, who was home from boarding school, to join in the game. Boy and dog would hang on to opposite ends of the piece of ash and swing hither and thither about the garden, each trying to shake off his opponent. Towards the end of the holidays Maurice remarked, "Sirius is getting damned strong. You can't tear the thing from him; you can't twist it from him." All this time Sirius had been carefully avoiding Diawl Du, but at last he felt ready. Though he was confident that his grip was much more powerful than it had been, and his head movements quicker and more precise, he would not trust to physical powers alone; cunning must be his mainstay. His strategy was planned with great care. He studied his chosen battle-ground, and rehearsed the crucial action which was to give him victory in the very scene of his former discomfiture, and under the eyes of Plaxy.

One afternoon when Plaxy had returned from school he hurried over to Glasdo, the farm where Diawl Du lived, and ostentatiously hung about till his enemy issued like a black avalanche from the farmyard gate. Sirius at once took to his heels, bolting for home. To reach the front door of Garth, which was ostensibly his objective, he had to make a right-angled turn through the yard gate. (Garth, it will be remembered, was an old farm-house.) As he checked himself to do this and swing through the gate, he glanced behind to see that

Diawl Du was at the correct distance. Then he raced round the yard in a great curve, arriving back at the gate, but at right angles to his original course through it, and hidden from Diawl Du by the wall. At that moment the collie swerved through the gate in pursuit, and Sirius with great momentum crashed into him on the left flank. Diawl Du rolled over with Sirius on top of him. Sirius gripped his throat, his teeth finding a much firmer hold than on the hard old spade handle. He hung on desperately, fearing that if he once let go the superior skill of the other dog would be his undoing. The collie's throttled screams and Sirius's own continuous muffled growl soon brought out the inmates of the house. Out of the corner of his eye, as he rolled over and over with his enemy, Sirius caught sight of Plaxy. The warm blood seeped into his mouth and threatened to choke him, but he hung on, coughing for breath. The saltness and odour of Diawl Du's blood, he afterwards said, turned him mad. Some pent up energy and fury in him was released for the first time. At the height of the struggle the thought flashed upon him, "This is real life, this is what I am for, not all that human twaddle." He gripped and tugged and worried, while Diawl Du's struggles became weaker, and the horrified human beings did their best to loosen his grip. They beat him, they threw pepper in his face so that he sneezed violently, but he did not let go. They fell upon him in a mass to hold him quiet while they tried to prise his jaws open with a stick. His own blood mixed with the collie's in his mouth, and he was surprised at the different flavour of it. Nothing that the family could do made him loosen his grip. Plaxy, desperate with horror, did her best to force her hands into his mouth. Then suddenly beside herself, she screamed. At last Sirius let go, and Diawl Du lay inert on the ground.

The victor stalked away, licking his blood-slippery lips, his spine still bristling. After taking a drink at the trough under the yard pump, he lay down with his chin on his paws to watch the proceedings. Elizabeth sent the children into the house for warm water, disinfectants, bandages, while she examined the wound. Presently Plaxy was holding the unconscious dog's head, while Elizabeth applied a large cotton-wool pad and wound the bandage round his neck. After a while

Diawl Du showed signs of life, moving his head slightly in Plaxy's hands. He produced the ghost of a growl, which ended in a whimper. Then they carried him inside and laid him before the kitchen fire with a drink of water beside him.

No one took any notice of Sirius, who still lay in the yard, stiff and sore; triumphant, but also rather bewildered and resentful. If she wanted him to have spunk, why didn't she come and praise him and pet him?

Presently Elizabeth came and started up the little car. When she had backed it into the road, she went in and, with Maurice's help, brought out Diawl Du in her arms, while the others prepared a place for him on the back seat of the car. When he was comfortably laid on a rug on the seat, she drove off to Glasdo.

The children turned towards Sirius. "Gosh!" said Maurice, "you've done it this time!" And Tamsy, "They'll have you shot as a dangerous animal." Giles contributed, "It was just murder." Plaxy said nothing but "Oh, Sirius!" He stared at her in silence, trying to analyse her tone of voice. Mainly it spoke reproach, and horror. But there was something else in it, perhaps exultation at his prowess, perhaps mere human superiority. Anyhow, what did he care? He lay still for a little longer with chin on paws, staring at Plaxy. At that moment Trix, the cat, came and rubbed herself against Plaxy's legs. Plaxy picked her up and hugged her. Sirius rose, his back once more bristling, and with a low noise between a snort and a growl he stalked with conscious dignity out through the gate.

The fight with Diawl Du was a turning point in the career of Sirius. He had tasted victory. He had got his own back. Never again would he be cowed by half-wit persecutors. But something more had happened than a calculated triumph. His deeper nature, his unconscious nature, had found expression. He had discovered something far more satisfying than human sophistication. These thoughts were not clear in his mind at the time; but looking back on the incident from a much later period, this was the form that he gave them.

Elizabeth warned him that, if he attempted murder again, there might be serious trouble. "Remember," she said, "to outsiders you are only a dog. You have no legal rights at all.

If someone decides that you are a nuisance and shoots you, he won't be had up for murder; he'll merely get into trouble for destroying a bit of our property. Besides," she added, "how *could* you do it? It was horrible, just animal." Sirius gave no response to this taunt; but taunt he felt it to be. He could both smell and hear her contemptuous hostility. Probably some suppressed and unacknowledged hate for her canine foster-child had found a sudden outlet. Sirius saw the folly and danger of his action clearly enough, but her last remark filled him with rage. In his heart he said, "To hell with them all!" Outwardly he gave no sign that he was even listening. He was sitting in front of the kitchen fire, and after Elizabeth's taunt he cocked up a hind leg and carefully, ostentatiously, groomed his private parts, a habit which he often used with great effect to annoy his women folk.

As the months piled up into years Sirius's self-confidence in relation to other dogs was greatly augmented. His increasing weight and strength combined with superior intelligence to give him not only freedom from persecution but acknowledged superiority over all the sheep-dogs of the countryside, who were all much smaller than the young Alsatian. His combination of size and cunning put him in a class apart. As for "spunk", the truth seems to be that throughout his life he remained at heart a timid creature who rose to a display of boldness only in desperation or when the odds were favourable, or on those rare occasions when the dark god of his blood took possession of him.

I cannot deal with his relations with animals of his own biological type without giving some account of his sexual adventures. Long before the fight with Diawl Du he had begun to be perplexedly interested in any bitch in heat that he happened to come across. Mostly they would have nothing to do with him, regarding him, presumably, as an overgrown puppy. But there was one large and rather elderly black bitch who seemed to find the callow young giant very attractive. With her he periodically indulged in a great deal of desultory love play. Thomas observed the antics of the couple with keen interest, because it soon became obvious that Sirius lacked the ordinary dog's intuitive aptitude for making full use of his opportunities. The two animals would race around, tumbling over one another in mock battle, obviously relishing the delectable contact of their bodies. But after a while Sirius would stand about foolishly wagging his tail, wondering what to do next. This aimlessness was of course a normal stage in the sexual development of dogs, but normally it soon led to copulation. Sirius, however, who as it happened had never observed another canine pair copulating, seemed permanently at a loss. It was not till he came upon his own beloved in the act of being taken by another dog, far younger than himself but more instinctive and more physiologically mature, that he discovered what it was that his body wanted to do.

Henceforth his amours were brought to a point in the normal manner. Physiologically he was still merely in the "school-boy" phase, and not very attractive to mature bitches. Nor was sex at this stage an obsessive passion with him. It was more important as a symbol of maturity than as an end in itself. Its natural seductiveness was much enhanced by its being "the done thing" for grown-up dogs. In comparison with Plaxy and even the elder children Sirius seemed sexually precocious, simply because his unrestricted amours afforded him experience and technique, while to the children everything of the sort remained for a long while almost unexplored territory.

In one respect Sirius found his love affairs miserably unsatisfactory, throughout his life. For the beloved of the hour, however delectable in odour and appearance and in bodily contact, was invariably from his point of view something less than a half-wit. She could not speak, she could not understand his spoken endearments. She could not share the adventures of his wakening mind. And when her heat was over she became devastatingly frigid and unattractive. The fragrance was gone; the moron mentality remained.

Thomas was greatly interested in Sirius's accounts of his love affairs; about which, by the way, he showed no reticence. To the question, "What is it that attracts you in her?" young Sirius could only reply, "She smells so lovely." Later in life he was able to say more. Some years later I myself discussed the matter with him, and he said, "Of course it's mostly the

luscious smell of her. I can't possibly make you understand
the power of it, because you humans are so bad at smells. It's
as though your noses were not merely feeble but colour-blind
But think of all that your poets have ever said about the delect
able curves and colours of the beloved, and how her appearance
seems to express a lovely *spirit* (often deceptively), and then
imagine the whole thing done in terms of fragrance. Morwen's
fragrance when she wants me is like the scent of the morning,
with a maddening tang in it for which there are no words.
It is the scent of a very gentle and fragrant *spirit*, but unfortunately the spirit of Morwen is nine-tenths asleep, and always
will be. But she smells like what she *would* be if she *were* really
awake."

"But what about her appearance?" I said. "Doesn't that
attract you?" "It attracts *me* a lot," he replied, "but ordinary
dogs take little notice of it. With them it's smell that counts,
and of course the touch of her, too. But it's the smell that
enthrals one, the maddening, stinging, sweet smell, that soaks
right through your body, so that you can't think of anything
else day or night. But her looks? Yes *I* certainly do care
about her looks. She's so sleek and slim and slick. Also her
looks help a lot to express the spirit that she *might* have been
if she had been properly awake, like me. But then you see *I*
have been made to notice appearances so much by being with
you sharp-eyed creatures. All the same, even for me her voice
is really more important than her looks. She can't talk, of
course; but she can say the sweetest, tenderest things with the
tone and rhythm of her voice. Of course she doesn't really
and clearly *mean* them. She says in her sleep, so to speak,
things that she *would* mean if she were awake."

But to return to Sirius's adolescence. Elizabeth had brought
up her children in the modern tradition. Living in the country
they were bound to learn a bit about sex from watching beasts
and birds. But since there was none of the still very common
guiltiness attached to sex in their minds, their interest in sex
was very desultory, and they took a surprisingly long time to
tumble to it. When Sirius achieved his first love affair, the
two younger members of the family, who were not yet at
boarding school, suspected nothing; but presently he began

to talk about it with obvious pride. Elizabeth had to use all her tact and humour to establish the convention that what was perfectly right and proper for Sirius was not to be indulged in by human children until they were grown up; and that anyhow one didn't talk about these things outside the family; and above all, not in Wales. The whole affair, she confessed to Thomas, was really rather awkward, and she only hoped she hadn't done more harm than good.

Plaxy had of course already had numerous childhood romances. Very early in her schooldays she had been violently in love with a little Welsh girl at the village school. Whether this should be regarded as a sexual sentiment or not, it was certainly an obsession. Sirius, for the first time in his life, found himself unwanted. Plaxy suddenly had no time for the games they used to play when school and homework were over; for she had always promised to do something with Gwen. She would not let him come with her when she went out with her friend, for (she said) Gwen would soon find out that Sirius could talk; and it was the whole family's most sacred taboo that outsiders must not discover yet that Sirius was something more than a super-sheep-dog. This was the secret which they had learnt to cherish as a tribal mystery. No one but the six members of the family knew about it, except Kate, who had long ago been accepted into the tribe. The other two members of the domestic staff, Mildred the nursemaid and the local girl, had both been regretfully dismissed in order that the secret might not be endangered. Sirius therefore saw the force of Plaxy's argument; but something in her voice told him that she was glad to have such a plausible excuse for leaving him behind. The sudden loss of Plaxy's companionship and confidence weighed heavily on the puppy. He did nothing but mope about the house and garden waiting for her return. When she arrived he treated her with effusive affection, but in her response there was often a note of absentmindedness or even indifference.

After a while this early romance faded out, and Sirius was reinstated. But other romances followed. When she was twelve Plaxy lost her heart to the local blacksmith's boy, Gwilim, who was eighteen. This was a one-sided affair, and

Plaxy saw little of him. She made Sirius her confidant, and he comforted her by protesting that Gwilim must be stupid not to love such a nice girl. Once he said, "Anyhow, Plaxy, *I* love you." She hugged him and said, "Yes, I know, and I love you. But I do love Gwilim. And you see he's my *kind*, and you're not. I love you differently; not less, but differently."

It was while Plaxy was pining for her brawny young black-smith that Sirius himself began to be seriously interested in the females of his own kind. Suddenly Plaxy found that her faithful confidant, who had always been ready to listen and sympathize, save during brief hunting expeditions, was no longer available. Often when she came back from school he was nowhere to be found. He failed to turn up either for homework or games or even meals. Or if he was present, he was mentally far away, and perfunctory in his sympathy. Once when she was telling him how marvellously Gwilim swung the hammer on to the red-hot iron, and how he smiled at her afterwards, Sirius suddenly sprang to his feet, stood for a moment sniffing the air, then bolted. Bitterly mortified, she said to herself, "He's not a real friend, after all. He's just a brute beast." (This expression she had recently learnt at school.) "He doesn't really understand, he doesn't really care." All this she knew to be quite untrue.

After her intermittent and always unrequited passion for Gwilim had dragged on for eighteen months, causing her much sweet sorrow and self-importance, she happened to come one day upon Sirius in the very act of love with his fragrant darling of the moment. On one occasion recently she had seen two dogs behaving in this odd way, but she had not seen Sirius doing it. She was surprised to find that it was a horrid shock to her. She hurried away, feeling unreasonably outraged and lonely.

It was two or three years after the affair with Gwilim that she made her first conquest. Conwy Pritchard, the post-master's son, was a much more responsive lover than the always friendly but never sentimental Gwilim. Conwy had a fight with another boy about her. This was very thrilling. She let herself be wholly monopolized by him. Sirius was once more neglected. When he himself happened to have an affair on, or

was crazy about hunting, he did not mind at all. At other times
he was often very lonely.

Moreover, during this enthralling intimacy with Conwy,
Plaxy's manner to Sirius sometimes showed an unwonted
harshness. It was as though she had not merely forgotten
about him, but resented his existence. Once he came upon the
youthful lovers walking in a lane, hand in hand. When she
saw him, Plaxy withdrew her hand and said in the way one
speaks to a mere dog, "Go home, Sirius!" Conwy remarked,
"Why does your father have to breed these fat-headed brutes?"
Plaxy laughed nervously, and said in a rather squeaky voice,
"Oh, but Sirius is a nice dog, really. Now off with you, Sirius.
We don't want you now." While the dog stood still in the road,
trying to analyse Plaxy's tone, to discover her precise emotional
state, Conwy made a move as though to pick up a stone, and
shouted, "Go home, you tyke." The strong silky mane rose
along Sirius's neck and shoulders, and he stalked ominously
towards Conwy, with head down, ears back, and the ghost of a
snarl. Plaxy cried out in a startled voice, "Sirius! Don't be
crazy!" He looked at her coldly, then turned and walked off
down the lane.

That evening Plaxy tried hard to make friends with Sirius,
but he would not respond. At last she said, and he could tell
that she was nearly in tears, "I'm terribly sorry about this
afternoon. But what could I do? I *had* to pretend you were
just an ordinary dog, hadn't I?" His reply disconcerted her.
"You wish I really was one, don't you!" A tear spilled out
of her eye as she answered, "Oh, Sirius, I don't. But I'm
growing up, and I must be like other girls." "Of course," he
answered, "just as I must be like other dogs, even though I'm
not really one of them, and there's no one of my sort in the
whole world." He began to move off, but she suddenly seized
him and hugged him, and said, "Oh, oh, you and I will be
friends always. Even if each of us wants to be away living
another life sometimes, we'll always, always, come back to
one another afterwards, and tell about it." "If it could be
like that," he said, "I should not be lonely even when you
were away." She smiled and fondled him. "Plaxy," he said,
"in spite of you being a girl and me a dog, you are nearest of

all creatures to lonely me." Sniffing lightly at her neck, he
added, "And the smell of you is more lovely really than the
crazy-making scents of bitches." Then with his little whimpering laugh he said, "Nice human bitch!" Plaxy blushed, but
she too laughed. She silently considered the phrase; then said,
"If Conwy called me a bitch he'd mean something horrid, and
I'd never speak to him again. When you say it, I suppose it's
a compliment." "But you *are* a bitch," he protested. "You're
a bitch of the species *Homo sapiens*, that Thomas is always
talking about as though it was a beast in the Zoo."

After the incident in the lane, Plaxy's affair with Conwy
went all awry. She saw him in a new light. He was an attractive
enough human animal, but he was nothing more. Apart from
his looks and his confident irresistible love-making, there was
nothing to him. The dog Sirius was far more human.

For a while Plaxy and Sirius maintained a very close intimacy. She even persuaded him to walk to school in the morning and bring her back in the afternoon, "to keep Conwy
from being a nuisance." Indeed the two were always together,
and never at a loss for talk. When Plaxy went to a party at
the village school, where there was to be dancing, Sirius was
of course lonely and bored, but he did not really mind. She
would come back. When Sirius went off for the day with
Thomas, it did not matter. Plaxy was lonely, but busy. And
when he came back he would tell her all about it. Even when
he went crazy over a new bitch she did not fundamentally
mind. She was secretly and unexpectedly jealous; but she
laughed at herself, and she kept her jealousy hidden. His love
affairs, she told herself, were no concern of hers, and they did
not really matter. Anyhow they were soon over; and she
herself was beginning to be interested in a boy she had met
at the dance, a young student, on holiday from Bangor.

At this time Plaxy was already (so I was told) developing
that rather queer gracefulness which became so striking in her
maturity. Whether by native composition or by constant
companionship with a non-human creature, or both, she
earned the remark of the local doctor's wife, "That child is
going to be a charmer, but somehow she's not quite human."
At school she was often called "Pussy," and there was indeed

a cat-like quality about her. Her soft hair and very large greenish blue eyes, her rather broad face, with its little pointed chin and flat nose, were obviously feline; so was her deliberate, loose-limbed walk. Sometimes when she was moody, and inaccessible to her own kind, her mother would call her "The cat that walked by itself." Not till long after I had married her did I tell her my own theory of her peculiar grace. It was, of course, the influence of Sirius, I said, that had created her "scarcely human" manner; but it was her latent antagonism to Sirius that had turned that manner cat-like. It was this character that enthralled him and exasperated him, and indeed all her admirers, from Conwy Pritchard to myself. There was one characteristic about her which particularly suggested an unconscious protest against Sirius, one which tended to be exaggerated whenever she was in conflict with him. This was the extraordinary delicacy and precision of the movements of her hands, both in practical operations and in gesture. It was as though her consciousness of herself was chiefly centred in her hands, and to a lesser degree in her eyes. This character of elegant "handedness" was something far stronger than mere felinity. It was reminiscent of those Javanese dancers who use their hands with such exquisite effect. It was at once human and "para-human," so that she seemed to me not so much cat as fay. She was indeed at once cat, fawn, dryad, elf, witch.

This description really applies to Plaxy in her early maturity, when I first met her; no doubt in childhood her peculiar charm was only nascent. But even at fifteen or sixteen the "scarcely human" grace was appearing, and was strongly attractive to the young males of her own species.

It was in this period, in fact when Plaxy was sixteen, that Elizabeth suggested to Thomas that it was high time for the child to go to boarding school. The others had gone at a much earlier age. Plaxy had been kept back partly to be an intelligent companion for Sirius. "But now," said Elizabeth, "she's much too wrapped up in him. She won't grow up properly this way. She's cloistered here in this lonely place. She needs to see more of her own kind." Thomas had been secretly planning not to send Plaxy to boarding school at all, partly for Sirius's sake, but also because the other three, he felt, had been rather deadened by it. "Cloistered!" he cried, "what about that damned nunnery where Tamsy was?" Elizabeth admitted that it had turned out rather badly, and added, "Anyhow, I thought we might send Plaxy to a more modern place, preferably co-educational. She doesn't mix enough with the boys."

Strange, or perhaps not strange at all, that both parents, though consciously modern in outlook, and on friendly terms with their children, were kept completely in the dark about their children's love affairs. They scarcely guessed that such things occurred!

I am inclined to think that there was another reason why Thomas was reluctant to send Plaxy away from home, a reason which, I suspect, Thomas himself did not recognize. Perhaps my guess is wrong, but on the few occasions when I saw father and daughter together, I felt that behind his detached and ostentatiously "scientific" interest in her lay a very strong feeling for his youngest child. And I suspect that he could not bring himself to face week-ends at Garth in her absence. Plaxy, on her side, was always rather aloof from her father, though quite friendly with him. She sometimes teased him about his mannerisms, for instance his habit of pursing his lips when he was puzzled. She was never infected by his passion for science, but when he was criticized she sometimes defended him with surprising ardour. For this reason, and in the light of subsequent events, it may be inferred that Thomas's submerged passion for her was reciprocated. Yet many years later, when Plaxy and I were married, and I was planning out this biography of Sirius with her, she ridiculed my suggestion that there was any strong feeling between her and her father, arguing that, like so many amateur psychologists, I was "always looking for a parent complex."

This book is about Sirius, not Plaxy. I should not mention the problem of Plaxy's relation with Thomas did I not feel that it may throw some light on her extraordinarily deep, though conflicting, feelings about Sirius, who was Thomas's crowning work, and the apple of his eye.

However this may be, Thomas was not easily persuaded to

let Plaxy go to boarding school. When at last he agreed in principle, and both parents began to search for a suitable school, he found weighty objections against all of them. However, in the end he accepted a certain co-educational and temperately modern establishment, situated conveniently near Cambridge.

The whole matter had, of course, been discussed with Plaxy herself, who was not easily reconciled to the prospect of what she called "going to prison." So great an upheaval in her life was bound to intimidate her. Moreover the thought came to her, "What will Sirius do without me?"

As though answering this unexpressed question, her mother said, "We think it's time for Sirius to get away for a bit too. He is to begin learning to be a sheep-dog."

Plaxy was in the end reconciled to going; and once she had made up her mind to it, she found herself sometimes strangely eager. This eagerness she could not help tracing to the prospect of being wholly a normal girl among other girls and boys. Evidently she was already suffering from a serious conflict over Sirius.

It was Thomas who talked to Sirius about the great change that was being planned. He began by saying that the time seemed to have come for Sirius to have an active life away from home. "I know quite well, of course, that I have no right to treat you as a mere dog, and that you yourself must settle your career; but you are young. In physical and mental growth, as in years, you are level with Plaxy, about sixteen. So the advice of an older mind may be helpful. Naturally I have my own ideas about your future. You are quite as intelligent as most human adolescents, and you have special advantages. I see you becoming one of the world's great animal psychologists and working with my crowd at Cambridge. But you mustn't get into the limelight yet. It would be very bad for you; and anyhow you have not had the right training yet, and of course mentally you are still too young. I think what you need now is a whole-time job as a sheep-dog, say for a year. I'll put you across as my 'super-super-sheep-dog.' I think I can fix you up with Pugh, and he will certainly treat you decently. You'll have a hard life, of course, but you need that.

And the whole experience should be interesting, and very useful to you later on. You must be careful not to give it away that you can talk; but you have had some practice at that game already. I'm afraid the job will be terribly dull at times, but most jobs are. For intellectual interest you will have to depend on your own resources. There'll be no chance of reading, but you will be able to make some very interesting observations of animal and human behaviour."

Sirius listened intently to this long harangue as he walked with Thomas on the crest of the Moel. At last he spoke, slowly and carefully; for Thomas was less practised than the others at understanding him. "Yes," he said, "I'm ready to have a shot at it. Do you think I should be able to come home fairly often?"

"Oh yes," Thomas replied, in an altered voice. "You probably haven't yet heard that Plaxy is going to boarding school. I'll tell Pugh the whole family will be very disappointed if you are not with us a lot during the holidays, because you are the family-dog, now that Gelert is dead. Pugh will arrange that all right." He added, "I'm afraid you and Plaxy will miss one another badly at first. But you will both get used to it. And after all you must live your lives separately some day, so you had better begin practising now."

"Yes, of course," said Sirius, but his tail drooped and he fell silent for a long time.

In fact only once did he speak. He suddenly asked, "Why did you make only one of me? It's going to be lonely being me."

Thomas told him that there had been a litter of "four of you," and that he alone had survived. "We have tried again many times," he said. "It's fairly easy to produce the Gelert sort, but you are a very different kettle of fish. We have two promising puppies coming on now, but they are too young yet for us to size up their powers. And there's a super-chimp, though of course she's no good to you. She's a problem, sometimes a nit-wit and sometimes too clever by half."

There was always a great bustle in the house when a child was being made ready for school. When it was the child's first term, the preparations were even more prolonged. Clothes had to be bought or made. Books, writing materials, sports gear, had all to be procured. As the day approached, Plaxy became more and more absorbed in her urgent affairs. Sirius wondered at her cheerfulness. It was supposed to be a gallant pose in the face of impending sorrow, but often it "smelt" genuine. There was little for him to do in the preparations, save for occasional messages, so he had far too much time to brood on the future. Plaxy's cheerfulness was, indeed, partly a cloak to cover her desolation at the prospect of leaving home and all that she loved. Had she been younger she might not have felt the break so badly. On the morning of her departure she happened to meet Sirius alone on the landing. She surprised him by dropping her bundle of clothes and kneeling down to hug him. With schoolgirl sentimentality but with underlying sincerity of feeling, she said, "Whatever becomes of me I shall always belong to you. Even when I have been unkind to you I belong to you. Even if—even if I fall in love with somcone and marry him some day, I shall belong to you. Why did I not know it properly until to-day?" He said, "It is I that am yours until I die. I have known it ever so long—since I bit you." Looking into his grey eyes and fondling the dense growth on his shoulder, she said, "We are bound to hurt one another so much, again and again. We are so terribly different." "Yes," he said, "But the more different, the more lovely the loving."

CHAPTER V

SHEEP-DOG APPRENTICE

ON the day after Plaxy went to boarding school Thomas took Sirius over to Pugh at Caer Blai. On the way he talked a great deal to the dog about his future, promising that when he had been with Pugh a year he should see something of the human world beyond the sheep country, and possibly settle in Cambridge. Sirius listened and consented; but he was an anxious and a sorrowing animal, and his tail would not stay proud.

One source of solid comfort lay in the fact that he knew
Pugh for a decent sort. Sirius classified human beings in
respect of their attitude to dogs; and even in later life he
found this a useful touchstone of human character. There
were those who were simply indifferent to dogs, lacking
sufficient imagination to enter into any reciprocal relation
with them. There were the "dog-lovers," whom he detested.
These were folk who sentimentalized dogs, and really had no
accurate awareness of them, exaggerating their intelligence
and loveableness, mollycoddling them and over-feeding them;
and starving their natural impulses of sex, pugnacity and
hunting. For this sort, dogs were merely animate and "pathe-
tically human" dolls. Then there were the dog-detesters, who
were either too highbrow to descend to companionship with
a dumb animal or too frightened of their own animal nature.
Finally there were the "dog-interested," who combined a
fairly accurate sense of the difference between dog and man
with a disposition to respect a dog *as a dog*, as a rather remote
but essentially like-minded relative. Pugh was of this sort.

At the farm they were greeted with an uproar by the two
super-sheep-dogs at present in Pugh's possession. The farmer
issued from the byre. He was a fresh-complexioned middle-
aged man with a scrubby reddish moustache and blue eyes
with a permanent twinkle. Sirius rather liked the smell of
him. He guessed the man must do a lot of laughing. They
were taken into the kitchen, where drinks were provided by
Mrs. Pugh, while the two men talked. Pugh had a good look
at Sirius, who was squatting on the floor by Thomas. "He's
really far too big for a sheep-dog, Mr. Trelone," said Pugh
in his singing Welsh voice. "He should be herding rhino-
ceroses, or not the little Welsh mountain sheep, anyhow.
But, my! What a head he has on him! If it's brain that counts,
Mr. Trelone, he must be a genius, isn't it! I can see it's he
that'll be running this farm and me running after the sheep
for him. Pity I'm so rheumatic!" Thomas admitted that
Sirius was pretty bright, for a dog. "He'll be useful. But don't
expect *too* much. After all, he's only a dumb animal." "Of
course," said Pugh, and then surprisingly he winked at Sirius.
"I have had experience of your dogs, Mr. Trelone, and fine

animals they are. There's Idwal here now. He's full of
strength, though he is twelve, which is very unusual for a
hard-working sheep-dog. Then there's the bitch you sent me
two years ago. Juno, we call her. My! She was quick to learn
the tricks of the trade! And now she has had that litter of six
by old Idwal. But the magic did not go into them from the
parents. They are six little fools. But I have sold them all for
a good price." "Well," said Thomas, "I told you not to
expect anything from the second generation." Pugh replied
with a sigh. "Yes, indeed, and you did, Mr. Trelone. I told
the purchasers what you said, but they would not believe it,
whatever; so what could I do but take the good price and tell
them they were fools." After lighting his pipe Pugh asked,
"And how old is this one, Mr. Trelone?" Thomas hesitated,
then said, "Fifteen, aren't you, Sirius?" The dog let slip a
"Yes," but Pugh apparently did not notice anything unusual
in his sudden grunt. "Fifteen! Holy Moses, Mr. Trelone,
but most dogs are dead long before that, and this one is not
much more than a puppy." Thomas reminded him that
longevity had been one of the aims of the experiment. "Well,"
said Pugh laughing, "if he will stay on with me he shall marry
my daughter Jane and take over the farm when I am gone.
But what is the name he answers to, Mr. Trelone, did you
say?" "I call him Sirius," said Thomas. Pugh pursed his
mouth and frowned. "That is not a handy name for calling
across the valley, is it!" He paused, puffing at his pipe, then
added, "Perhaps, Mr. Sirius, you will permit me to call you
by some other name. How would Bran do?" Sirius had tilted
his head over on one side, as though he were vainly trying to
understand this remark, obviously addressed to him. Thomas
said, "That's fine. He'll pick it up in no time."

Sirius's despondency was increased by the discovery that
even his name was to be taken from him. Surely, he thought,
he would be changed into a new being. Nothing whatever of
the old life was to be left to him but the memory of it. At
home, though he had grown up in the custom of sharing
ownership of most things with Plaxy, each of the two young
creatures had possessions of their own. Nearly all their toys
had been held in common, but when Plaxy had gone to the

village school she had also begun to acquire personal property connected with her new life—books, pens, pencils and many little nondescript treasures gained through intercourse with her fellows. Sirius also had begun to collect a few personal possessions, though far fewer than Plaxy; for, owing to his lack of hands, there were few things that he could use. There were certain ancient treasures preserved on a shelf in the minute room that had been allotted him—a rubber bone, a lump of gleaming white quartz, a sheep's skull, several picture books. And there were later-acquired possessions—more books, and music, his three writing gloves and several pens and pencils.

In his new life he had to be even more propertyless than St. Francis, for he was just a dog, and whoever heard of a dog with property? Fortunately property meant little to him; he had a propensity towards communism, due perhaps to his strong canine sociality. It should be remembered, however, that though dogs in many ways show a far more social disposition than human beings, in some respects they have a keen sense of personal ownership, for instance over bones, bitches, human friends, and localities. For Sirius, at any rate, to be completely stripped, even of his precious writing gloves, was indeed to be reduced to the status of a brute-beast. And now they intended to take away his very name. Speech, too, was of course stolen from him by the simple fact that no one on the farm could understand him. Nor was he to be able as a rule to understand them, for among themselves the Pughs talked Welsh.

Sirius's attention had wandered from the conversation, but it was recalled when Thomas rose to leave. All three went out into the yard. Thomas shook hands with Pugh, then patted Sirius, and said "Good-bye, old man. You stay there." Sirius feigned perplexity, made as if to follow Thomas, was shooed back and retreated with a puzzled whimper.

In the afternoon Pugh took Sirius and Idwal to a high valley, on the slopes of which some of his sheep were grazing. He gave a word of command in Welsh. Idwal raced off and began to round up the sheep. Sirius looked anxiously at Pugh. The command was repeated, this time along with his new name,

"Bran." He shot away to help Idwal, who was moving round behind the sheep in a great semi-circle, so as to bunch them towards Pugh down in the valley. Sirius tumbled to the situation at once, and decided to start at the opposite horn of the semi-circle and meet Idwal in the middle. Automatically each dog took charge of his own arc. Idwal's, however, was much wider than Sirius's, partly because the less experienced dog had to spend time in retrieving sheep that he had allowed to slip away up the hill, partly because Idwal was the faster animal. The operation continued till all the sheep on the hill-side had been brought down into the hollow where Pugh was standing. He said a Welsh word, and Idwal at once squatted, panting. Sirius followed suit, anxiously trying to fix the word in his memory.

Pugh then put the two dogs through sundry manœuvres with the sheep, folding them in a stone pen, fetching them out, taking them in a bunch along the valley, separating them into two equal groups, scattering them again, picking out a particular individual at which Pugh pointed with his stick. All this was done with commands in Welsh, aided by various kinds of whistling. After a while he issued commands to Idwal alone, keeping Sirius at his side. Idwal was made to single out a particular wether and hold it with his eye. He crept up to within a few feet of it, flat on the ground like a snake, all the while staring fixedly at it. Then he lay still, belly to earth, legs ready for sudden action, nose stretched out on the grass in front of him, tail on the grass behind him. The wether stared back, or made incipient movements, which Idwal checked by mere gestures. The animal just stood patiently waiting, or fidgeted with mild exasperation. Obviously it was not really afraid. It was used to this sort of game, and it recognized in Idwal's eye a command that must be obeyed.

Sirius knew that he was witnessing the famous sheep-dog trick of control by "the eye." Idwal evidently had developed "the eye" almost to perfection.

Idwal was then put through other manœuvres, which Sirius anxiously watched. Presently it was his turn to perform. The novice had strained every nerve to follow the proceedings, but he found himself badly at sea. Not only did the sheep constantly slip past him, causing Pugh to bellow with amiable rage, but also he found that fatigue was preventing him from managing his body with precision, so that he often stumbled over rocks or into holes. His great head became increasingly heavy, so that any slight slip might bowl him over like a shot rabbit. In addition to all this there was the language difficulty. Again and again Sirius found himself completely at a loss while Pugh repeated some strange Welsh noise in a frantic *crescendo*, and Idwal whimpered impatiently at his side. If only the man would talk English, thought Sirius.

But when it came to the exercise of holding the sheep by the power of the eye, Sirius found to his delight that he was by no means incompetent. Of course the process needed perfecting. Once or twice the sheep nearly broke away. It evidently did not feel itself as masterfully held as it did under Idwal, but it recognized Sirius's authority. Pugh was obviously pleased.

Presently Pugh worked the two dogs together again, but issued different commands to each by name, and also in a different tone of voice for each. Sirius had to get accustomed to acting promptly to the shriller tone, whether his name, Bran, was mentioned or not; and to ignore the deeper tone which was meant for Idwal.

At last the lesson was over. Pugh walked back along the grassy valley with the two dogs at his heels. Sirius was more tired than he had ever been before, "dog-tired," as we say. His tail hung, his head almost touched the ground. The under surface of his body was caked with bog-mud. His feet were sore, his head ached. With despair he looked forward to a whole year of this sort of thing, with no companion but the sub-human dogs and the remote Pugh. Perhaps he would forget language altogether, and when he met Plaxy again he would indeed be a dumb animal. But, worn out and despondent as he was, he was able to summon his fundamental doggedness, and promise himself that he would not be beaten by this new life. And when he caught Pugh's eye quizzing him with friendly ridicule because of his abject appearance, he stuck up his tail and wagged it, at the same time grinning, as though to say, "Oh, I have spunk all right, you'll see." This unmistakably human response startled Pugh, and set him thinking.

When they reached the farm, the two dogs were given the remains of the family midday dinner. After they had devoured this they were put into an outhouse for the night. Under the straw bedding there was a rough stone floor. It seemed to Sirius that he had hardly lain down and gone to sleep when he woke up to the sound of Idwal whining at the shut door. Sunlight streamed through the chinks.

During the following weeks Sirius was given constant work with the sheep, and he soon began to get the hang of the job. With practice he wasted less energy on retrieving his mistakes, and arrived home less tired. He was successfully learning not only the Welsh commands but the names of the fields. One day Pugh took both dogs far up among the hills to inspect the sheep on the remote high pastures and teach Sirius the names of the hillsides, streams and cwms. Here he was in familiar country, for he had often walked in this direction with Thomas. At one point the tour brought him to a bwlch within a couple of miles of his home. He even seemed to catch a faint characteristic whiff of it on the wind, but this was probably a delusion.

It did not take long for Sirius to gain sufficient experience to carry out orders unattended. For instance he could be sent to search all the bracken areas for sick sheep; for when sheep feel ill they grow fearful of their disapproving fellows, and so they hide themselves in the bracken, where, if they are not found, they may die through lack of attention. Sirius knew also how to help a bogged or crag-bound sheep to free itself. He would carefully tug at it, till the extra force enabled it to struggle into safety. And he could catch a sheep and throw it, and hold it down for Pugh or his man to inspect.

The power of his "eye", too, was greatly improving. In this matter dogs vary between excessive gentleness towards the sheep and excessive ruthlessness. Idwal was on the whole ruthless, sometimes making the sheep unduly nervous and restless. Sirius, on the other hand, was often too mild by disposition, so that his authority was not established until he had deliberately learnt a firmer policy. The difference of natural style appeared also in the whole method of the two dogs.

Idwal was of the "obstinate" type, insisting on doing everything in his own way. If Pugh prevented him he would raise his tail defiantly and simply trot off the field of action, "refusing to play." It was to Pugh's credit that on these occasions he generally gave in, with humorous vituperation, knowing well that Idwal could be trusted to do the job efficiently in his own style. Sirius, on the other hand, was of the "biddable" type. He was desperately anxious to learn, and had little faith in his own intuition. Shepherds regard this type of dog as less brilliant in the long run than the other, since they lack the conviction of genius; but it soon became clear to Pugh that Bran's docility was not due to a servile disposition. When he had learnt his lesson he often introduced novelties which greatly improved the method. Yet even when he had become an expert with sheep, he was always ready to pick up new tips from observation of other dogs at work.

Sirius could be sent out into the hills alone to select a required bunch of sheep from the flock, whether young ewes or "hoggs" (young sheep before their first shearing) or wethers; and he could bring them down from the hills to the farm without human aid. All this was real super-sheep-dog work. In order to make full use of his clever animals Pugh had arranged all his gates with latches that a dog could open or shut.

As autumn neared, the time came for bringing groups of lambs or of old or unhealthy ewes down from the mountains to be taken away for sale. This task Pugh entrusted almost entirely to Idwal and Sirius, helped sometimes by Juno. But that bright creature was of a distressingly unstable nature, and was often incapacitated by convulsions. The dogs would travel over the high moors, picking out the appropriate animals, sometimes losing them again in the cloud, and recovering them by scent, finally bringing them in a bunch along the turfy track in the high valley. All Pugh's sheep bore a red mark on the rump, but this, of course, was invisible to the colour-blind dogs. In addition the sheep bore three little slits in the left ear to mark them as Pugh's. This was invaluable to Idwal and Sirius, as a confirmation of the distinctive smell of the Caer Blai flock. Any sheep that had strayed into Caer Blai territory from a neighbouring run was soon detected and piloted home. In addition to the common smell of the flock, by the way, each individual sheep had its own peculiar odour. It did not take Sirius more than a few weeks to recognize every sheep in the flock by its smell, or even by its voice. Occasionally the dogs found a sheep that had been damaged, and then one of them had to set out to the farm to fetch Pugh. There was a recognized way of barking to signify "damaged sheep"; another, less excited, meant "sheep undamaged but crag-bound and inaccessible"; yet another meant "dead sheep."

The collecting of sheep for sale was a process which occurred now and again over many weeks. When the lambs or ewes had been brought down from the moors they had to be taken by train, or in lorries hired for the purpose, to the auction sales in the lower country. The dogs accompanied them, and Sirius thoroughly enjoyed these excursions into the great world. It was a pleasure merely to hear the English language spoken again, and to find that he could still understand it.

When the sales were over and autumn was well under way, the main task of the dogs was to guard the high valley pastures from the sheep. It is often the custom of mountain sheep to sleep on the heights and come down in the morning to the richer grazing; but in the autumn they must be prevented from doing this because the valley grass will be more urgently needed in the winter. In the autumn, too, the ewes must be prevented from grazing in marshy places, lest they should become infected by liver fluke. And autumn is a time for dipping the whole flock. As Pugh had many hundreds of sheep, this was a great undertaking, and the dogs were desperately hard worked for many days, bringing the sheep down in batches and driving them into the pen, where Pugh or one of his helpers could seize each animal in turn and force it into the dip. Sirius was pleased to find that he stood up to the strain of this great undertaking as well as Idwal, though he was not at this stage quite so fast or quite so agile.

Presently came another task. The ewe lambs had to be collected and sent to a lowland farm so that they might escape the grim conditions on the mountains during winter, the savage weather and poor food. Not till the following May would they be brought home.

In spite of all this hard work, there were days when the dogs had nothing to do but hang about the yard or accompany Pugh on his rounds, or run messages to the village. A little stationery-cum-newspaper shop in the village used to attract Sirius. Outside were posters from which he gained the most sensational news. Sometimes he put his paws on the window-sill and read the headlines of the papers displayed within, or the titles of the little rank of cheap novels. In the village he met other dogs. They gave him no trouble, because he was by now very large and "hard as nails." Out of loyalty to Thomas he tried to study the psychology of these animals; but apart from simple temperamental differences, they were men-tally all depressingly alike. The most obvious differences between them had been imposed by human conditioning. Some were disposed towards friendliness with all human beings, some were cold to strangers but obsessively devoted to their masters, some habitually fawned, some cringed.

One day in the village Sirius came upon a fine young bitch in heat, a red setter. Suddenly life was worth living once more. Her odour and touch intoxicated him. In their love-play they careered about the open space in the village while Pugh was in the pub. (Pugh seems to have had an idea that super-sheep-dogs would be cruelly bored if they were forced to sit with him inside.) The consummation of this union took place under the lascivious eyes of two schoolboys and an unemployed quarry-man.

Henceforth Sirius had a constant hunger for the village and the bitch. He was tempted to run away from the farm and have all he could of her while she was still in the mood; but he did not, because he had once seen a dog on a neighbouring farm thrashed for absenting himself from duty. Sirius was determined that he would never do anything to incur such an indignity. He had never been thrashed in his life, though occasionally hit or kicked in anger. To be deliberately thrashed seemed to him to be a mortal insult to his dignity as an intelli-gent and self-respecting person. If Pugh ever tried it on him, Pugh must be killed on the spot, whatever the consequences. But Pugh never did. Pugh belonged to the school of sheep-dog owners who pride themselves on obtaining obedience by kindness rather than ferocity. Sirius never saw him use violence on any dog. Probably he would never have beaten Sirius even if Sirius had given him serious provocation, for he had a firm though vague conviction that the new dog was somehow more than a dog, even more than a super-dog.

Several incidents had aroused this suspicion. Once he sent Sirius to the village with a basket and a ten-shilling note to fetch a pair of boots which the cobler had repaired. The dog duly brought back the boots and the change. When he arrived in the yard, Pugh, who was in the darkness of an outhouse, saw Sirius take out the boots and study the money in the basket. After looking puzzled for some time he trotted back along his tracks, nosing the ground. Presently he came on a small object which he managed with great difficulty to pick up. With obvious satisfaction he brought it back with him. When he dropped it into the basket it was visible to Pugh as a small brown disc, in fact a penny. Sirius then brought the basket to Pugh. It contained the boots, the receipted bill and the change, which consisted of two half-crowns, a florin, and seven pennies. Pugh was not so fanciful as to suppose that the dog had actually counted the change and checked it by the bill, but at least he must have spotted the difference between six pennies and seven.

Another incident made Pugh suspect that there was something "human" (as he put it) about this dog. The farmer had a few cows and a fine young bull. Sirius had once been prodded by a cow, and he had heard alarming stories about bulls. From time to time a cow was brought from one or other of the neighbouring farms to be served by the Caer Blai bull. On these occasions the dogs had to enter the paddock, round up the bull, and bring it down the lane into the farmyard for its love-making. When the deed had been done, the dogs drove the bull back to its paddock. Sirius was always very nervous, and did his stuff very badly. Idwal would face the bull with fierce persistence, and slip away from its lowered horns in the nick of time; but Sirius was far too anxious to keep his distance. The bull discovered that Sirius was a coward, and formed a habit of chasing him.

Pugh, by the way, was struck with the different ways in

which the two dogs behaved when bull and cow were brought
together in the farmyard, generally surrounded by a small
group of interested men and boys, while the women kept
discreetly indoors. Idwal nosed about the yard or lay down
to rest. Sirius watched the whole performance with the same
cheerful interest as the human spectators. It was evident that
his interest was sexual, for when the bull effected his clumsy
embrace, the dog himself gave unmistakable signs of sexual
excitement.

But the incident which impressed Pugh most, and made him
suspect that Sirius's intelligence was as quick as a man's,
occurred in connection with the bull's habit of taking the
offensive against the cowardly Sirius. Pugh had gone to the
village with Idwal. Owen, the hired man, was ploughing in a
remote field. Somehow the bull managed to break out of its
paddock into the lane. It trotted down into the yard, saw
Jane with a basket of washing, and approached her, snorting.
Always a nervous girl, she screamed, dropped the basket and
slipped into the stable. The bull spent a few minutes tossing
the clothes, then made off down the lane. Meanwhile Mrs.
Pugh had made a tentative sortie from the house. Then Sirius
appeared, and raced down the lane after the bull. He did not
overtake it till after it had reached the main road. Then he
silently rushed at it, and seized its tail. With a roar the bull
swung round, but Sirius had let go, and was retreating towards
the lane, barking. The bull followed him, and he led it back
to the farmyard and into its field. It was now rather blown,
but Sirius led it round and round the field, till its ardour was
cooled. The less anxious it was to follow him, the more bold
grew Sirius. When it came to a standstill, he rushed in and
nipped its hind leg. The reinfuriated beast chased him once
more, but was soon exhausted. This process was repeated
several times, till Sirius noticed that the two women had put
some strands of barbed wire across the gap in the hedge. Then
he retreated, with a proud tail, leaving a bull that was thoroughly
cowed. Henceforth Sirius was always able to deal with the
bull or any other cattle.

Some time after this incident Sirius did something which was
far beyond super-sheep-dog capacity.

Throughout his first term he was desperately lonely. He longed for his own people, and most of all for Plaxy. If only he could write a letter! But he had no writing-glove, and no stationery. And anyhow the task of putting a stamp on a letter had always defeated him.

He knew he could write a few words very badly by holding a pencil in his mouth; if he could find one, and paper. He had once seen Pugh take out pen, ink and paper from the drawer in the oak dresser. One day, when Mrs. Pugh and Jane were milking, he slipped into the kitchen, opened the drawer, and found in it several sheets of paper, also envelopes, a pen, an ink-pot, and a pencil with a broken point. He stole a sheet and an envelope. Pen and ink seemed too complicated, and the pencil was useless, so he left these, and took merely an envelope and paper to the dog's outhouse. He put them in an old packing case under some straw.

There was now nothing for it but to wait until someone should need to sharpen the pencil. He seized every opportunity to sneak into the kitchen and look into the drawer. Meanwhile he spent much thought in planning exactly how he would write his letter, and what he would say. Sometimes he practised. Holding a splinter of slate in his mouth, he scribbled on the slate doorstep. The process was difficult, because his nose was always in the way, and he could not see what he was doing; and generally the slate-splinter snapped.

At last, after many days, he found that the pencil had been sharpened. He took it away to the outhouse.

Not till several days later did Sirius find an opportunity of writing his letter. In spidery capitals it said, "Dear Plaxy, I hope you are happy. I am lonely without you, terribly. Love, Sirius." With great care he addressed the envelope, hoping that his memory was trustworthy. He had serious difficulty in folding the paper and putting it into the envelope. Then he licked the gummy-edge, closed it, and held his paw on it. He had intended to post it unstamped; but the thought that Plaxy would have to pay threepence, double postage, on it distressed him so much that he decided to wait in the hope of finding some stamps in the drawer. When at last a sheet of six three-halfpenny stamps appeared, he ran off with them and set about trying to detach one. First he held the sheet between his paws and pulled with his teeth. The stamp tore across the middle, and the bit in his mouth stuck to his wet teeth, so that he could not get rid of it. Flustered by this experience, he decided to think the problem out more carefully. He hit on a plan. He held the envelope down with his paw and licked the right-hand top corner. Then with extreme care he took up the stamp-sheet in his teeth and laid it on the envelope so that one of the corner stamps was roughly in the right position. This was difficult, because as usual his nose was in the line of sight. He let go, and inspected the result. The stamp was crooked, and not wholly on the envelope. Hastily he lifted it off again and replaced it, well on the envelope. Again he inspected it, then carefully pulled it into better position. Then he pressed it on with his paw. When he thought the gum was dry, he held the sheet of stamps down with his paw and gently pulled the letter with his teeth. The letter came away, with the stamp intact, and part of the next one projecting over the edge. This he trimmed off with his teeth. He then restored the mangled sheet of stamps to the drawer. Not till he came back to the letter did he notice that the stamp was upside down.

He hid his letter under the straw and waited till his next errand to the village. This did not occur till some days later. It was fairly common for him to be sent with letters to the post, but on this occasion his own was the only one. He trotted off with his basket and an order for the grocer; and his letter. He went straight to the post office, put down his basket, took out the letter, raised himself against the wall, and slipped the precious document into the box.

This was no unusual sight in the village. Dr. Huw Williams, who was passing, scarcely noticed it; but when, next day, he met Mr. Pugh and wished him good day, he mentioned the incident, complimenting him on his dog's intelligence. Now Pugh had sent off no letter that day. He wondered whether his wife had written to her mother in Bala, or if Jane had entrusted Bran with a love-letter. This possibility disturbed him, for though by nature a friendly man, prone to treat people with respect and trust, he was no modern parent. When he reached home he made inquiries. Mrs. Pugh and Jane both denied that they had given Bran a letter. Pugh went to the drawer and saw that the stamps had been badly mauled. One was missing, and two others were torn. In a burst of indignation he charged his daughter with clandestine correspondence, theft, lying and clumsiness. Jane defended herself with vigour, and added, "Go and ask Bran whose letter it was." That sarcasm put a wild idea into Pugh's head. He went to the drawer again and picked up the pencil. There were tooth-marks on it—Bran's or his own? Fantastic doubt!

CHAPTER VI

BIRTH-PANGS OF A PERSONALITY

TO Sirius, Plaxy's first term at boarding school seemed endless, but in due season the holidays loomed near. Sirius had counted the days by putting a pebble a day in the old packing-case. One day, when he had collected almost the right number of pebbles but was expecting two or three more days of labour, he returned with Pugh and the other dogs from the moors, with early snow on Pugh's hat and the dogs' backs, and encountered Thomas in the yard. Sirius rushed at him and nearly knocked him down with a wild welcome. After both men had shaken the worst of the snow from their clothes, Pugh took Thomas into the kitchen. Sirius knew that he was not supposed to go into the house when he was in a mess; but, after a violent shake, in he went. Mrs. Pugh smiled indulgently.

Thomas asked Pugh about Sirius's success as a sheep-dog, and was given a good report. Sirius had proved himself as hardy as Idwal, and far more cunning and responsible. But he was not always quite "on the spot." He was a bit of a day-dreamer. He was sometimes caught napping. A sheep might escape from the flock and run away before Sirius woke to the situation. It was "as though he had been thinking of something else." After making the report Pugh nodded knowingly at Thomas, who merely changed the subject. Before they parted, Pugh insisted on handing over to Thomas ten shillings less fourpence halfpenny. This sum he described as Bran's earnings, "less a small item of expenditure." Saying this, he stared hard at Sirius and winked. The dog hastily looked away, but could not prevent a snort of surprise and a tremor of the tail. Thomas tried to refuse the money, but Pugh insisted.

The journey home through driving sleet was a journey to heaven. Thomas explained that he and Elizabeth had come home a couple of days early to get the house ready before Plaxy and Giles arrived from boarding school. Tamsy and Maurice, both of them undergraduates, were visiting friends.

Sirius recounted some of his experiences. "It has all been very good for me, I know, but I really don't think I *can* go on with that life any longer. I should go mad with loneliness. No talk, no books, no music. And all the while knowing the world is so big and strange beyond the farm. Plaxy will leave me far behind."

This speech came as a shock to the not very imaginative Thomas. He remarked cautiously, "Oh, it's not quite as bad as all that, is it? Anyhow, we must talk it over carefully." Sirius knew from his tone that he was rather put out about it, and that there would be trouble.

Elizabeth greeted Sirius as one of her children, hugging him and kissing him. He showed none of his former boisterousness, but gave a tremulous little whine of painful joy.

Next day Giles arrived, and in the evening Plaxy. Thomas took the car to the station to meet her, Sirius sitting beside him. Out of the train stepped the long-legged schoolgirl in her school hat and coat. Having kissed her father, no doubt with her customary rather distant affection, she squatted down to hug Sirius. "I got your letter," she whispered, "but I couldn't answer, could I?" Of course she couldn't. Sirius savoured the well-known voice with delight; but with an undertone of anxiety, for school life had changed it.

During the first part of the holidays Sirius simply enjoyed being home again. He scarcely noticed the two disquieting facts that had obtruded themselves right at the beginning.

Thomas would not let him off his sheep-dog apprenticeship; Plaxy was changed.

For a week or so he was content to live the old family life, which, though by no means entirely harmonious, did afford to every member the invaluable experience of belonging to a true community. There was always talk going on, and Sirius after his long isolation felt a great need for conversation. There were many walks with members of the family, and several long expeditions up Moelwyn, the Rhinogs, Arenig. But what Sirius now craved most was indoor life, with reading, music, talk, and all the little affairs that fill the day.

After a day or two of almost entirely social life he began to take up once more some of his old private occupations. Not only did he read as much as his eyesight would let him, and experiment a good deal in music; he also contrived adventures in his private art of odour. This he did by collecting all kinds of materials that had striking or significant smells, and blending them in saucers. Sometimes, much to the amusement of the family, he laid his materials out in a long trail round the garden path, and then followed it from beginning to end, giving tongue in a weird diversified chant that was neither human nor canine. After these olfactory adventures he was often very silent and remote. Sometimes they seemed to put him in the mood for hunting, for he would disappear for many hours, returning tired and dirty. Not infrequently he brought back a rabbit or hare, or even a wild duck or grouse, handing it over to Giles to prepare for cooking. But often he brought nothing, and behaved as though he himself had gorged.

Not much of his time was spent in solitary occupations, for he craved social intercourse more than ever, chiefly with Plaxy. Gradually it dawned on him that when she and he were out together they did not always find the careless intimacy which formerly had never failed them. Sometimes neither of them seemed able to think of anything to say; sometimes Sirius found himself bored with Plaxy's stories of school life; sometimes she seemed to have lost interest in all the things that formerly they had enjoyed together. Sirius expected not only that she would have out-distanced him in knowledge of school subjects, which of course she had, but also that she would be

more keenly and persistently interested in the life of the mind.
But she was nothing of the sort. She was mainly absorbed, it
seemed, in her school companions, with all their loves and
hates; and in the teachers, male and female, who were playing
so large a part in her new life. When he asked her to teach
him some of the wonderful things that she must have learnt
during the term, she said she would, some time; but always
she found some excuse to postpone the lesson. At last there
came a time when no excuse was available. She was idling in
an easy chair petting the cat, Smut, who was purring heartily.
Sirius, whose thirst for knowledge was at this time more
insistent than discriminate, suggested that she should tell him
what she had learnt during the term about the Cavaliers
and Roundheads. Cornered, she blurted out, "Oh, I just *can't*
swot in the holidays." He did not ask her again.

It was not that they were any less fond of one another. On
the contrary, each craved the other's society; but always there
was a faint mist of remoteness between them. And occasionally
open antagonism occurred, as when Plaxy ostentatiously doted
upon Smut, half in jest, half in earnest, calling him "my black
panther," affirming that she was a witch, and witches always
had black cats as their companions, and never clumsy dogs.
But antagonism was rare. More often there was a faintly
awkward friendliness. At this time Plaxy developed a maiden
shyness in relation to Sirius. He was bewildered, for instance,
by her new and to him quite inexplicable reluctance to respond
to their familiar urinary tune by singing the antistrophe that
signified assent, and crouching to relieve herself. Although this
new shyness was only a passing phase, it was to recur whenever
Plaxy was feeling too much involved with Sirius.

In fact her estrangement from him was partly a reaction
against her deep-rooted entanglement with him. But he, who
was far more conscious of her aloofness than she was herself,
attributed it to the fact that she had outstripped him both in
learning and in experience of human people, while he had
stagnated at Caer Blai. Once or twice, however, when she had
gently twitted him with being interested in nothing but learning, he wondered whether it was she that was stagnating. He
had conceived a real passion for learning, for finding out about

the great world, and understanding the miracle of human nature and the minor miracle of his own unique nature. The arid weeks behind him and the arid weeks to come filled him with a thirst not only for intelligent companionship but also for intellectual life. His proximity to the sub-human perhaps made him over-anxious to prove that even the loftier ranges of the human spirit were not beyond him.

It was during these holidays that another and a long-established source of alienation between Plaxy and Sirius took on a new form and a more disturbing effect. Even in earlier days Plaxy had developed a peculiarly keen interest in seeing. As a child she had often shown disappointment and exasperation with Sirius for his failure to share this delight with her. She would rhapsodize over the colour and shape of a speedwell, or of hills receding hazily one behind the other in a cadence of russet to purple. Once she had innocently called upon him to admire the golden elegance of her own young arm. On all such occasions his response was perfunctory, since vision was never for him a gateway to heaven. Even of Plaxy's arm he could say only, "Yes, it's lovely because it has the look of a handy tool. And it smells good, like the rest of you, and it's good to lick." From childhood onwards Plaxy had amused herself with pencil and paint box, and at school her gift for colour and shape had won her much praise from the drawing mistress. In the holidays she spent a good deal of time looking at reproductions of famous pictures, and in discussing art with her mother. Even more absorbed was she in drawing schoolgirls in blatantly graceful poses, and in painting the view of the Rhinogs from her bedroom window. Sirius found all this fuss over the looks of things very boring. He had tried hard to develop a taste for pictorial art, but had failed miserably. Now that Plaxy was so absorbed in it, he felt "left out." If he took no notice of her creations she was disappointed. If he praised them, she was irritated, knowing quite well that he could not really appreciate them. Yet all this visual interest, which at bottom, no doubt, was a protest against Sirius, she also longed to share with him. Thus did these two alien but fundamentally united creatures torture one another and themselves.

As the end of the holidays approached, Sirius's anxiety about his future increased. He took every opportunity of tackling Thomas on the subject. But Thomas always managed to turn the talk in some other direction. When at last the time came for Plaxy to return to school, it was assumed that Sirius would return to Caer Blai. When Plaxy said good-bye to him, she begged him to go back with a good grace. She herself, she said, hated leaving home. But he knew quite well from her voice and her tingling smell that, though in a way she did hate it, in another way she was glad and excited. But he—well, in a way he too was glad, surprised though he was at this discovery. He was glad to get away from the mist that had come between him and Plaxy; and also because a mist had come between him and the whole of his beloved home life. What was it? Why was there this remoteness. What was it that kept rising between him and all his dearest things, making him defiant and wild? Was it just that he wanted a fragrant bitch, a sweet though stupid companion of his own kind, instead of these stinking humans? Or did he need something more? Was it the ancestral jungle beast that sometimes woke in him? His farewell to Plaxy was seemingly all affection and sorrow. She never guessed that another and an alien Sirius was at that moment yawning himself awake, finding her company tiresome and her smell unpleasant.

There followed a term of bitter weather and heavy work with the sheep. All the dogs were now kept busy stopping the sheep from going up to the heights for the night, for fear of snow. This meant staying with them till dark whenever snow seemed likely. Sometimes, without warning, heavy snow would fall on the tops during the night, and then dogs and men would have to go up in the morning to bring the flock down into the valleys. Generally there is far less snow in Wales than in the more northerly mountain districts, but a run of severe winters caused the dogs much toil and a good deal of danger. On several occasions, up and down the district, dogs and even men were lost in the snow. Sometimes sheep were completely buried under snowdrifts. Only a dog could then find them; and often only a man with a spade could rescue them. Sometimes the snow covered both high and low pastures. So long as it remained soft, the sheep could scrape it away with their feet and feed on the grass below. But when the surface was hardened by frost following thaw, this was impossible, and then hay had to be taken out to them. This was a job for Pugh or his man with a cart and the old mare, Mab. But the dogs, being super-dogs, were expected to report on the condition of the snow. If it was hard, they would come home to scratch and whine at Pugh's feet.

Sometimes when Sirius was out on the hills alone in the winter dawn, examining the condition of the snow and looking for sheep in distress, the desolation of the scene would strike him with a shivering dread of existence. The universal carpet of snow, the mist of drifting flakes, the miserable dark sheep, pawing for food, the frozen breath on his own jaws, combined to make him feel that after all *this* was what the world was really like; that the warm fireside and friendly talk at Garth were just a rare accident, or perhaps merely a dream. "The whole world is just a dreary accident, with a few nice accidents mixed up in the mass." He had still to learn that there was something far worse than bitter weather with the near prospect of food and comfort, far worse even than his bitter loneliness at Caer Blai; and that the most horrible things in the world were all man-made. It was perhaps well that he did not yet realize the depth of man's folly and heartlessness, for if he had done so he might have been turned against the dominant species for ever. As it was, he attributed all evil to accident or "fate," and in fate's very indifference he sometimes found a certain exhilaration. Plodding home through the snow one day (so he told me long afterwards) he had a kind of inner vision of all living things, led by man, crusading gallantly against indifferent or hostile fate, doomed in the end to absolute defeat, but learning to exult in the battle, and snatching much delight before the end. And he saw himself as a rather lonely outpost in this great war, in which victory was impossible, and the only recompense was the sheer joy of the struggle. But by the very next day, so he said, his mood had changed from self-dramatization to an amused acceptance of his little-ness and impotence.

Before the lambing season Pugh went over all his ewes to

cut locks of wool away from their udders, so that their lambs should not swallow wool and clog their stomachs. This simple process itself meant a great deal of work for men and dogs, but the actual lambing meant a great deal more. The flock had to be met at dawn on its way down from the heights. During the day the men would be hard at work, but the dogs would often be idle. Pugh noticed that Bran was far more interested than ordinary dogs and even super-sheep-dogs in the process of birth. This was one of the many signs that convinced him that Bran was really a sort of man-dog. Pugh had gradually formed a habit of giving Bran fairly detailed instructions in English, and they were always accurately carried out. He still had no idea that Bran himself could talk, and he kept his convictions about the dog's nature strictly to himself. But he increasingly treated him as an assistant rather than as a chattel, an assistant who was particularly bright and responsible, but lamentably clumsy through lack of hands. All Sirius's clever arrangements for fetching and carrying, for pouring from tins and bottles, and so on, failed to compensate for his grievous handlessness. One useful operation that needed dexterity he could do. He could drive Mab, the old mare, whether with the spring cart, the heavy cart, the roller or the harrow. Ploughing inevitably remained beyond him. And of course he could not load a cart with turnips or hay or manure, and so on. Nor could he manage the simple task of harnessing the mare. Buckles defeated him.

When, at the end of the school term, Elizabeth came to fetch Sirius home, his joy was tempered by a self-important doubt as to how Pugh would manage without him.

During these holidays he busied himself in intellectual work. Taxing his eyesight, he even plunged into Wells's *Outline of History* and *The Science of Life*. He also pestered members of the family to read poetry aloud to him, and passages from the Bible. He was very sensitive to the rhythm of verse and prose, and of course to the musical quality of words; but vast tracts of literature meant nothing to him, save as verbal music, because his subconscious nature had not the necessary human texture to respond to them emotionally, nor had he the necessary associations in his experience. His strong feeling for personality led him at one time into an obsession with Browning. Later came a more lasting interest in what he called "the poetry of self and universe." Hardy at one time fascinated him. The early Eliot intoxicated him with new rhythms and with a sense of facing the worst in preparation for a new vision. But the vision never came. Instead came orthodoxy. Sirius longed for that vision. He hoped for it from the younger moderns; but though he was even younger than any of them, they meant little to him.

Music was ever for Sirius a more satisfying art than poetry. But it tortured him, because the texture of his own musical sensibility remained alien to the human. He felt that he had to choose between two evils. Either he must express himself with full sincerity but in utter loneliness, unappreciated by dogs or men; or, for the sake of his underlying brotherhood with man, he must violate his finer canine sensibility, and discipline himself to the coarser human modes, in the hope that somehow he might express himself adequately to man in man's own musical language. For this end he was anxious to absorb as much human music as possible.

His relations with Plaxy at this time were uneasy. While he was obsessed with the life of the mind, she was obsessed with personal relations. The loves and hates of school were still far more important to her than book-learning. And her school life was utterly different from Sirius's hard and anxious life on the farm. It might have been expected that in these circumstances dog and girl would find little in common; and indeed superficially there was little enough. On their walks they were often silent, while each pursued a private train of thought. Sometimes one or the other would hold forth at some length, and the soliloquy would be punctuated by sympathetic but rather uncomprehending comments by the listener. Occasionally this mutual incomprehension caused exasperated outbursts.

Their discord was often increased by a tendency on Plaxy's part to express her vague sense of frustration in subtle little cruelties. Very often the cattish torture of Plaxy's behaviour was unconscious. For instance, at times when she was subconsciously resentful of his emotional hold over her, the affectionate ragging which they sometimes indulged in would change its character. Not knowing what she did, she would twist his ear too violently, or press his lip upon his teeth too hard. Then, realizing that she had hurt him, she would be all contrition. More often her felinities were mental. Once, for example, when they were coming down the moel during a brilliant sunset, and Plaxy was deeply stirred by the riot of crimson and gold, of purple and blue and green, she said, not remembering how it must wound her colour-blind companion, "Sunsets in pictures are so tiresome, but only boors and half-wits are not stirred by real sunsets."

Apart from this infrequent and often thoughtless exposure of her claws, Plaxy kept up the manner of friendliness even when secretly she was straining away from him; for fundamentally each respected the other's life and was thankful for the other's society. The roots of these two alien beings were so closely intertwined that in spite of their divergence each needed the other. One unifying subject of common interest they always had, and they often talked about it. Both these sensitive young creatures were beginning to puzzle about their own nature as persons. Both, for very different reasons, were revolting against the purely scientific assumptions of their home, according to which a person was simply the psychological aspect of a very complex physical organism. Plaxy was feeling that persons were the most real of all things. Sirius was more than ever conscious of the inadequacy of his canine body to express his super-canine spirit. The word "spirit" seemed to them to epitomize the thing that science left out; but what precisely ought to be meant by the word they could not decide. Plaxy had come under the influence of a member of the school staff for whom she had conceived a great admiration. This quick-witted and sensitive young woman taught biology, but was also a lover of literature. It seems to have been her influence, by the way, that first made Plaxy clearly feel that, however important science was, for herself not science but literature was the way to full mental life. The young teacher had once said, "I suppose I ought to believe that Shakespeare was *just* a highly developed mammal, but I can't *really* believe it. In some sense or other he was—

well, a spirit." This remark was the source of Plaxy's juvenile dalliance with the word "spirit"; and then of Sirius's.

The young dog was now seriously worrying about his future. Sheep-farming was not without interest, now that he was helping Pugh in a more human way; but it was not what he was *for*. What *was* he for? Was he *for* anything? He remembered his desolate impression on the snow-clad moors that the whole world was just a purposeless accident. Now, he somehow could not believe it. Yet the all-wise Thomas said no one was *for* anything, they just *were*. Well, what could a unique creature like him, a sheer freak, find to *be*? How could he discover peace of mind, of spirit? Thomas did not see why he should worry. Thomas had a nice slick programme for him.

One evening when the others had gone to bed, man and dog were left in the sitting-room in the course of one of those long talks which had been so great a factor in the education of Sirius. They were sitting before the fire, Thomas in one of the easy chairs, Sirius luxuriating on the couch. Thomas had been telling him of the progress of his research, and explaining the latest theory about the localization of mental powers in the brain-centres. He was pleased at the dog's shrewd questions, and had said so. Sirius, after a pause in which he absently licked a paw while gazing into the fire, said, "Even by human standards I really am fairly bright, am I?" "Indeed you are," was the prompt reply. Sirius continued, "You see, I don't seem able to think properly. My mind keeps wandering. I start out to think about something, and then suddenly, with a jolt I wake up to find I've been thinking about something else instead; and often I can't even remember what it was, or even what the first subject was. It's frightening. Do you think I'm going mad? It's like—going off on the trail of a rabbit and then being led aside by a hare, and then streaking off on the smell of a fox, and twisting and doubling on the trail till all of a sudden you find yourself up against water, and no trail at all. And then you say to yourself, 'How on earth did I get here? What in hell was I doing?' Human beings don't think that way, do they?" Thomas laughed with delight. "Don't they!" he said. "I certainly think that way myself, and I'm not exceptionally scatter-brained." Sirius sighed with relief, but continued, "Then there's another thing. Sometimes I manage to follow a trail of thought quite well for a long time, in and out, up and down, but always with my mind's nose on the trail; and then suddenly I find—well, the weather has changed and given it all a different meaning. It was warm and bright, but now it's cold and dank. No, worse than that! It was fox, and now it's cat, so to speak, or just dull cow, or horrible menagerie tiger. No, *it's* the same but *I* have changed. I wanted it desperately, and now I don't. There's an entirely new me. That's frightening, too." Thomas reassured him. "Don't worry, old thing!" he said. "It's just that you're a rather complicated person, really, and there's too much diversity in you to be easily systematized."

Sirius once more licked his paw, but soon stopped to say, "Then I really am a *person*, not just a laboratory animal?" "Of course," said Thomas, "and a very satisfactory person, too; and an excellent companion for *this* person, in fact the best I have, apart from one or two colleagues." Sirius added for him, "And Elizabeth, I suppose." "Of course, but that's different. I meant man-to-man companionship." Sirius pricked his ears at that phrase, and Thomas laughed at himself. Said the dog, "Then why apprentice me to a sub-human job, which is bound to dehumanize me?" "My dear Sirius," replied Thomas with some heat, "we have had all that out before, but let's try to settle it now, once for all. It's true you have a first-class human intelligence, but you are not a man, you are a dog. It's useless to train you for some human trade, because you can't do it. But it's immensely important to give you some responsible practical work until the time comes for you to join us at Cambridge. You are not to be an imitation man. You are a super-super-dog. This sheep-dog life is very good for you. Remember you are not yet seventeen. There's no hurry. Your pace is Plaxy's, not Idwal's. If you grow up too quick, you'll fossilize too quick. Stick to sheep. There's a lot in that job, if you give your mind to it. When you come to us at the lab we want you to have had experience of a normal dog's way of life."

Inwardly Sirius said, "Blast the lab!" but to Thomas he

said, "I *have* been putting my mind into the job. And as a matter of fact it's not just sheer dog's work now. Pugh has been giving me a lot of man's work to do. He knows I am different from Idwal. But—well, that sort of work, though it *is* largely man's work, does deaden the mind. And the mind —is *me*. I'm not human, but also I'm not canine. Fundamentally I'm just the sort of thing you are yourself. I have a canine clothing, just as you have a human clothing, but *I*— I am"—he paused and looked warily at Thomas—"a spirit, just as you are." Thomas snorted, and presently his smell went rather sour. Then almost in the tone of a liberal-minded parent expostulating with a child that had said something "rude," he remarked, "Why use that silly meaningless word? Besides, who has been putting such ideas into your head?"

Sirius did not answer this last question. Instead, he said, "There's something in me very different from my canine body. If *you* had a dog's body instead of a man's, you would grasp that as clearly as I do. You couldn't help it. You would feel like someone trying to typewrite on a sewing machine, or make music with a typewriter. You would never mistake the sewing machine for *you, yourself.*"

"I see what you mean," said Thomas, "but the conflict is not really between your spirit and your canine body; it's between the canine part of your body and the super-canine part, that I gave you."

There was silence in the room for a full minute. Then Sirius yawned, and felt the warmth of the fire on his tongue. He said, "That sounds so sensible; and yet, though I'm only seventeen and only a dog, I can smell there's something wrong with it. It's only just a bit more true than the 'soul' dope that the parsons give—the Rev. Davies, for instance, when he called on us, and tried to convert you to Methodism, while you tried to convert him to scientific method. Do you remember? He caught me staring too interestedly at him, and he said I looked as if I was more open to persuasion than you were yourself, and it was a pity, almost, that God hadn't given *me* a soul to be saved."

Thomas smiled, and rose to go to bed. As he passed Sirius he gave his ear a friendly pull, and said, "Oh, well, nearly all great questions turn out in the end to be misconceived. Probably both our answers are wrong."

Sirius, getting down from the couch, suddenly realized that he had been once more side-tracked from his purpose, which was to discuss his future. "One thing is sure," he said, "My job is not just sheep, and it's not to alternate between being a sheep-dog and being a super-laboratory-animal. It's the spirit."

Thomas came to a halt. "Oh, very well," he said gently, respectfully, but with a faint ridicule that did not escape Sirius. "Your job's the spirit." Then after a pause he added with friendly sarcasm, "We must send you to a theological college."

Sirius gave a snort of indignation. He said, "Of course I don't want the old religious dope. But I don't want just the new science dope either. I want the truth." Then, realizing that he had said the wrong thing, he touched his master's hand. "I'm afraid I'm not working out according to plan," he said. "But if I am really a *person* you shouldn't expect me to. Why did you make *me* without making a world for me to live in. It's as though God had made Adam and not bothered to make Eden, nor Eve. I think it's going to be frightfully difficult being me."

Thomas laid his hand on the dog's head. The two stood gazing into the dying fire. The man said to the dog, "It's my fault that you are more than a dog. It's my meddling that woke the 'spirit' in you, as you call it. I'll do my best for you, I promise. And now let's go to bed."

CHAPTER VII

WOLF SIRIUS

THOMAS succeeded in persuading Sirius to complete his year with Pugh, assuring him with Machiavellian subtlety that it would be an invaluable "spiritual training." And it was. It was a Spartan, an ascetic life; for Sirius accepted all the ordinary sheep-dog conditions. At times it was a life of

grim hardship and overwork. Men and dogs returned from
their labour dead tired, and fit for nothing but supper and
sleep. But there were other times when there was little to be
done that did not necessitate human hands. Then Sirius used
to lie about pretending to sleep, but in fact trying desperately
to think about man and himself, and the identity of the spirit
in them, a task in which he was singularly unsuccessful.

Since Pugh was by now fairly well in the know about Sirius,
Thomas had arranged that during his last term the dog should
have more or less regular hours, like a human worker, so that
he could frequently go home and put in a little study. The
word "study," of course, was not mentioned, but Pugh agreed
with a knowing wink.

Expeditions over the high hills were becoming rather much
for the ageing Welshman, so he handed over more and more
responsibility to Sirius. He arranged with the saddler to make
two pairs of small panniers which could be strapped on to the
dogs' flanks. These he filled with lotions, medicines, bandages.
Sirius could now travel far afield and doctor sick sheep without
Pugh having to accompany him. He would set off with Idwal,
who now accepted him as a leader, and spend the day inspecting
the whole flock. When they had rounded up a bunch of sheep
into some remote moorland pen, Sirius would examine each
one of them for foot-rot or fly-strike. Any animal that showed
restlessness, or kept trying to nibble at its own back, was
probably infected with fly-strike. Sirius was sufficiently human
to dislike exposing the grubs with his own teeth, and cleaning
out the superficial wound with his tongue; but the work had
to be done. By keeping a sharp watch on the flock, and
tackling the earliest symptoms himself, he was able to reduce
to a minimum the number of advanced cases which demanded
attention from man's exploring fingers. But inevitably a few
were not found till they were deeply infected. These had to be
taken away for human treatment. Very rarely Sirius came on
sheep lying down, neither ruminating nor sleeping, and with
great open wounds seething with grub. For these he had to
fetch human aid at once, or they would soon die. Pugh, by the
way, had put all the drugs and ointments into tins with clip-on
lids which Sirius could open without excessive difficulty.

When the shearing season arrived the whole flock had to be brought down in batches, and put into pens to be tackled each in turn by one of the half-dozen shearers who were going the round of all the flocks in the district. The actual shearing was a job which Sirius would never be able to do. Nothing but human hands or some mechanical device could ever divide a sheep from its fleece. Sirius would stand about watching the manual dexterity of the shearers with fascination and sadness. The sheep, on its haunches between the knees of the man, would sometimes struggle, generally when its skin was nipped and little red stains appeared on the cream of its inner wool; but in the main the blades peeled off its coat as though merely undressing the creature. The gleaming inner surface of the fleece, as it was rolled back upon its own drab exterior, was a wave of curd. When the operation was over, the naked, angular beast would spring away bleating with bewilderment.

Throughout the last few months of his year with Pugh, Sirius was much absorbed in his work; but also he was in a state of suppressed excitement, and of conflict. He delighted in the prospect of release from this servitude, yet in spite of himself he regretted that the connection must be broken. He had become thoroughly interested, and he had a real affection for Pugh. It seemed mean to desert him. And though Cambridge promised novelty and a great diversity of human contacts, he was sufficiently imaginative to realize that town life might not suit him at all.

There was also another and a deeper conflict in his mind, one which was increasingly troubling him. It was the endless conflict over his relations with the dominant species of the planet. Never did he cease to feel that man and he were at once poles asunder and yet in essential nature identical. At this early stage the trouble had not come clear to him. He could not yet focus it. But to explain his obscure and still largely inarticulate distress, his biographer must set forth Sirius's plight with a clarity which he himself had not yet attained. Men were many and he was one. They had walked the earth for a million years or more, and they had finally possessed it entirely. And he? Not only was he himself a unique product of their cunning, but the whole race of dogs were their creation. Only the wolf was independent. And wolves were now no more than a romantic relic that man would never again seriously fear. Little by little, through their million years, men had worked out their marvellous human way of living, culminating in civilization. With those enviable hands of theirs they had built themselves their first crude forest shelters, then settlements of huts, then good stone houses, cities, railways. With nicely correlated hand and eye they had made innumerable subtle implements, from microscopes to battleships and aeroplanes. They had discovered so much, from electrons to galaxies. They had written their millions of books, which they could read as easily as he could follow a trail on a damp morning. And some few of those books even he must read, because they had the truth in them, a bit of it. He, by contrast, with his clumsy paws and imprecise vision, could never do anything worthy of the brain that Thomas had given him. Everything worth while in him had come from mankind. His knowledge, such as it was, they had taught him. His love of the arts, of wisdom, of the "humanities"! God! Would that wisdom lay rather in "caninities"! For him there was no possible life-aim except to help on in some minute way the great human enterprise, whether through the humble work of sheep-tending or the career that Thomas had planned for him as a museum piece and a tenth-rate scientist. For him there could be no wisdom but man's alien wisdom; just as for him there could be no real loving but the torturing business of loving these infinitely alien human creatures. Or would Thomas some day produce others of his kind for him to love? But they would be so young.

It was indeed mankind that had shown him what love was, with their gently ministering and caressing hands and their consoling voices. His ever-trusted and caninely revered foster-mother had loved him always as her own child; or only with so slight a difference that neither she herself nor her Plaxy but only he with his keen ears and nose could detect it. For this difference he could feel no resentment. It was not indeed strictly a difference of love at all but of animal maternal attraction. Then Thomas, yes Thomas also had shown him what love was, but in a different aspect, in the aspect of "man-to-man" intelligent companionship. Of course Thomas really loved his science far more. Probably he would be ready to submit his creature to any torture, physical or spiritual, for the advancement of his science, of his creative work. But this was as it should be. God himself, if there was a God, might be like that. Might he? Might he? Anyhow, Sirius could understand this attitude. It was not with Thomas nor with Elizabeth but with Plaxy that he had found the essence of love, the close mutual dependence and sharing. Yet strangely it was often the thought of Plaxy that wakened the other mood in him, in which he rebelled against humanity's dominance.

Throughout the summer at the farm he brooded a great deal about his relationship with Plaxy. When the term was over and they met again, he found that time and difference of experience had increased the gulf between them. They still needed one another and gravitated towards each other, but they ever strained apart for the fulfilling of their divergent lives. Strange indeed was his relation to Plaxy! So alien were they in native propensity, yet so united in common history and in essential spirit. But now so divergent, like stars that have swung very near together out of space to fly apart towards opposite poles of the heaven. Altogether, how he loved her; and how, in another mood even while loving, he hated her!

The native odours of Plaxy were not naturally attractive to him, as was the intoxicating scent of a bitch. In nature, in the jungle, the characteristic human smell would probably have repelled him, like the stink of a baboon. Certainly it was an acquired taste, but he had acquired it so long ago and so thoroughly that the love of it had become a second and fuller nature to him; so that by now, though the sweet maddening smell of a bitch might at any time irresistibly draw him away from Plaxy, always he must return to her. She, he felt, must ever be the centre of his life and he of hers; and she knew it. Yet their lives must inevitably fall apart. There was no common future for them. Even now, how tiresome was her schoolgirl prattle, how boring her unfulfilled schoolgirl romances! (Why ever had the human race developed this ridiculous attitude to sex? How it disgusted him!) And those heartless artificial scents that she had begun to use, perversely wishing to cover her wholesome, and to him by now lovely, natural odour!

But there were times when the natural odour of Plaxy filled him with disgust. Then, all human beings stank in his nostrils, but Plaxy his darling most of all. Sometimes when he was lying in the yard waiting for orders, watching the old cock treading one of his harem, or Jane setting off in her best clothes to Dolgelly, or Mrs. Pugh carrying pails of milk to the dairy, or one of the hired men shifting muck out of the pigstye, he tried hard to analyse his feelings about the human species, and the causes of his own fluctuation between adoration and contemptuous resentment. He recognized that the species that had produced him (more or less for fun) had on the whole treated him pretty well. The specimens that he knew best had on the whole been kindly. All the same he could not but resent his present servitude. Even Pugh, who was fundamentally decent, treated the dogs essentially as chattels. When they happened to be in the way they were just booted out of it; always with that ingrained rough friendliness of Pugh's, but still it was exasperating. Then there were the village people. Many of them showed an unaccountable spite, kicking him or hitting him for no reason whatever, when Pugh was not looking. At first he thought they must be Pugh's enemies, or Thomas's; but no, they were just letting off some secret pent-up vindictiveness against a living thing that could not hit back. Most dogs had been thoroughly trained to take these cuffs and kicks meekly, but Sirius often surprised his assailants by vigorous retaliation.

One cause of Sirius's incipient contempt for human beings was the fact that since they thought he was "only an animal," they often gave themselves away badly in his presence. When they were observed by others of their kind, they maintained the accepted standard of conduct, and were indignant if they caugh anyone falling short of that standard; but when they thought they were not being watched, they would commit the very same offences themselves. It was, of course, to be expected that in his presence they should pick their noses (how he chortled at their unconscious grimaces) or break wind, and so on. What roused his contempt was their proneness to insincerity. Mrs.

Pugh, for instance, whom he had once seen licking a spoon instead of washing it, indignantly scolded her daughter for doing the very same thing. And the hired man, Rhys, who was a great chapel-goer, and very righteous about sex, would often, when he was alone, with only Sirius present, do unprintable things to relieve himself of sexual pressure. Not that Sirius saw anything wrong in such behaviour, but the insincerity of the man disgusted him.

This insincerity of the dominant species, he decided, was *one* of the main causes of those sudden uprushings of rage and physical repugnance which sometimes possessed him. At these times the human odour became an intolerable stench. He came to recognize this revulsion as a sign that his "wolf nature," as he called it, was waking. In this mood all the acquired meanings of smells seemed to evaporate, and their natural qualities smote him with exquisite delight or horror. If he was at home he would go out from the oppressive stench of the house to clean his nose with deep sniffs of the fragrant moorland air. A great loathing of man would seize him. He would perhaps plunge into a stream to wash away the pollution, or roll in sweet cow dung. Then he would go hunting, carefully avoiding every human being, irrationally feeling that the hand of man was everywhere against him. Most often his quarry was a mere rabbit; but with sufficient luck and intelligence he might take a mountain hare. The snap of his jaws on the spine, the yielding flesh, the rich blood welling into his mouth, went to his head like alcohol. He felt his spirit washed by the blood of the quarry, washed clean of humanity with all its itching monkey-inquisitiveness, all its restless monkeying with material things and living things and living minds. To hell with wisdom and love and all cultural dope. The way of life was to hunt, to overtake, to snatch, to hear the sharp scream, to wolf the crushed flesh and bones. Then a drink and a rest in the moorland sunshine, alone, at peace.

During his last month with Pugh, Sirius suffered a distressing alternation of moods. Sometimes he was wholly wrapped up in care of the sheep, sometimes he longed for the life of the mind, sometimes he felt the strange uprush of the wolf's nature in him.

One day, after attending to some sheep that had been badly struck by fly, he was haunted by the stinging smell of the lotions that he had applied. They turned him savage. Why should he be the menial of these dunder-headed ruminants? Gradually the wolf-mood took complete possession of him. It was a free afternoon for him, and he should have gone home to read. Instead he cantered off among the hills till he reached a certain distant "foreign" sheep-run beyond Arenig Fach, a miniature Table Mountain far to the east. There he sniffed the wind and cast about with nose to earth till he found the trail he wanted. He had not followed it long before the quarry stood before him, a great ram with royal head and a neck heavy with muscle. Sirius checked, and stood looking at the beast, which also stood, sniffing the wind, pawing the ground. Suddenly the dog felt the human, the humane, in him coming uppermost again. Why murder this fine creature? But it was man's creature, and it epitomized all the tyranny of the sheep-dog's servitude. He rushed at the ram, who met his onslaught with lowered head and flung him off. There followed a long battle. Sirius was gashed in the shoulder. He persevered, however, running in again and again till at last he was given a chance to seize the ram by the throat. Desperately it tried to throw him off, crashing about among the heather and rocks; but Sirius hung on, remembering his battle with Diawl Du. The ram's struggles became feebler, as Diawl Du's had done. At last they ceased. Sirius let go. His tail tucked itself between his legs. He looked about to see if any human being was in sight. Then he looked at the dead ram. Human pity, horror, disgust, welled up in him. But he fought them down, remembering that he was hungry. He began tearing off great shreds of the hide, bracing his feet against the ground. Then he dragged at the warm flesh, and gorged himself. At last he slunk away.

It was sheer luck that Sirius was never charged with this crime. It so happened that another sheep-dog from a farm near by had run amok and killed several sheep; so the ram was attributed to him. But Sirius, when his wolf-mood had passed and he realized the full significance of his deed, lived in terror of detection. There was the tell-tale wound on his shoulder.

But after all this might have been made by an old nail on a
fence.

During the rest of his time with Pugh, Sirius devoted himself
conscientiously to the sheep, treating them with new solicitation
and tenderness. When at last Thomas came to fetch him away
and Pugh made his final report, the old man said, "Yes, indeed,
Mr. Trelone, it is a wonderful dog he is, and I don't know how
I shall do without him. This summer he is like a mother to
the sheep, so loving he is in his ways with them. And they are
all in great health because he has watched over them so
closely, and tended any that would be poorly before it ever
showed any sadness for itself. If only he were a man, Mr.
Trelone, I would have my daughter marry him for the sheeps'
sake. But she has set her heart on a two-legged animal, a
draper's assistant that has not half the brain of this dog, though
he is no fool in his own business. So now I must look round
and take some other young man into partnership, since Mr.
Bran insists on going." He looked at Sirius with a rueful and
affectionate grimace, then continued, "But surely to goodness,
Mr. Trelone, when you make another dog like this one you
will not again forget that hands are as needful as a brain. I
have often broken my heart for Bran when I have watched him
trying to use his mouth to do the things I do so easily with
these great clumsy paws of mine. Yes, you must give the next
one hands, isn't it, Mr. Trelone."

Unexpectedly, when Sirius was once more at home, the wolf-
mood became more insistent than ever. With Pugh he was
generally absorbed in some bit of practical work, and had little
time to brood; but at home during that summer holiday his
future was all uncertain and had to be discussed; and Plaxy
was present, with her familiar spell and her increasing remoteness.

Right at the outset, on the walk home from Caer Blai, Sirius
had broached the subject of his future. "Well," said Thomas
with a guarded voice, "first you need a good holiday at home.
Then I thought we might do a walking tour with my young
colleague, McBane, in the Lake District, where you would see
a different style of sheep-farming. Then you might enter for
some of the Cumberland sheep-dog trials, just to surprise the

local people a bit. Then it will be time for you to come into
residence at the laboratory, so that we can begin a whole lot
of fine experimental work on you, physiological and psychological. You'll find it all very interesting, and of course your
active co-operation will be needed throughout. You will learn
a lot that way. Little by little, we shall train you to be a
research worker in animal psychology. If you turn out well we
may be glad to publish some of your stuff. Then, of course,
scientists of all sorts passing through Cambridge will want to
see you. So you will have a very interesting life, and you will
be the cynosure of every scientific eye. I hope to God it doesn't
turn your head and make you an insufferable prig." Sirius
remained silent. Presently Thomas continued, "Oh, yes, and
when we can spare you I think you might put in a few weeks
now and then on sheep again, either at Pugh's or elsewhere.
In time we shall probably have done all the research we need
of you, and then—well, you will probably come on to our staff
as a permanent member."

"I see," said Sirius, and said no more. He thought about it
all the way home. He thought about it by day and by night,
and about other matters that were disturbing him.

One of these matters was of course his relationship with
Plaxy. Shortly after she came home she learned that she had
won a scholarship for one of the Cambridge colleges. Her
subject, by the way, was English literature. It had been
Thomas's wish that she should become a doctor, but she had
steadily veered away from science towards the arts, thus (according to my theory) asserting her independence against the father
whom she secretly admired. The study of literature at Cambridge is scientific in temper, and in working for her scholarship Plaxy, I suggest, had both asserted her independence and
been true to her father's moral code. She had worked hard
for her scholarship, and now for a time she put the life of the
mind behind her. Sirius, on the other hand, after his hard
labour with Pugh, proposed to spend all his spare time on the
life of the mind. He had been hoping for her collaboration.
Plaxy, however, was unusually silent and remote. Superficially
she was as friendly as ever, and would often go for walks
with him. But they were silent walks; and the silence, though

apparently she did not notice it, oppressed him. She did not seem really interested in his problems. Even the great problem of his future, though she often encouraged him to speak of it, did not *really* interest her. And she spoke less and less of her school life, because it took so much explaining. Thus nearly all their talk centred round family or local affairs and the natural phenomena of a Welsh summer. This was easy and happy, but Sirius felt that it did not get them anywhere.

One day in mental agony he said, "Plaxy, why have you gone dead on me? I do so want us to be happy together!" She answered, "Oh, I know I'm sometimes a pig to you. The trouble is I'm terribly worried just now, and I can't think of anything else." "Tell me about it," he said; but she replied, "I *can't*. It's too complicated. You wouldn't understand. How could you? There's nothing in your life to help you to begin to understand. No, I'm sorry, but somehow I *can't* tell you. It's—it's just a *human* thing."

It was not the words that offended him so much as the faint tone of superiority in the voice. The wolf-mood, which had been brewing in him ever since his conversation with Thomas, came violently into action. The smell of this human female beside him suddenly lost all its loveliness and became a repugnant stink. Sidelong he looked at her. Instead of seeing the dearest face in the world, he saw the uncouth hairless features of a super-ape, in fact of that species which so long ago had broken in his ancestors to be their slaves in body and soul.

"Sorry," he said. "I didn't want to butt in." He was startled at the snarl in his own voice, and surprised (and oddly resentful) that she did not notice it. All the way home they walked in silence. At the gate she touched his head with her hand, and said, "I'm sorry." He answered, "That's all right, I wish I could help." The snarl was still in his voice, hidden under gentleness. She did not hear it. Her touch sent conflicting tremors down his back, for it was at once the touch of his darling and the touch of the super-simian tyrant.

At the doorway the human smell of the house raised his gorge. She entered. Longing to restore community with her, he actually licked her hand as she passed in; and while he did so, he felt to his horror his lips curl themselves back, baring his teeth for action. She vanished into the house. He turned away, sniffing the fresh air.

He cantered ruthlessly across a flower-bed, leapt the garden wall, and swung easily up the hillside with his tail streaming out behind him.

That night he failed to return home. There was nothing unusual in this, and no one was anxious. On the following night also he was absent. Thomas was disturbed, but concealed his anxiety under annoyance, for he had planned a long walk with Sirius for the next day. On the third night also there was no Sirius. Pugh had not seen him, nor had he put in an appearance at any of the neighbouring farms, nor in the village. Thomas was now alarmed; and Plaxy, thinking of their last meeting, felt remorse for her coldness.

The whole household was organized as a search party, with Idwal and another super-sheep-dog, who were borrowed for the occasion and made to smell Sirius's sleeping-basket before setting out on the search. Since there was no news of him in the cultivated regions, it seemed probable that he had taken to the moor. The searchers spread out fanwise in allotted directions.

It was Plaxy who found Sirius, late in the afternoon. Coming round a buttress, she saw him standing over the carcass of a little moorland pony. She had approached up wind, and Sirius had not seen her. He began tugging savagely at the hide of the mangled neck, tearing it away from the flesh. His legs were driven deep into the bog in the effort to get a solid purchase. His tail curved under his belly. His jaws and shoulders were smeared with blood, and peaty mud was splashed all over him. A great pool of blood and mire spread from the pony's throat. There had evidently been a wild struggle, for the pony's flanks were torn and the bracken and grass were trampled.

Only for a second did Plaxy watch, unobserved and horror-stricken. Then she gasped out, "Sirius!" He let go and faced her, licking his crimson lips and muzzle. The two gazed at each other, she into the eyes of a wolf, he into the white, nude, super-simian face of his ancestral tyrant. His back bristled. A snarl twisted his lips. A low growl was all his greeting.

She was thoroughly frightened and nauseated, but also she realized that some desperate art was needed to save him from ruin. And in that moment (she afterwards said) she realized for the first time the strength of the bond between them. She advanced towards him. "Sirius, *darling*," she cried, surprising herself no less than him, "what ever will become of us now?" Miserably she approached him, with the bog squelching over her shoe-tops. His growl became more threatening, for the beast in him was jealous for its quarry. His ears lay back. His teeth were more crimson than white. She felt a weakening at the knees, but plodded towards him, and stretched out a hand to touch the savage head. As she did so, she caught a nearer view of the carcass, and suddenly she vomited. When the paroxysm was over, she sobbed out, "*Why* did you have to do it? I don't understand. Oh, they'll want to kill you for it." She sat down on a damp tussock and gazed at Sirius, and he at her. Presently he turned on the carcass and tore at the flesh. Plaxy screamed, leapt up and tried to drag him off by the collar. With a roar he turned on her, and she was flung back on to the boggy ground with the great beast standing over her, and the cold boggy water oozing about her shoulders. Their eyes were close together. His breath smelt of blood.

Some people in desperate moments have a knack of doing the right thing. Plaxy is one of them. "My dear," she said, "you are *not* a wild beast, you're Sirius. And you don't really want to hurt me. You love me, you know you do. I'm your Plaxy." His lips crept back over his teeth. His growl died out. Presently, with a little whimper he delicately kissed her cheek. Stroking his throat, she said, "Oh, my poor darling, you must have been mad"; then, as she rose to her feet, "Come, let me clean you up a bit."

She took him to the edge of the boggy pond, and with a bit of moss for a sponge she wiped the blood from his muzzle and his neck and shoulders. While she was doing so she said, "*Why* did you have to do it? *Why* did you have to leave us? Was I *very* horrid to you that day?" He stood silent, passive to her ministrations, with his tail still tight under him. When he was more or less clean of blood, she kissed his forehead, then straightened herself. She walked over to the carcass.

"Poor pony," she said. "He's like our Polly that we used to ride on when Giles and I were little. Do you remember how you used to kiss her nose, nearly getting yourself fallen over?" A sudden tortured whimper was his answer. Then she, still gazing at the pony, said in an altered voice, "If we leave this mess to be found, they won't rest till they have tracked you down, and then? If only we could bury it in the bog! We had better go home and tell Thomas."

On the long walk home she tried to make Sirius tell her all about it, and suddenly she realized that he had never said a word since she had found him. "Tell me, tell me!" she implored. "Oh, do at least say something. What's the matter with you?"

At last he spoke. "You wouldn't understand. There's nothing in your life for you to judge it by. It's just—a canine thing." This echo of her own words startled and pained her. "Oh, I'm terribly sorry," she said, "I *was* horrid." But he said, "It wasn't all your fault. I was going wild before that."

The rest of the search party had arrived home before them. Sirius was given a hearty but anxious welcome. He took it coldly. Refusing his supper, he retired to bed. Plaxy at once told her story to Thomas, who was at first indignant and then increasingly interested, though of course alarmed for Sirius's safety. Next day he traced the owner of the pony and told him the whole story, attributing the murder to "a new, untrained experimental super-sheep-dog of mine." He paid up twice the value of the pony.

The killing of the pony was one of the turning points in Sirius's career. It clarified his relations with Plaxy, and it made Thomas realize that Sirius was being seriously strained, and would have to be treated carefully.

A couple of days later Plaxy and Sirius found themselves talking more freely to one another than had been possible for many months. It began by her telling him about that "human" matter which she had formerly withheld. Consideration for Plaxy forbids me to publish its details, which are anyhow irrelevant to my theme. Let it suffice that Plaxy had allowed herself to become entangled with a young man for whom she felt a strong sexual attraction but no great respect; and that in these circumstances the shameless promiscuity of Sirius's own sex life seemed to her to render him an impossible confidant. But the pony incident had made her realize more clearly how much her intimacy with Sirius mattered to both of them. She felt compelled to do her utmost to restore confidence. Sirius on his side told her of the conflict which was racking him, the alternating moods of respect and loathing for humanity. "You, for instance, are sometimes the dearest of all things in the world, and sometimes just a horrible monkey that has cast a filthy spell on me." She answered at once, "And *you* are sometimes just my father's experimental dog that I have somehow got tangled up with and responsible for, because of *him*; but sometimes you are—*Sirius*, the part of Sirius-Plaxy that I love." A faint change in her fragrance made him realize the warmth of her feeling far better than her words could do, or even the shy frankness of her voice.

Thomas made a point of lecturing Sirius on the folly of killing ponies, but the lecture gradually changed into a discussion about the causes of the wolf-mood in him. At the crisis of this talk Sirius cried, "Unless you help me to be *myself*, you will force me to be—a sham wolf." Thomas countered this with, "And *what* must you be to be 'yourself'?" After a long pause Sirius said, "I don't know, yet. But I must be given a chance to find out. I must be helped to look round at the world. I shall not see much of it if I just alternate between sheep and your laboratory. You see, I feel I have my *own* active contribution to make to—well to human understanding. I can't be just a passive subject for experiments, or at best a tenth-rate research worker. There's something I *must* get clear in my own mind, and when I have got it clear, then I must get it across somehow to mankind." Thomas softly whistled. "Sounds as though you wanted to be a sort of canine messiah to men!" Sirius moved restlessly and said, "No, I'm not as silly as all that. I don't feel superior at all, far from it. But—well, my point of view is so utterly different from man's, and yet at bottom the same. In making me you made something that sees man from clean outside man, and can tell him what he looks like." Thomas was silent, considering this, and Sirius presently added, "There's another point. When I feel I'm not going to be able to be my true self, or not allowed to try to be it, the whole human race turns foul in my nose, and I just go wild. Everything blacks out. I don't know why, but there it is."

Thomas was by now thoroughly aware that his policy for Sirius had been too simple. He undertook to modify it. On the following day he talked it all over with Elizabeth. "What a fool I was," he said, "not to foresee this psychological trouble! I don't think I ever *really* realized that if things went wrong with *this* experiment I couldn't just wash my hands of it all, and start again; any more than a surgeon can wash his hands of an operation that has gone wrong. I feel as God ought to have felt towards Adam when Adam went wrong— morally responsible. The devil of it is that, though moral feelings are mere subjective feelings, you can't ignore them."

After a long discussion Elizabeth and Thomas decided on a new programme for Sirius. He should come to the Laboratory, as planned; but also he should be "shown round a bit" by Elizabeth, so that he could "begin to get the hang of this crazy human world," He would go about simply as her dog, meeting her friends in Cambridge and elsewhere, listening to their talk. She would also help him to do a bit of sight-seeing, if it could be arranged—slums, factories, docks, museums, concerts. This could be done at odd times, from the lab. He could also, with Thomas's aid, make proper use of Cambridge as an educational centre. Thomas would suggest lines of study and get him books from libraries. All this might help him to see more clearly what he could do with his life.

When Thomas explained the new plan to Sirius, he ended with a caution. If Sirius did wander about the country with Elizabeth, he must be very careful not to give the show away. He must behave simply as her dog. No one must suspect him of being able to talk, no one but the people in the know at the laboratory. "But why?" protested Sirius. "Surely it's time I came out into the open. I can't go on pretending for ever." Thomas insisted that the time had not yet come for publicity. "We must have you firmly established in the scientific world before the commercial world can get hold of you. Otherwise some unscrupulous tough, out on the make, will try to kidnap you and run you into some foreign country to show you off for money. Then you really would be a slave for the rest of your life." Sirius snorted. "Let' em try, that's all." Thomas pointed out that a choloroform cloth would put him out of action very effectively, till they got him away. "Don't think it's just my fancy," Thomas added. "There are some guys on your track already, and it's time I warned you. Only yesterday two townee people called here to inquire about buying a super-sheep-dog. I put them off because I didn't like the look of them. Told them I had no animal ready. They said they had seen one in Trawsfynydd posting a letter, you in fact. Wouldn't I sell you? They offered £30, £40, and gradually raised it to £250. This was fantastic for a super-sheep-dog, so I began to be suspicious. Well, those fellows have been hanging about here since then, so look out. And remember, chloroform."

Some weeks later, when Sirius had almost forgotten about this story, an attempt was actually made to kidnap him. He had been out hunting, and was returning by his usual route, which passed over a stile in a wall about a hundred yards or so above the house. He was on the point of climbing over the stile when he caught a whiff of something strange. It was sickly-sweet and pungent. He remembered chloroform, and checked. Now unfortunately for his assailants his meditations on the way home from the chase had been sombre. He had been brooding on his subjection to the human race, and so he was in a mood for retaliation. He leapt the stile and crashed into two men, who were waiting for him. They had not expected him to come over like a shell from a gun, exploding on impact. Both men were knocked flying, and in the struggle which followed Sirius got his teeth in the throat of one of the men before the other could apply the chloroform cloth. The choking smell forced him to let go and attack his other assailant. Number one, however, was temporarily out of action, so Sirius had to deal only with number two and the chloroform. The taste, or rather the idea, of human blood had roused the wolf-mood in Sirius. He became just an animal fighting its natural enemy-species. The man did his best with the chloroform, but though Sirius had a few strong whiffs he managed to avoid its full power. Meanwhile the noise of battle had roused Thomas, who was down below in the garden at Garth. He pounded up the hill shouting. The damaged man had risen to his feet to help his colleague, but when he saw Thomas he made off. The other had succeeded in doping Sirius enough to make him no longer dangerous; but he too, when he heard Thomas, clambered to his feet, with blood streaming from his face, and took to his heels, leaving the dog already three parts doped and quite unable to give chase. Both men reached the cart track where they had left their car, and drove off as fast as the bumps would permit. Thomas made no attempt to follow them. Instead, he went to Sirius and gripped his collar, lest the dog should recover in time to pursue his enemies.

Shortly after this incident Thomas took Sirius by car to the Lake District for the projected walking tour with his young colleague, McBane. His main object was to familiarize McBane with Sirius, and particularly to give him an opportunity of learning to understand the dog's speech before undertaking work on him at the Laboratory. Incidentally Sirius was also given an opportunity to see the north country sheep-dogs at work. The party also attended an important sheep-dog trial. Thomas had been persuaded by McBane to enter Sirius as a competitior. Sirius had on several occasions acquitted himself brilliantly at trials in Wales, under Pugh; but Thomas knew nothing of the technique. It very soon became obvious to judges and spectators that the master was no shepherd, while the dog was more brilliant than any dog ought to have been. It did not matter how ineptly Thomas gave his orders; Sirius ignored them and carried out the desired operation with every refinement of skill. Finally it was discovered that Thomas was the famous producer of super-sheep-dogs. He received many offers to purchase Sirius, but laughingly refused. The would-be purchasers had to be content to have their names entered on the waiting list for future dogs.

CHAPTER VIII

SIRIUS AT CAMBRIDGE

WHEN the holiday was over, Thomas took Sirius to Cambridge. A private bed-sitting-room had been prepared for the wonder-dog within the precincts of the Laboratory, near a room which Thomas occupied himself. The senior members of the staff were introduced to Sirius as "man to man," on the understanding that they must keep the secret and behave in public as though this dog were only a rather specially bright super-sheep-dog.

Sirius was at first very happy at Cambridge. The bustle of city and university, though rather bewildering, was stimulating. During the first few days he spent much time in wandering about the streets watching the people, and the dogs. The abundance of the canine population surprised him, and so did the extraordinary diversity of breeds. It seemed to him incredible that the dominant species should keep so many of the dominated species alive in complete idleness, for not one of these pampered animals had any function but to be the living toy of some man or woman. Physically they were nearly all in good condition, save for a common tendency to corpulence, which in some cases reached a disgusting fulfilment. Mentally they were unwholesome. How could it be otherwise? They had nothing to do but wait for their meals, sink from boredom into sleep, attend their masters or mistresses on gentle walks, savour one another's odours, and take part in the simple ritual of the lamp-post and the gate-post. Sexually they were all starved, for bitches were few, and jealously guarded by their human owners. Had not the canine race been of sub-human intelligence, they must one and all have been neurotics, but their stupidity saved them.

Sirius himself had often to act the part of these sub-human creatures. When Elizabeth took him out to visit her friends he allowed himself to be petted and laughed at, or praised for the "marvellous intelligence" that he showed in "shaking hands" or shutting the door. Then the company would forget him completely, while he lay stretched out on the floor in seeming boredom, but in fact listening to every word, and trying to get the hang of some conversation on books or painting; even furtively stealing a glance at drawings or bits of sculpture that were circulated for inspection.

Elizabeth did her best to give Sirius a fair sample of life in a university city. It became a sort of game with her to contrive means to insinuate him into meetings and concerts. After the simple subsistence life of the sheep-country, Cambridge filled him with respect for the surplus energies of the human species. All these great and ornate buildings had been put up stone by stone, century by century, with the cunning of human hands. All these articles in shop-windows had been made by human machinery and transported in human trains, cars and ships from the many lands of human occupation. Perhaps most impressive of all to his innocent mind was the interior of a great library, where, by patient intrigue, Elizabeth managed to effect an entry for him. The thousands of books lining the walls brought home to him as nothing else had done the vast bulk and incredible detail of human intellectual tradition. He stood speechless before it all, his tail drooping with awe. As yet he was far too simple-minded to realize that the majority of the volumes that faced him, shoulder to shoulder, were of little importance. He supposed all to be mightily pregnant. And the naïve belief that he could never attain wisdom until his poor eyes had travelled along most of those millions of lines of print filled him with despair.

Thomas had decided that the time had come to let out the secret of Sirius's powers to a carefully selected public. A number of his scientific and academic friends must be allowed to make the dog's acquaintance and form their own opinions of his ability, on the understanding that the truth must not yet be published. His policy was still to keep the greater public from sharing the secret, lest the forces of commercial stunt-manufacture should be brought to bear on his work, and possibly wreck it.

He arranged for Sirius to meet a few eminent persons in the University, mostly zoologists, biochemists, biologists of one sort or another, but also psychologists, philosophers, and philologists, who would be interested in his speech, and a few stray surgeons, painters, sculptors and writers who happened to be among Thomas's personal friends. These meetings generally took place after a lunch in Thomas's rooms. Over the meal Thomas would tell the party something about his experiments and the success of the super-sheep-dogs. Then he would lead on to his more daring research, and describe Sirius as "probably quite as bright as most university students." When lunch was over, the small company would settle in easy chairs with their pipes, and Thomas, looking at his watch, would say, "I told him we should be ready for him at two o'clock. He'll be along in a minute." Presently the door would open and the great beast would stalk into the room. He did not lack presence. Tall and lean as a tiger, but with a faint suggestion of the lion's mane, he would stand for a moment looking at the company. Thomas would rise to his feet and solemnly introduce his guests one by one to Sirius. "Professor Stone, anthropologist, Dr. James Crawford, President of —— College," and so on. The guests generally felt extremely ill at ease, not knowing how to behave, and often suspecting that Thomas was playing a trick on them. Sometimes they remained stolidly seated, sometimes they rather sheepishly rose to their feet, as though Sirius were a distinguished human newcomer. Sirius looked steadily into the eyes of each guest as he was introduced, acknowledging him with a languid movement of his great flag of a tail. He would then take up his position in the centre of the company, generally squatting down on the hearth-rug. "Well," Thomas would say, "first of all you want to know, of course, that Sirius really can understand English, so will someone ask him to do something?" Often the whole company was so paralysed by the oddity of the situation that it took a full half-minute for anyone to think of an appropriate task. At last the dog would be asked to fetch a cushion or a book, which of course he straightway did. Presently Thomas would carry on a conversation with Sirius, the guests listening intently to the strange canine speech, and failing to understand a word of it. Then Sirius would say a few simple words very slowly, Thomas translating. This would lead on to a general conversation in which the guests would often question the dog and receive the answer through Thomas. Not infrequently Sirius himself would question the visitors, and sometimes his questions were such that Thomas was obviously reluctant to pass on. In this way the guests received a clear impression of a strong and independent personality.

And in this way Sirius himself gradually reached certain conclusions about these distinguished specimens of the dominant species. One characteristic about them perplexed him greatly. It was such a deep-seated thing that they themselves did not seem to be aware of it. One and all, they undervalued or misvalued their hands. Many of them, in fact all but the surgeons, sculptors, painters, and research workers, were wretchedly clumsy with their hands, and by no means ashamed of it. Even those whose work involved manual skill, the surgeons, sculptors and so on, though they were so skilled in their own specialized technique, had often lost that general handiness, that manual versatility, by which their species had triumphed. On the whole they were helpless creatures. Hands were for them highly specialized instruments, like the bird's wing or the seal's flipper, excellent for some one action, but not versatile. Those that came on bicycles never mended their punctures themselves. They could not sew on their buttons or mend their socks. Moreover even these specialized geniuses of the hand had to some extent been infected by the general contempt for "manual toil," which the privileged class had invented to excuse their laziness. As for the writers, academics, lawyers, politicians, their unhandiness and their contempt for mere manual dexterity were amazing. The writers couldn't even write properly. They fell back on the cruder activity of pressing typewriter keys. Or they simply dictated. Sirius had heard that in Old China the scholar class let their finger-nails grow fantastically long so that their incapacity for manual work should be obvious. Think of the millions of cunning hands thus wasted! How he despised these regressive human types for the neglect and atrophy of the most glorious human organ, the very instrument of creation; and for infecting with their contempt for manual skill even the manual workers themselves, on whose practical dexterity the whole structure of civilization was founded! Artizans actually wanted their sons to "rise" into the class of "black-coated" workers. What would not Sirius himself have achieved if he had been given even the clumsy hands of an ape, let alone the least apt of all these neglected human organs!

The first few weeks at Cambridge were indeed delightful for Sirius. Every morning some bit of research was done upon him at the Laboratory, with his interested co-operation. Sometimes it was a case of studying his motor or sensory reactions, sometimes his glandular responses to emotional stimuli, sometimes his intelligence, and so on. X-ray photographs had to be made of his skull, gramophone records of his speech. With the co-operation of a psychologist he himself planned to write a monograph on his olfactory experiences, and another on his power of detecting human character and emotional changes by scent and tone of voice. Psychologists and musicians studied his musical powers. His sex life had also to be recorded.

In addition to all this strictly scientific work, in which Sirius collaborated with his human observers, he planned to undertake two popular books entirely on his own. One was to be called *The Lamp-post, A Study of the Social Life of the Domestic Dog*. The opening passage is interesting for the light which it throws on Sirius's temperament. "In man, social intercourse has centred mainly on the process of absorbing fluid into the organism, but in the domestic dog and to a lesser extent among all wild canine species, the act charged with most social significance is the excretion of fluid. For man the pub, the estaminet, the Biergarten, but for the dog the tree-trunk, the lintel of door or gate, and above all the lamp-post, form the focal points of community life. For a man the flavours of alcoholic drinks, but for a dog the infinitely variegated smells of urine are the most potent stimuli for the gregarious impulse." The other projected book, *Beyond the Lamp-post*, he kept a dead secret. It was to be autobiographical, and would express his philosophy of life. These works were never completed; the second was scarcely even begun, but I have found the random notes for it extremely useful in writing Sirius's biography. They reveal a mind which combined laughable naïvety in some directions with remarkable shrewdness in others, a mind moreover which seemed to oscillate between a heavy, self-pitying seriousness and a humorous detachment and self-criticism.

It was flattering to Sirius to be the centre of so much interest; and it was very unwholesome. Inevitably he began to feel that his mission was after all simply to be his unique self, and to allow the human race respectfully to study him. Far from retaining the humility that had oppressed him on his visit to the library, he now swung away towards self-complacency. As his presence became more widely known, more people sought his acquaintance. Thomas received innumerable invitations from outside the chosen circle, persons who had evidently heard vague rumours of the human dog and were eager to verify them. When Sirius was out in the streets people often stared at him and whispered. Thomas strongly disapproved of his going out by himself, lest attempts should be made to kidnap him. The anxious physiologist even went so far as to hint that unless his precious charge agreed never to go out without a human escort he would have to be confined to the Laboratory. This threat, however, infuriated Sirius; and Thomas recognized that, if it were carried out, all friendly co-operation would cease. The best he could do was to engage a detective to follow the dog on a bicycle whenever he went out of doors. Sirius conceived a humorous dislike of this individual. "He's rather like a tin can tied to my tail, he and his clattery old bike," said Sirius; and henceforth always referred to him as "Old Tin Can." The game of giving Old Tin Can the slip or leading him into awkward situations became Sirius's main outdoor amusement.

Contrary to his original intention Sirius spent the whole of that autumn term at Cambridge. Though he was often very homesick for the country, and nearly always had a headache and often felt seedy, he found Cambridge life far too fascinating to surrender. Several times he did, indeed, suggest to Thomas that he ought to be moving on; but Thomas was reluctant to break off the research, and Sirius himself was too comfortable to find energy to press the matter.

Very soon the Christmas vacation was upon him, and he went back to Wales with Thomas, Elizabeth, and Plaxy. Once more on the hills, he discovered that he was in a sorry state of physical decay, and he spent much of his time trying to restore himself by long hunting expeditions.

During the spring term Sirius was less happy. The glamour of Cambridge had begun to fade, and he was increasingly restless about his future; the more so because Cambridge was like a habit-forming drug. By now he obtained only a mild satisfaction from it, yet it had got into his blood and he could not bring himself to do without it. He had arrived in Cambridge, an anatomical study of bone and muscle. A soft, inactive life, which included far too many delicacies received in the houses of admiring acquaintances, had already blurred his contours with a layer of fat, and filled out his waist. Once when he met Plaxy in the street, she exclaimed, "Gosh! You're going fat and prosperous, and you waddle like a Pekinese." This remark had greatly distressed him.

Along with physical decay went a less obvious mental decay, a tendency to sink into being a sort of super-lap-dog-cum-super-laboratory-animal. His disposition became increasingly peevish and self-centred. There came a day when a serious difference occurred between Sirius and McBane. Thomas's lieutenant had prepared a piece of apparatus for a more minute research into Sirius's olfactory powers. Sirius protested that he was not in the mood for such an exacting bit of work to-day; his nose was in a hypersensitive state and must not be put to any strain. McBane pointed out that, if Sirius refused, hours of preparation would be wasted. Sirius flew into a whimpering tantrum, crying that his nose was more important than a few hours of McBane's time. "Good God!" cried McBane, "you might be a prima donna."

Thomas had been surprised and pleased at the way in which Sirius had settled down to his new life. It seemed as though the dog had outgrown his romantic cravings, and was reconciled to becoming a permanent property at the Lab. But in his second term, though Sirius was still superficially able to enjoy his work, on a deeper level of his mind he was becoming increasingly perturbed and rebellious. This life of ease and self-gratulation was not at all what he was "meant for." The mere shortage of physical exercise made him miserable.

Sometimes he cantered a few miles along the tow-path, but this was very boring; and he was always oppressed by the knowledge that the faithful detective was following on a bicycle. He could not force himself to run every day. Consequently he was generally constipated and disgruntled. He felt a growing nostalgia for the moors, the mists, the rich smell of the sheep, with all its associations of hard work and simple triumphs. He remembered Pugh with affection, and thought how much more real he seemed than these dons and their wives.

He was vaguely aware too of his own moral decay. It was increasingly difficult for him to do anything that he did not want to do. Not that he was incapable of all mental effort, for he still generally carried out his intellectual work with conscientious thoroughness. But then, he happened to like that. What he was failing to do was to control his ordinary selfish impulses in relation to his human neighbours. He was also growing less capable even of prudential self-regard.

For instance there was the matter of bitches. Of the few bitches that he encountered in the Cambridge streets, most were anyhow too small for him, and many had been treated with a preparation which disguised the animal's intoxicating natural odour, and made potential lovers regard her as a filthy-smelling hag. He insisted to Thomas that, since in Cambridge there was practically no scope at all for love-making, bitches must be provided for him. It was not to be expected that a vigorous young dog should be able to do without them and yet maintain his mental balance. So a succession of attractive females was procured for him. These creatures were brought in turn and at appropriate times to his rooms in the Laboratory; and the whole matter was treated as part of the prolonged and complicated scientific study in which he was co-operating. The Laboratory, by the way, had analysed the chemistry of the odours which were sexually stimulating to Sirius, and could choose seductive animals for him with considerable success. But, his appetite instead of being assuaged, increased. Almost daily they brought a young bitch to his room, yet he was never satisfied. Indeed he became more and more lascivious and difficult to please. Thomas urged him to take himself in hand, otherwise his mental vitality would be sapped. Sirius agreed to do this, but failed to carry out his promise. And now a note of sadism crept into his love-making. Once there was a terrible commotion because in the very act of love he dug his teeth into the bitch's neck.

This incident seems to have frightened Sirius himself, for a change now came over him. Dreading the dark power that seemed to rise up within him and control his behaviour, he made a desperate effort to pull himself together. He also determined to leave Cambridge at once and go back to Wales for a spell with the sheep. Thomas reluctantly agreed that he had better go, but pointed out that he was in no condition to undertake sheep work again without some weeks of severe physical training. This was all too true. The best that could be done was that Thomas should arrange with Pugh to take him for a month not as a sheep-dog but as a paying guest. This plan was much discussed, but somehow Sirius could not bring himself to such an ignominious course. In default of a better policy he simply stayed on at Cambridge till the end of the term. There followed an Easter Vacation in Wales, given over wholly to physical training in preparation for a spell of sheep-tending in Cumberland. But as no satisfactory arrangement could be made for him, the lure of Cambridge proved in the end too strong, and he returned with Thomas for the summer term.

In the familiar environment the old way of life proved fatally easy. Laboratory work, meetings with Thomas's scientific or academic friends, a great deal of desultory biological and other scientific reading, a certain amount of philosophy, the writing of his monographs and notes for *The Lamp-post* and *Beyond the Lamp-post*, select parties at which he was lionised by the wives of dons, the perennial shortage of exercise, a succession of bitches, all this told upon his health and loosened his character. He developed more and more the prima donna disposition. He became increasingly self-centred and self-important. Yet all the while, deep in his heart, he felt completely disorientated and futile, spiritually enslaved to the will of man.

At last, when he felt in himself a return of sadistic impulses, he was seized with such a terror of sheer madness that he once more gathered all his moral strength together for a great recovery. He set himself a course of strict self-discipline and asceticism. He would have no more bitches. He would cut down his food by half. Sometimes he would fast; and "pray to whatever gods there be." He would take exercise. He would co-operate conscientiously with the Laboratory staff in their researches on him. He would once more tackle his literary work; for even this, which had for long been his one remaining active interest, had recently been dropped.

For a while he did indeed live a more austere life, punctuated by bouts of wild self-indulgence; but presently his resolution began once more to fail, and he found himself slipping back into the old ways. Terror seized him; and a desperate loneliness in the midst of his social contacts. He felt a violent need for Plaxy, and sent her a note, asking her to come for a good walk with him.

Plaxy gladly made an appointment with him, but the day was not a success. She was naturally very absorbed in her university life; and though Sirius was in a manner a member of the same university, their experiences did not overlap. Lectures, essays, meetings, dances, and above all her new friendships filled her mind with matter that was remote from Sirius. At first they talked happily and freely, but there was no depth of intimacy between them. Several times he was on the verge of blurting out his troubles; but to say, "Oh, Plaxy, help me, I'm going to hell," which was what he wanted to say, seemed somehow preposterous. Moreover, as the day wore on, he began to suspect from a faint change in her odour that she was growing subconsciously hostile to him. He had been talking to her about the bitches. It was then that her scent had begun to take on a slight asperity, though in speech and manner she remained quite friendly. Towards the end of the day a gloomy silence fell upon them both. Each tried to dispel it with light talk, but vainly. When at last they were on the point of parting, and Plaxy had said, "It was nice to be together again," Sirius registered in his own mind the fact that her odour had been growing mellower as the parting approached. "Yes, it's good indeed," he said. But even as he said it the human smell of her, though unchanged in its sensory quality, began to nauseate him.

In order to return to the Laboratory he had to cross the town. He strolled off, without any positive desire to reach his destination, or indeed to do anything else. As he drifted along the streets, he felt stifled by the surrounding herd of the grotesque super-simians who had conquered the earth, moulded the canine species as they trimmed their hedges, and produced his unique self. Feelings of violent hatred surged up in him. A number of significant little memories presented themselves to his embittered mind. Long ago in a field near Ffestiniog he had come upon an angel-faced little boy taking baby thrushes out of a nest and skewering them one by one on a rusty nail. More recently in a Cambridge garden he had watched a well-dressed woman sitting on a seat and fondling a dog's head. Presently she looked about as though to see if she was being observed. There was no one but Sirius, a mere animal. Still stroking the dog with one hand, she reached out with the other and pressed her lighted cigarette end into the creature's groin. This streak of sexual cruelty in human beings horrified Sirius all the more because he himself had indulged in something of the sort with his bitches. But he persuaded himself that this aberration in him was entirely due to some sort of infection from man, due, in fact, to his human conditioning. His own kind, he told himself, were not by nature cruel. Oh, no, they always killed as quickly as possible. Only the inscrutable and devilish cat descended to torture.

It was all due to man's horrible selfishness, he told himself. *Homo sapiens* was an imperfectly socialized species, as its own shrewder specimens, for instance H. G. Wells, had pointed out. Even dogs, of course, were self-centred, but also far more spontaneously social. They might often fight for bones or bitches, and they persecuted one another for the glory of dominance; but when they *were* social they were more wholeheartedly social. They were much more ready to be loyal absolutely, without any secret nosing after self-advantage. So he told himself. They could give absolute, disinterested loyalty; for instance to the human family that claimed their pack-allegiance, or to a single adored master, or to the work that was entrusted to them. The sheep-dog didn't expect to get anything out of his job. He did it for the work's sake alone.

He was an artist. No doubt some men were as loyal as any dog, but Cambridge life had taught Sirius to smell out self-regard under every bit of loyalty. Even Plaxy's affection for him seemed in his present mood merely a sort of living up to a pattern for her precious self, not real self-oblivious love. Or take McBane. Was it science or the budding great scientist, Hugh McBane, that really stirred him? Sirius had noticed that he smelt most excited and eager whenever some little personal triumph was at stake. Then there were all those prominent people that he had met at Thomas's lunch parties—biologists, physicists, psychologists, doctors, surgeons, academics, writers, painters, sculptors and God-knows-what-all. They were so very distinguished, and all so seeming modest and so seeming friendly; and yet every one of them, every bloody one of them, if he could trust his nose and his sensitive ears, was itching for personal success, for the limelight, or (worse) scheming to push someone else out of the limelight, or make someone in it look foolish or ugly. No doubt dogs would be just as bad, really, except when their glorious loyalty was upon them. That was the point! Loyalty with dogs could be absolute and pure. With men it was always queered by their inveterate self-love. God! They must be insensitive really; drunk with self, and insensitive to all else. There was something reptilian about them, snakish.

Long ago he had idealized humanity. His silly uncritical, canine loyalty had made him do so. But now his practised nose had found out the truth about the species. They were cunning brutes, of course, devilishly cunning. But they were not nearly so consistently intelligent as he had thought. They were always flopping back into sub-human dullness, just as he was himself. And they didn't *know* themselves even as well as he knew himself, and not half as well as he knew them. How he knew them! He had been brought up in a rather superior family, but even the Trelones were often stupid and insensitive. Even Plaxy knew very little about herself. She was so absorbed in herself that she couldn't see herself, couldn't see the wood for the trees. How often she was unreasonable and self-righteous because of some miserable little self-regard that she herself didn't spot. But *he* spotted it all right, oh yes! And she could be cruel. She could make him feel an outcast and a worm, just for spite.

What enraged him most of all about human beings, and particularly the superior ones that he met in Cambridge, was their self-deception. Every one of them was quite different really from the mask that he or she presented to the world. McBane, for instance. Of course he really *was* devoted to science, up to a point, but more so to himself; and he daren't admit it, even to himself. Why couldn't he just say, "Oh, I know I'm a selfish brute at heart, but I try not to be"? Instead, he pretended to have a real sheep-dog loyalty to science. But he didn't really *use himself up* for science. Perhaps he might some day, just as Thomas did. Some day he might be ready to die for science even. But if he did, he would really be dying not absolutely for science, but for his own reputation as a devoted scientist.

Oh God! What a species to rule a planet! And so obtuse about everything that wasn't human! So incapable of realizing imaginatively any *other* kind of spirit than the human! (Had not even Plaxy failed him?) And cruel, spiteful! (Had not even Plaxy had her claws in him?) And complacent! (Did not even Plaxy really, in her secret heart, regard him as "just a dog"?)

But what a universe, anyhow! No use blaming human beings for what they were. Everything was made so that it had to torture something else. Sirius himself no exception, of course. Made that way! Nothing was *responsible* for being by nature predatory on other things, dog on rabbit and Argentine beef, man on nearly everything, bugs and microbes on man, and of course man himself on man. (Nothing but man was really cruel, vindictive, except perhaps the loathly cat.) Everything desperately struggling to keep its nose above water for a few breaths before its strength inevitably failed and down it went, pressed under by something else. And beyond, those brainless, handless idiotic stars, blazing away so importantly for nothing. Here and there some speck of a planet dominated by some half-awake intelligence like humanity. And here and there on such planets, one or two poor little spirits waking up and wondering what in hell everything was for, what it was all about, what they could make of themselves; and glimpsing in

a muddled way what their potentiality was, and feebly trying
to express it, but always failing, always missing fire, and very
often feeling themselves breaking up, as he himself was doing.
Just now and then they might find the real thing, in some
creative work, or in sweet community with another little spirit,
or with others. Just now and then they seemed somehow to
create or to be gathered up into something lovelier than their
individual selves, something which demanded their selves'.
sacrifice and yet gave their selves new life. But how pre-
cariously, torturingly; and only just for a flicker of time!
Their whole life-time would only be a flicker in the whole of
titanic time. Even when all the worlds have frozen or exploded,
and all the suns gone dead and cold, there'll still be time.
Oh, God, what for?

CHAPTER IX

SIRIUS AND RELIGION

AS Sirius walked home to the Laboratory after his day with
Plaxy, brooding on the shortcomings of man, and his own
loneliness, and the indifference of the universe, he began to
slip into the wolf-mood. Frustration always tended to have
this effect on him, and he was feeling desperately frustrated.
He longed for self-expression, and could find no means of
attaining it. When he was a puppy he had decided that he
would be a general, deploying his human troops with superhuman skill, charging with them to superhuman victory.
Ludicrous, impossible dream! Later he had determined to be
an explorer of the Siberian Tundra or prairies (a country that
he thought suited to his powers); but how could a dog take the
necessary gear with him without causing excitement among the
human inhabitants? Or perhaps Australian sheep-farming
would suit him, or some kind of hunting career in the north
of Canada. No, by now it was all too clear that nothing would
suit him, nothing was possible but to be a super-lap-dog-cum-
super-laboratory-animal.

Yet always there was a strange nagging "something" within him which said, "Get on with it! You have unique powers. There is only one of you, and you exist to make your contribution to the world. Find your calling. It is difficult for you, no doubt, but you must find it or be damned." Sometimes the voice said, "For you, humanity is the pack. You are not one of them, but they made you and you are *for* them. And because you are different you can give them a vision which they can never win for themselves." Could he, after all, fulfil his task, perhaps, through music? Grandiose fantasies assailed him. "Sirius, the unique canine composer, not only changed the whole character of human music, importing into it something of the dog's finer auditory sensibility; he also, in his own incomparable creations, expressed the fundamental identity-in-diversity of all spirits, of whatever species, canine, human or super-human."

But no! It could not be. Man would never listen to him. And what reason had he to suppose that he had the genius to strike his music into the deep incomprehensible heart of man?

On the way back to the Laboratory Sirius heard the familiar nagging voice, calling him to express the "spirit" in him. He greeted it with an inward snarl. What could he possibly do about it? Nothing. He was a misfit, a mistake. He ought never to have occurred.

He felt an increasing impulse to run amok in the street. Life was no good to him. Why not throw it away, why not kill as many as he could of these ridiculously bedecked, swelled-headed apes, until they managed to destroy him? "I won't, I won't," he kept saying to himself. "Even if they *are* apes, or forked worms, they are the same stuff really as I am." Fleeing from himself, he broke into a trot, a canter, a real gallop, needing the seclusion of his own room. There, he paced up and down for many hours, far into the night. These hours form a crucial point in his life, so I shall quote from the account which he himself wrote down on the following day; turgid stuff, but significant of his unwholesome state.

"I walked and walked, rubbing my shoulder painfully against the wall every time I turned, snapping at the curtain as I passed it. This was affectation; I was dramatizing myself as a caged beast. The colleges and churches chimed, quarter by quarter. The noise of passing cars died down as the night advanced. I kept remembering with fury the smell of Plaxy, dear and loathsome; and the scent of my last bitch, so sweet, but false, promising a lovely spirit that did not exist. Then the sudden presence of Idwal's friendly smell, and of a flock of sheep, drenched with mist. The smell of Pugh, sweaty and excited. Of frost, of a summer day, of wind from the sea, of the change of wind from west to east. Trails of rabbit and hare. The infuriating stink of cat. Fox, rich and subtle. The menagerie. Chloroform, and the two toughs that had attacked me. The faint, throat-tightening smell of suffering which sometimes seems to come from the part of the Lab where I have never been.

"Below all this flood of smells there was an undercurrent of sounds; tones of human voices, and dog voices; bleating of sheep and lambs; the wind, whimpering or furious; snatches of human music, and themes of my own singing.

"My whole life seemed to crowd in on me in smell and sound; and touch also, for I felt Plaxy's hand on my neck, and the cracking of bones between my teeth, and the soft flanks of a young setter that I had loved long ago in Ffestiniog.

"Visual shapes came too, but dimly, unsteadily. Sometimes I glimpsed Thomas with pursed lips, considering me; sometimes Plaxy smiling.

"While these memories presented themselves to me, thoughts also kept racing and jostling one another through my mind, chiefly terrified and resentful thoughts about man's power over me, and my own failure to be master of my fate. How could I ever save myself from the breakdown that had already begun in me? What help was there anywhere for me? Thomas did not really understand the creature he had made. Elizabeth was always ready to hear my troubles and comfort me; but somehow she turned them all into child's troubles. And Plaxy was now so far away. It was 'the spirit,' we had said, that mattered. It was 'in the spirit' that we were eternally together. But now? Had we meant anything real at all by 'the spirit'? I wondered. After all we were just animals, with some degree of intelligence; animals of different species, doomed never really to be at one with each other, always in discord, and now drifting inevitably apart.

"Why, why was everything so sweet in promise and yet always in realization bitter?

"But presently, as I paced up and down the little room, a queer thing happened. It was as though my wandering imagination came upon a new quality, different from all that I had ever known; yet one which was also more familiar and intimate than the smell of Plaxy in the mood of love, more piercing sweet than bitches, more hunt-worthy than the trail of a fox.

"No, I must not romanticize. This is a scientific report. No new sensory quality really came to me. But something happened in my mind which I can't describe in any other way. If it was a fragrance at all, it was the fragrance of love and wisdom and creating, of these for their own sake, whether crowned with success and happiness or not. It was this fragrance, which somehow came to me with such a fresh poignancy that it was something entirely new to me. It was this fragrance, trailed across the universe, winding in and out of all its chasms and interstices, that had so often enticed me; but now in my excited state it presented itself to me so vividly that I had to dramatize it to myself as a new quality, neither odour nor sound nor visible form, but most like an odour to be pursued.

"And I did pursue it. I stopped pacing, and lay down with my forelegs stretched before me; and I laid my chin along them. Ignoring all the other remembered scents, I pursued this strange new trail, with the flying feet of inner attention. And as I followed, the trail became stronger, clearer, more exquisite. Sometimes it escaped me, but casting back I recovered it. Sometimes my strength failed, and as I flagged the trail grew fainter. But I gathered myself together again for the chase, and as I pursued, lessening the distance between myself and the quarry, the scent grew clearer and more compelling.

"At last a terrible thing happened. As I drew nearer, the quality of the heavenly quarry seemed to change. Though its exquisite sweetness remained, drawing me on, a new, pungent tang, a stinging, choking, bitter, exquisite and terrifying perfume, was mixed with it. There was something in it that made my mind reel, as the chloroform had done; and something

fierce, like the mighty smells of tiger and lion, but with a grim-
ness that no earthly smell ever had. I could not give up the
chase. With staggering mind I still clung to the trail. The
thing that I was hunting must surely be the source of all fragrance in the universe, and all horror also. And I was famished
for the thing. I must, must reach it; though in the end surely
not *I* should devour *it*, but *it* would devour *me*. Surely the
thing that I was crazily hunting must be the very thing that men
called God, the dear and beautiful and dread.

"At last it was as though the quarry turned at bay and over-
whelmed me. Remembering, I cannot recapture that moment
of agony and bliss, the agony of my slaughtered self, the bliss
of the freed spirit in me. It was as though—how can I put it?—
as though the trail which had first promised the most succulent
prey, and then the most formidable but spell-binding enemy,
had led after all not to the universal Tiger but to the universal
Master, the superhuman master whom my super-canine nature
so desperately needed to take possession of me and steady me
with his claim for absolute loyalty and service.

"That supreme moment passed. I can remember only that
when it passed I found peace such as I had not known before
and shall never, I believe, quite lose. The whole universe now
presented itself with a new quality, as though my monochrome
vision had suddenly gained the glory of colour. But the colours
that I saw were not of sensation. They were the colours that
are seen by the eye of the spirit. All the things and people that
I had seen hitherto in the plain greys of ordinary life were now
enriched with a great diversity of the new quality which I am
calling colour, so that they gained a new meaning, much as
sounds gain a new meaning in speech or music. I saw them all
in their own true colours and suffused with the music of the
whole. And even now, on the day after my glorious moment,
which is lost save for its afterglow in my mind, I still see everything coloured by the light of the spirit."

There followed a postscript.

"All this was written on the day after my vision, if vision
it was. And now another day has passed. I have read it over,
and I see that it does not describe at all the thing that happened
to me. It is sentimental verbiage. It does not recapture the

experience for me, it blurs it. But I am certain that something big really did happen to me. And the proof shall be shown in my life. I will take charge of my life. I will drift no more. I will still be true to science, but I will be true to my new light also. I will be a sceptic about everything but one thing, which does not admit of scepticism (once one has clearly seen it), namely that it does indeed matter to be as quickened a spirit as possible, and to live for the quickening of the spirit everywhere. In fact I am going to be the hound of the spirit. Me? Lazy, excuse-finding me? That's a good joke, isn't it! Looking at the matter with scientific detachment, I am sure I shall be adrift again before the week is out. Well, even if I *am*, the thing that happened the night before last will make a difference. And looking at it all in the light of the thing—no, by God! I shall never be adrift again! Not fundamentally."

With much misgiving Sirius dutifully offered this document to Thomas. Would he be amused, or annoyed? Or would he take it with all his aloof scientific detachment as a psychological datum? Sirius never discovered what Thomas really felt about it. The great physiologist was respectful, almost diffident; and hoped Sirius did not object to having the document typed in triplicate, "for the Laboratory records, and to show to a few of my friends, if you don't mind."

This seemingly mystical experience awakened in Sirius a new interest in religion. Through one of Thomas's guests he stumbled on the literature of mysticism, and was soon devoting a great deal of his time to St. Catherine of Siena, St. John of the Cross, Jacob Boehme, the Vedanta, and so on. It was Thomas who had to procure these works for him; and the task made Thomas smell acrid and disapproving, even though in word and deed he remained sympathetic.

Sirius now conceived a great desire to discuss religion with some sincere and orthodox religious person. No such person, it seemed, was among Thomas's circle of trusted friends who might be admitted into the secret of Sirius's intelligence. They were all either strictly scientific in the narrow sense or inclined to say "One feels in one's bones that there must be *something* in religion, but God knows what." Contact with these people merely increased Sirius's desire to pursue the matter, without helping him.

Sometimes he would hang about the doors of chapels and churches, to watch the congregation enter or leave the building, or to strain his hypersensitive ears to catch reverberations of the music, the prayers, the lessons and the sermon. The fact that as a mere dog he was not allowed into the sacred building increased his sense of exile and inferiority, and his readiness to believe that in spite of the critics it was within those walls that man attained his highest range of experience.

On one occasion his hunger for the truth was so great that he could not restrain himself from a very foolish act. It was summer time, and there was a heat wave. He had been watching the worshippers entering a little Methodist Chapel. Contrary to custom, the doors were not shut before the service began. Emotional prayer and vigorous singing flooded out upon him. To his refined sensibility the music was crude and the execution vulgar, but these very imperfections increased for him the feeling that music was here only a hastily executed symbol of some ulterior experience. A poem might be sincere no matter how hastily it had been scribbled. Jarred by the barbaric sound, yet fascinated, Sirius drifted step by step into the porch and across the inner threshold. He had entered during a prayer. The minister's eyes were reverently closed. His tone of voice was unctuous and complacently servile. With the conventional intonation of penitence and worship, but without any inner experience of them, he affirmed the sinfulness of the whole human race, and confidently, flatteringly, asked his God for forgiveness and eternal bliss for himself and his flock. The backs of the bowed congregation appeared above the pews like the backs of sheep in a pen. But their smell on that hot day was all too human.

When the prayer was ended the minister opened his eyes. He saw the great dog standing in the aisle. Pointing dramatically at Sirius, he exclaimed, "Who has brought that animal into God's House? Put it out!" Several black coats and striped trousers moved towards Sirius. They expected him to retire before them, but he stood his ground, his head and tail erect, his back bristling. A faint growl, rather like distant thunder, made the assailants hesitate. Sirius looked round the building. All eyes were turned on him, some outraged, some amused.

He turned slowly to retrace his steps. The ejectors cautiously advanced. One of them said, "Good dog! Go home!" but another began to chivvy him with an umbrella, and rashly tapped his haunch. Sirius leapt round with a bark that echoed through the bare chapel, and his pursuers retreated a pace. He stood looking at them for a few moments, amused at his easy triumph. The hair on his spine subsided. He vaguely waved his tail, and turned towards the door. Then a mischievous idea took possession of him. At the door he once more faced the congregation, and in a clear, accurate, though wordless, voice he sang the refrain of the hymn that had been sung before he entered. As he turned to leave the building a woman screamed. The minister in a rather strained voice said, "Friends, I think we had better join once more in prayer."

On another occasion he marched beside the drums of the Salvation Army, sometimes forgetting himself so far as to add his voice to the trumpets. The open air service gave him, he told Thomas, an irrational sense of salvation. What appealed to him most was one of the hymns, sung with immense gusto. "Washed in the blood of the Lamb," was its theme. He could not resist joining in the singing, though softly. He could not see how the imagery of the hymn agreed with the religion of love, but somehow it had a strange power over him. He vaguely and quite irrationally felt it as unifying all the tenderness of his life with all the wolf in him. He scented again the seductive reek of his killed ram and his killed pony. Somehow the haunting conflict between pity and blood-lust seemed to be resolved. His guilt was washed away. There was no sound reason for this; he just felt it. He and these human animals somehow unloaded their sins upon the Lamb, and found a crude ecstasy of community one with another, and all together. They abased themselves into the personified spirit of the group. The intoxicated minds gave up all attempt to think clearly and feel precisely, and yielded to the common mentality; which somehow seemed to be universal, cosmical, the personified "togetherness" of all individual spirits in all the worlds. Thus he felt, as the barbaric tune soaked through his brain. Yet to another part of his mind the blasting of the trumpets, the thundering of the drums and the lusty human singing seemed as remote as the howling of an alien species in the jungle. Not in this way, said the protesting part of his mind, not in the remission of clear thought and feeling for the sake of the mere warmth of togetherness, could one find the essential spirit, identical in himself and in these humans. Only in the most articulate, precise self- and other-consciousness was the thing to be found; for instance on those rare occasions of spiritual accord with Plaxy, when through their very difference and distinctness they discovered their underlying identity. Yes, and in another manner he had sometimes found that thing, with Thomas, when their two intellects had moved together up the steep path of some argument, Thomas always leading, till they had reached together some pinnacle from which, it seemed, they could view the whole universe.

CHAPTER X

EXPERIENCES IN LONDON

ONE day Sirius demanded very urgently that Thomas should arrange for him to meet a few of the outstanding religious people of Cambridge. "But I don't know any," said Thomas. "They're not my line. And anyhow I wouldn't trust them not to blab." Sirius was not to be put off; and finally it was agreed that Elizabeth should help him to satisfy his curiosity about religion, and at the same time show him London. She had a cousin who was a parson in the East End. He could be taken into their confidence, and the two of them could perhaps visit him.

The Rev. Geoffrey Adams, now well advanced in middle age, was one of those clerics who had cared more for his parishioners than for self-advancement. Long ago he had undertaken a slum parish, and he had stayed there ever since. His life had been spent in comforting the sick and the dying with assurances of peace hereafter, in fighting local authorities on behalf of hard cases, and in agitating for playgrounds, free milk for mothers and children, and decent treatment for the unemployed. Throughout the country he had something of a reputation as a fighting parson, for on several occasions his indiscreet championship of the oppressed had brought him up against the state or his ecclesiastical superiors. Nearly all his parishioners admired him, some loved him, very few attended his services.

Elizabeth wrote to Geoffrey, telling him about Sirius, and asking if she might visit him, with the wonder-dog. He replied that he was desperately busy, that religion was not a thing to be got merely by talking about it, but that if they came to the East End he would show them round, and they might see a little of it in action.

Elizabeth took Sirius by train to King's Cross, a tiresome journey for the dog, as he had to travel in the luggage van. They spent the afternoon walking about the more prosperous end of the metropolis, for Sirius's edification. Oxford Street, Regent Street, Piccadilly and the parks gave Sirius a new impression of the multitude and power of the human race. What an amazing species it was, with its great buildings, its endless streams of cars, its shop-window displays, its swarming foot-passengers, with their trousered or silken legs! He could always detect the familiar sheep smell in the tweed; and in the fur coats there were still odours of the menagerie. Sirius had many questions to ask Elizabeth, but of course they dared not talk, for fear of rousing curiosity.

After a while Elizabeth was tired with all the walking, and wanted her tea. It was difficult to find a café where the great dog was acceptable, but after a while they settled beside a little table. Sirius, of course, lay on the floor, and was much in the way of the waitresses. Elizabeth gave him a bun and a slop-basin full of sweet tea. While she smoked, he watched the company. Someone was overheard to say, "That dog's expression is almost human."

After they had refreshed themselves they went eastwards by tube, and emerged in an entirely different world, the down-and-out world that Plaxy had often described to him. He was amazed by the contrast of *homo sapiens* in affluence and *homo sapiens* in penury. Young men hung about aimlessly at pub-corners. Dirty-faced children and shabby curs played in the

gutters. Both the smell and the voices of the passers-by gave
Sirius an unmistakable impression of defeat and resentment.
He walked beside Elizabeth with alert and anxious eyes and
heavy tail. This line of country threatened to be too much for
him. The only familiar and comforting thing about it was the
variety of odours left by his own kind at the foot of each lamp-
post. The rest was overwhelming, not only because of the
oppressive stink of man, but because it was a stink of man in
abject anxiety. The western crowd had smelt mainly of
cosmetics, perfume, soap, fresh tweed, tobacco smoke, moth
balls and the slaughtered beasts whose furs they had stolen.
There was also, of course, a strong undertone of human
sweat, mostly female, and of all the other physical odours,
including now and then an unmistakable whiff of sexual
excitement. But in the eastern crowd the smell of crude
human bodies dominated everything else; and it was on the
average different in quality from the smell of the western
bodies. In the prosperous region the odour was mainly of
wholesome physique, but in the poorer region there was a faint
but definite and very widespread smell of ill-health, rising
sometimes (for his keen nose) to one or other of the repellent
stenches of disease. There was another difference, too. Even
in the west there was a tell-tale smell of peevish discontent; but
in the east, where frustration was far more poignant, the same
smell of discontent was stronger, and often accompanied by the
acrid stink of chronic but suppressed rage.

Sirius, of course, had come across sordid town areas before,
but never before had he imaginatively realized the extent of
man's degradation in Britain. So this, he kept saying to himself, is what man has done to man, this is the average condition
of the proud tyrant species. Its fundamentally self-regarding
intelligence and its inadequate feeling for community has led
it to this. The West End cared not a damn for the East End,
and both, in their several ways, were frustrated.

The Rev. Geoffrey Adams received his visitors with some
embarrassment. He had no idea how to treat Sirius, and even
ordinary dogs he felt to be rather remote and incomprehensible.
However, he soon learned that this great beast must be treated
more or less as a human being; and he showed a surprising

quickness in recognizing that Sirius's strange noises were an attempt at the English language. He accounted for his aptitude by saying, "I come across so many queer lingos at the docks." Then, realizing that this remark might seem disrespectful, he looked anxiously at Sirius, who moved his tail slightly in sign of friendliness.

Elizabeth had intended that they should spend a couple of nights with Geoffrey and then return to Cambridge, but Sirius was determined to stay on by himself, if Geoffrey would have him. For here was an aspect of mankind about which he knew nothing, and he could not begin to understand it in a couple of days. Geoffrey had been at first rather sceptical and even offhand about Sirius's search for religion, but some of the dog's remarks during their first interview, interpreted by Elizabeth, had roused his interest, particularly his statement that the heart of religion was love, and nothing else mattered. Here was a truth that called for elaboration and qualification. Geoffrey was also much intrigued by Sirius's real capacity for song, for the cleric was musical, and something of a singer himself. This was an added reason for his unexpectedly warm encouragement of Sirius's suggestion that he should remain in the East End for a while.

It was arranged that the dog should stay with Geoffrey for a week. Actually he remained much longer, He masqueraded as Geoffrey's dog, going with him among the parishioners whenever possible. Often, of course, he had to be left behind. Geoffrey could not take him to share death-bed scenes or difficult interviews with town councillors. But on most pastoral visits cleric and dog would set out together, and on the doorstep Geoffrey would ask, "May I bring in my dog? He's quite friendly." Sirius's amiable expression and waving tail would nearly always gain him a welcome.

In this manner he saw much of the conditions in which the less fortunate members of the dominant species lived. He also listened to many a conversation on matters practical or spiritual. Sometimes Geoffrey would greatly amuse his friends in the parish by including Sirius in the conversation, and Sirius to their delight would "reply." No one, of course, suspected that these little performances were genuine; but the Rev.

Adams's queer dog was well received in all but the most unimaginative families. Children were specially accessible, for Sirius allowed them to ride him and maul him, and often showed "an uncanny understanding" of their talk and games. One boy of twelve insisted that Sirius's own talk was not sham at all, and that he himself could often understand it. Geoffrey affirmed, "Of course it's real," then knowingly smiled at the grown-ups.

Sometimes Geoffrey's duties took him to a canteen or mission-hall in dockland, sometimes to a Men's Club, where, followed by the observant Sirius, he would pass from room to room exchanging greetings with the members. Sometimes the parson took a turn at darts or billiards, or watched a boxing match. Once, with Sirius carelessly stretched out on the floor, he gave a talk on "Housing."

It did not take long for Sirius to discover that there were many different reactions to Geoffrey in this club. A few members regarded him with resentment and suspicion; and expressed their spleen by furtive persecution of his dog. Others, while respecting Geoffrey's kindliness and sincerity, regarded him and his religion as survivals from a prehistoric world. A few curried favour by professing conventional piety. One or two, for whom Geoffrey showed a special bantering affection, were for ever trying to convert him to atheism. The arguments, on both sides, rather shook Sirius's faith in the intellectual honesty of the dominant species, for on both sides the calibre of the reasoning was sometimes laughably poor. It was as though neither side really cared about mere logical cogency, because both had already made up their minds. Of all the club members, not one, it seemed to Sirius, was a sincere Christian in Geoffrey's sense of the term; though many were deeply influenced by Geoffrey's personality.

Sometimes Geoffrey took Sirius into the actual land of docks. The strange odours of foreign merchandise greatly interested him. They afforded him, he said, not only information about the goods themselves but something of the atmosphere of the lands from which they came. They enabled him to "travel by nose." He was greatly intrigued also by the new varieties of human odour associated with coloured people.

Negroes, Lascars, Chinese, each had their distinctive racial scent, and in contrast with these the smell characteristic of Europeans distinguished itself in his mind.

On one occasion Geoffrey and Sirius came upon a minor riot. The dockers were on strike on account of the sacking of one of their number for political reasons. Blackleg labour was introduced, and the local men attacked the interlopers. Geoffrey and Sirius arrived at the height of the trouble. A large crowd of men was preventing a smaller crowd from going to work. Stones and bottles were thrown. A blackleg was knocked unconscious, and lay in the mud with a bleeding forehead. Geoffrey hastened to him, with Sirius at his heels, the wolf-mood rising. As Geoffrey bent over the stricken man, some of the dockers reviled him for helping their enemy. Someone even threw a stone, and Sirius took up a position between Geoffrey and the crowd, with bared teeth and a terrifying growl. Geoffrey did not take the men's hostile action meekly. In fact, for the first time Sirius saw him lose his temper. "Fools!" cried the parson. "I'm on your side, but this man is as precious to God as any of us." At this point God's damaged treasure recovered consciousness and rose to his feet, using most ungodly language. Then the police arrived in considerable force, drew their truncheons, and charged the dockers, most of whom fled. A few put up a fight and were arrested; two were picked up unconscious.

Before going to bed that night, Geoffrey and Sirius, as was their custom, talked over the affairs of the day. This time Sirius was deeply interested. He had long ago discovered that the human species was not at one with itself, and that authority was not always sympathetic with the common people, but the scene at the dock entrance had brought this home to him. According to Geoffrey the aim of the strike was to make a stand against gross victimization; and yet the police, though their action had been legally correct, had shown unnecessary brutality.

The world that Sirius now lived in was bewilderingly different from both his two other worlds, North Wales and Cambridge. The three worlds were inhabited by such diverse creatures that he could almost believe them three different species. Country people, intellectuals, dockers! Mentally they were far more alien to one another than dogs, cats and horses. Yet, of course, the difference was really all imposed by environment. Well, for the present he was wholly occupied in studying his third world; the others faded imperceptibly into dreamlands. For some weeks he was far too interested in the East End to look back on those other worlds; but at last there came times, chiefly when Geoffrey was busy on committee work, when he found himself hankering after open country and the smell of the sheep. For at these times there was nothing for him to do but wander about the streets watching the rather shabby crowds, listening to their monkey chatter, smelling their slightly unhealthy and frustrated odour, and feeling himself utterly alien to them. Then he would begin to worry about his future. What was to become of him? In Wales he was just a sheep-dog and a chattel; in Cambridge, a curiosity. In London? Well, at least, he was a student of the human species. But what could he ever *do*? It was his nature to *give* himself absolutely to some work; but to what work? To mere sheep-tending? To science? Why, of course, to the spirit. But how? His despondency was largely due to constipation. Do what he would, he could not get enough physical exercise in a town, and he could not help eating far too much for an inactive life. Worse, his soul was constipated. He was always taking in mental food and never doing anything with it.

One day as he was strolling past the entrance to a railway station, he noticed a display of large framed photographs advertising holiday resorts. One of them was a magnificent picture of moorland with mist driving over it. There was a little llyn, and one or two sheep. Waves splashed seductively on the stony shore. In the background the mountain rose darkly into the cloud. The immediate foreground was all tussocks of grass and heather, inviting his legs to action. He stood for a long time looking at this picture, letting the feel of the moors soak into him again, getting the smell of them. He caught himself actually working his nostrils to take the sheep's scent. Were they Pugh's or a neighbour's? It was all so real. And yet so far away and dreamlike. He could scarcely believe that he would ever be there again. Sudden panic seized him.

Then Sirius came to a firm resolution about his future. Science or no science, spirit or no spirit, he would spend his life in that sort of country, not in slums, nor in universities. That alone was his line of country. That was the only world he could ever really live in. Somehow in that world he must express whatever potency it was that was always straining in him to find exercise. But how?

On Sundays Geoffrey was always very busy, and Sirius was of course excluded from his sacred duties. The dog generally took the opportunity of securing a bit of much-needed exercise, cantering off into Epping Forest. On Sunday evenings Geoffrey often seemed dejected and old. Sirius had observed that few people entered the church for any of the services. Unfortunately Geoffrey, though respected and loved by so many, could not attract a large congregation. This incapacity he regarded as a failure in his religious duty. He did not realize, but Sirius did, that the influence of his personality reached far beyond the range of his official ministrations, and that he had given to thousands the essence of religion, though they could not accept from him the ritual and doctrine which, though symbolically true for a past age, was quite out of keeping with the spirit of our times. Some of Geoffrey's warmest admirers were persons who never attended his church or even counted themselves Christians. Of those who did attend, a few were of course sincere believers in the Christian myth as "gospel truth." Others came because they vaguely felt the need of some kind of religious life. They recognized in Geoffrey a truly religious spirit, and he assured them that they ought to join in communal worship. But the living example which he gave them in his life of practical love was somehow not clarified or strengthened by his church services. Geoffrey had no power to infuse the services with the ardent religious passion which he himself felt; and this failure it was which filled him with a gnawing doubt of his own sincerity.

These conclusions Sirius boldly announced to Geoffrey in their many talks over meals or late in the evenings. The ageing priest was saddened by them. He could not for a moment contemplate the possibility that his rituals and doctrines had only symbolical truth, though he could and did doubt his own

sincerity as a servant of God. He was saddened that men
should be so blind as to doubt the literal truth of Christian
doctrine, and specially sad that his friend Sirius should be so
blind. For between priest and dog there had rapidly developed
a deep mutual respect and affection. They had told one
another much of their personal lives, and in particular of their
religious searchings. To Geoffrey it seemed that Sirius's vague
yearnings and rigorous agnosticism formed only an utterly
inadequate shadow of religion. To Sirius it seemed, of course,
that Geoffrey's religion was an incongruous tissue of true
value-intuitions and false or meaningless intellectual proposi-
tions. Sirius had spoken of his love for Plaxy as "at heart a
religious love for the universal spirit." He had also told of his
strange vision in Cambridge. On one occasion he had said,
"I see, indeed I *know*, that in *some* sense God is love, and God
is wisdom, and God is creative action, yes and God is beauty;
but what God actually *is*, whether the maker of all things, or
the fragrance of all things, or just a dream in our own hearts,
I have not the art to know. Neither have you, I believe; nor
any man, nor any spirit of our humble stature." Geoffrey
merely smiled sadly and said, "May God in His time show you
the truth that His Son died to manifest."

On another occasion Sirius challenged Geoffrey about
immortality. They had been discussing for some while when
Sirius said, "Now take me! Have *I* an immortal soul?"
Geoffrey replied at once, "I have often wondered about you.
I *feel*, indeed, that you are an immortal spirit, and I earnestly
prayed that God should grant you salvation. But if you are,
and if He does, it is a miracle which I cannot interpret."

Sirius had come to Geoffrey in the hope of finding the true
religion. At Cambridge, in spite of all the free and fearless
intelligence, there had obviously been something lacking,
something that he greatly needed, though Cambridge regarded
it as something almost indecent. He had thought it must be
simply "religion," and he had come to London to find it.
And in Geoffrey he had, indeed, found it. There could be no
doubt that Geoffrey had a firm hold on the thing that Cambridge lacked, that Geoffrey was the very embodiment of
"religion" in action. But—but—one couldn't have Geoffrey's

religion without violating all that one had learnt at Cambridge, all the constant loyalty to intelligence that was the best thing in Cambridge. In a way it was easy to cling to faith and betray intelligence, though Geoffrey's active faith was no easy-going affair. It was easy, too, to cling to intelligence and abandon faith, like McBane, for instance. But was there no way of being equally loyal to both? Vaguely it began to appear to Sirius that there was, but that it involved both keener intelligence and more sensitive religious feeling than either of the other courses. Passion for "the spirit," the awakened way of living, whatever its fortune in the universe, passion for the spirit, stripped of all belief and comfort save the joy of that passion itself—this, expressed in a life of devoted action, like Geoffrey's, this was the only, the true religion. But poor Sirius felt dismally that this was beyond him. He just hadn't the guts. He hadn't either the intelligence or the passion. If only the spirit itself would seize him and set fire to him! But then—he was not prepared. He was not really inflammable. There was too much damp fog drenching all his tissues.

The friendship of the parson and his dog was the source of much comment in the district; the more so when it became known that the Rev. Adams was sometimes to be heard talking to the great animal as though to a human being. The dear old man, they said, was growing more eccentric than ever. Some declared simply that he was crazy. But presently rumour had it that real conversations did take place between man and dog, and that there actually was something mysterious about Sirius. The devout said he was either possessed by the Devil or was an angel in disguise. The scientific wiseheads said it was all quite simple, the dog was a biological sport.

The climax came when Sirius made a dramatic appearance in church. He had for long been secretly planning to gain Geoffrey's consent to this, partly because he wanted to witness one of Geoffrey's services, partly because it rankled to be shut out from the most solemn activity of the human species, and treated as an inferior animal. Geoffrey, of course, felt that he ought not to permit a brute to enter the holy place. His curate would have been outraged, and so would the congregation. But he had been much impressed by Sirius's superb singing

voice, and Sirius had subtly induced him to toy with the idea
of allowing his canine friend to sing a wordless anthem from
behind the vestry door. When they were at home together,
Sirius made a point of practising some of Geoffrey's favourite
"sacred" music.

With much misgiving, and a sense not of sin but of naughti-
ness, Geoffrey finally agreed to allow Sirius to sing at a Sunday
morning service, unseen, from behind the vestry door. The
great day arrived. Dog and man walked to the church, the
priest explaining to the canine singer the point in the service
at which the anthem should occur. "Keep well behind the
door," he said. "This is a bold step for me, Sirius. If they
find out there will be trouble."

When the couple reached the gate of the little church, Sirius
paused for a moment, looked up at Geoffrey rather anxiously,
and then deposited a few drops of golden fluid on the gatepost.
With a rather nervous laugh Geoffrey said, "You might have
relieved yourself somewhere else." "No," answered Sirius.
"It was a religious act. I have poured my libation in honour
of your God. And I have relieved my spirit of impurity. I am
lightened for the chase, the pursuit of the divine quarry by
song."

When the service was about to begin, the verger noticed that
the parson had left the vestry door open. He stepped over to
shut it, but Geoffrey waved him away with his hand.

At the appropriate point in the service Geoffrey announced,
"You will now hear a wordless anthem sung by a dear friend
of mine who will remain unnamed and unseen." Sirius's
strong pure voice, unaccompanied, then filled the church.
Geoffrey listened with delight at its power and delicacy of
expression. It seemed to him that in this music lay the truth
that he himself had striven all his life long to express in word
and deed. And now a dog, interpreting a great human composer (it was Bach) was saying it unmistakably, though without
words. Many of the congregation also were deeply moved.
The few musical members were impressed and mystified, for
the execution was accurate, and it expressed with severe restraint a deep and subtle passion. But what perplexed them
was the curiously non-human quality of the voice. Was it

perhaps some cunning instrumental imitation of a man's voice, or of a woman's? The range, they said, was too great for either. If it was indeed a singer, why did he or she not appear? Throughout the following week rumour was busy. A great singer, it was said, had consented to do this thing for Mr. Adams on condition that his identity was not revealed. The pious secretly believed that the great singer was not a man but an angel from heaven. Such was the decay of faith, however, that fear of ridicule prevented all but a few simple souls from openly proclaiming this belief.

Next Sunday there were far more people than usual at the morning service, though not enough to make the church look full. The newcomers obviously had come out of mere curiosity. In his sermon Geoffrey scolded them for it. There was no anthem.

Not till the following Sunday, which was to be Sirius's last before returning to Cambridge, did he sing again. His earlier success had made him long for another opportunity, and he wished to face the congregation. This was to be the beginning of his message to the human species. He would sing them something of his own composition. It must be something intelligible to human ears, and indeed to a good proportion of this simple congregation. It must be something which would help them to feel again the essential truth in their own religion, and the unimportance of its mythology.

Geoffrey was reluctant to let Sirius perform again, because too much of a "sensation" had aready been caused. But he longed to hear that great voice filling his church once more. And his natural sincerity inclined him to let the singer be seen as well as heard. Moreover, though he knew there would be trouble with the bishop and some of the congregation, he felt that he was under an obligation to welcome his canine friend in God's house. Further, he secretly relished the prospect of shocking his earnest young curate.

Sirius spent several mornings out in Epping Forest, trying over many of his compositions. Though he kept out of view, as far as possible, his strange voice caused several people to seek him out. Whenever anyone discovered him, he let his song turn imperceptibly into a normal canine baying, so that the intruder supposed that the musical quality had been an illusion.

At the morning service Sirius sang from behind the vestry door. But the music was very different from that of his previous performance. All the meaningful intonations of the human voice and all canine ullulations seemed to enter into this alien yet intelligibly musical, this sweet yet rather frightening, sound. It ranged from a thundering growl to a high clear piping, almost as of singing birds.

I am not myself sufficiently sensitive musically to judge whether "interpretation" of music is legitimate. In Geoffrey's view, though he was intensely interested in music for its own sake, the supreme function of this art, as of all other arts, was as a medium of religious expression. Hence his eagerness to have Sirius sing in his church, and his intention to interpret the song to his congregation. Sirius, too, held that interpretation was legitimate, though in the hands of the imperfectly musical it often became ludicrous. I have heard him insist that, in so far as music ever had a "meaning" beyond the immediate and exquisite value of the sound-pattern itself, its "meaning" must be simply an emotional attitude. It could never speak directly about the objective world, or "the nature of existence"; but it might create a complex emotional attitude which might be appropriate to some feature of the objective world, or to the universe as a whole. It might therefore create religious feelings. Its "interpretation" in words would then involve describing those features of the universe which should evoke those feelings.

In this sense the strange music that Sirius put forth in Geoffrey's church spoke of bodily delight and pain, and of the intercourse of spirits. It expressed through the medium of sound, and transformed into universal symbols, the particular spirits of Thomas, Elizabeth, Plaxy and Geoffrey himself. It spoke of love and death, of the hunger for the spirit, and of Sirius's own wolf-mood. It spoke of the East End and the West End, of the docker's strike and the starry heaven.

All this it did at least for Sirius himself. To most of the congregation it was an inconsequent mixture of music and noise, and moreover a mixture of the recognizably, comfortably pious and the diabolical.

Geoffrey in his sermon tried to tell the congregation what the strange song had meant to him. "The singer," he said, "must have known love in his own experience and recognized it as good absolutely. He must also have known the presence of Satan, in the world and in his own heart."

In the evening service, when Geoffrey had announced the anthem, he added, "This time the singer will appear in the church. Do not be outraged. Do not think that a trick is being played on you. The singer is my dear friend, and it is good that you should know that God can still work miracles."

Out of the vestry strode the great beast, black and frosty-fawn. Head and tail were proudly erect. Grey eyes keenly watched the congregation. There was an audible gasp of surprise and protest, then dead silence. It was as though the power of "the eye," which the Border Collie used so successfully on sheep, was now being used by Sirius upon a whole human flock. He had made his entry with very solemn feelings; but the spectacle of these spellbound human sheep greatly tickled him, and he could not resist turning his head towards Geoffrey and giving him a very human wink with the eye that was hidden from the congregation. After this lapse, which shocked Geoffrey, Sirius pulled himself together. His mouth opened, displaying the white fangs that had recently killed ram and pony, and gripped the throat of a man. The church was then flooded with Sirius's music. Geoffrey seemed to hear in it echoes of Bach and Beethoven, of Holst, Vaughan Williams, Stravinsky and Bliss, but also it was pure Sirius. Most of the congregation, on a far lower musical level than their pastor, and a far lower human level also, were merely intrigued by its novelty. Some were sufficiently sensitive to be disturbed and revolted by it. A few conscious musical modernists probably decided that it was a bad imitation of the real thing. One or two, perhaps, were stirred more or less in the manner that Sirius intended. The performance lasted quite a long time, but the audience remained throughout still and attentive. When it was finished Sirius looked for a moment at Geoffrey, who returned his questioning gaze with a smile of admiration and affection. Sirius crouched down, muzzle on paws, tail stretched out along the ground. The service proceeded.

Geoffrey began his sermon by trying to interpret the music, warning his congregation that it might legitimately mean different things to different people, and that to the composer-singer his interpretation might seem very wrong. The congregation were startled. Were they expected to believe that the animal that had produced the music had also composed it, that what they had witnessed was not simply the result of brilliant circus-training but actually a miracle?

Geoffrey affirmed, rightly or wrongly, "The song gave me a view of humanity from outside humanity, from the point of view of another of God's creatures, and one that both admires and despises us, one that has fed from our hands and has also suffered at our hands. By means of echoes of the great human composers mingled with themes reminiscent of the wolf's baying and the dog's barking and howling, the singer conjured up his vision of humanity. And what a humanity it was! With God and Satan, love and hate together in its heart; with cunning surpassing all the beasts, and wisdom too, but also utter folly; with fabulous power, turned as often as not to Satan's will!" Geoffrey spoke of the luxury of the rich and the misery of the workers all over the world, of strikes and revolutions, of the ever-increasing threat of a war more terrible even than the last war. "And yet in our personal lives love is not unknown. In the song, as in my own knowledge, I seem to hear it said that love and wisdom must triumph in the end, because Love is God."

He looked down at Sirius, who was showing signs of protest. Geoffrey continued, "My friend does not agree with that part of my interpretation. But that is indeed how the climax of his song affected me."

He paused, then ended his sermon with these words: "I am growing old before my time. I shall not be able to carry on much longer. When I have gone, remember me by this Sunday. Remember that I once, by God's grace, was able to let you witness a very lovely miracle."

Not many of the congregation imagined even in that summer of 1939 that in a few months not only the ageing priest but many of the congregation themselves would be lying crushed under the East End buildings, or that the little church would become a blazing beacon for enemy planes.

At the end of the service Sirius walked out behind Geoffrey, and before the congregation had begun to leave the church he hurried off in the direction of Geoffrey's home. Soon after the parson had returned, Elizabeth arrived (according to plan) to take Thomas's canine masterpiece back to Cambridge.

During the following weeks Sirius received letters from Geoffrey talking of the excitement in the neighbourhood. Journalists had pestered him, but he had refused absolutely to give them any information. The church was filled on the following Sunday, but Geoffrey surmised that only a small minority had come for religion. Indeed he very soon realized that a daring act which he had undertaken with innocent motives was appearing to the public as no better than a piece of gross self-advertisement. His ecclesiastical superiors reprimanded him, and might well have deprived him of his office, had it not been for the passionate loyalty of his supporters in the parish.

When Thomas was told of the incident, he was at first annoyed, but the humour of it won him over to forgive Sirius for his escapade.

CHAPTER XI

MAN AS TYRANT

IN the summer of 1939 the clouds of war were already gathering over Europe. Everyone was living in dread of the future or hoping against hope that by some miracle the storm would after all not break. Sirius had never taken much interest in the international situation, but now, like so many others, he was forced to be interested. Thomas also was merely bored at the prospect of war. He wanted to carry on his work unhindered, and he feared that war would make this impossible. Of course, if the clash came, we should have to do our damnedest to win; but if only the fool politicians had been more intelligent and honest there would never have been any trouble. This was roughly Sirius's attitude also, except that in addition he felt a rising fury against the dominant species, which had been given such power and such opportunity, and yet was making such a sorry mess of its affairs.

During the summer vac the Trelone family spent only a few weeks in Wales. It was a clouded holiday, for there was no escape from the international situation. Thomas was embittered, and Elizabeth desperately saddened. Tamsy, who had been married some months earlier, spent her week in Wales brooding over the newspapers and the wireless set. Maurice, now a don at Cambridge, argued a great deal with Tamsy about Hitler's chances. Giles was very quiet, adjusting himself to the idea that he would soon have to fight. Plaxy ignored the war-clouds completely, and went out of the room whenever the subject was raised. Sirius concentrated on recovering physical fitness after Cambridge and London.

When war broke out Sirius was on a Cumberland sheep farm learning the ways of the Lakeland shepherds. Sirius's Cumberland experiences were valuable, but painful. Thwaites, who was by no means typical of the fine Lakeland type, turned out to be a harsh and unreasonable master. He showed Sirius an aspect of humanity with which he had never before had personal, contact to any appreciable extent. Sirius suspected Thwaites at the outset because his own dog, Roy, a Border Collie, avoided him whenever possible, and cringed when spoken to. In Thwaites's relations with Sirius some quite irrelevant and probably forgotten conflict seems to have found expression. He conceived an uncontrollable dislike for the dog, perhaps because of a strong suspicion that Sirius was no ordinary super-sheep-dog, and was privately judging his character very ruthlessly. Whatever the cause, Thwaites soon began to treat Sirius with crude harshness. I find it difficult to excuse Thomas for his gross carelessness in choosing him as Sirius's instructor. Thomas was always surprisingly insensitive about the psychological aspect of his great experiment; or perhaps not insensitive but unimaginative. But on this occasion his failure to secure decent conditions for Sirius was so flagrant that I am inclined to attribute it to deliberate purpose. Had he determined to afford the dog some first-hand experience of the more brutal aspect of humanity? If so, his purpose was only too well fulfilled.

Anyhow, Thwaites constantly indulged his spite against Sirius, ordering him to carry heavy loads in his mouth, forcing on him all sorts of tasks which only a human hand could perform efficiently, overworking him with awkward jobs that were obviously unnecessary, and laughing bitterly at him in conversation with his neighbours.

At first Sirius was rather pleased to have the experience of contact with a human being of brutal temper. Hitherto his immediate human environment had been on the whole too amiable to be a fair sample. He needed to know what man was like in his harsher modes. There was soon trouble, because Sirius did not cringe when Thwaites gave orders. Instead, he carried out his task with calm efficiency. This provoked the man to curse him on the flimsiest pretext; and when he did so, Sirius would gaze at him with cold and ostentatious surprise. This, of course, made matters worse. In time, Thwaites's harsh voice and the whole atmosphere of the place began to get on Sirius's nerves. The milder human contacts in Wales, Cambridge and London began to fade out of his consciousness, and he found himself feeling that Thwaites was the typical man. Obscurely he dramatized himself as the champion of his own kind against the tyrant race. Thwaites's great cruel hands symbolized for him the process by which the ruthless species had mastered all the living creatures of the planet. Irrationally Sirius, though a hunter who had again and again inflicted agony and death, felt a self-righteous indignation against the sheer cruelty of man. Compassion for the weak, which had been inculcated in him by his own human friends, now turned him against humanity itself.

Thwaites had several times threatened Sirius with his stick, but had always thought better of it, sobered by the dog's great size and a dangerous look in his eye. As time passed, the man's irrational spite against the dog increased. But the incident which caused the final catastrophe was an attack not on Sirius but on Roy. A few days before Thomas was due to come and

fetch Sirius away there was some difficulty with a bunch of
sheep that Roy had brought into the yard. Thwaites caught
the collie a sharp blow on the haunch. Sirius turned on
Thwaites in fury and knocked him down; then, remembering
himself, he withdrew and watched the man pick himself up.
Roy promptly disappeared from the scene. It was a fixed
principle with Thwaites that when dogs were rebellious one
must thrash them into subjection, which meant in his view
thrashing them almost to death. He called to his hired man,
"Anderson, the brute's gone savage, come and help me teach
him." There was no answer. Anderson was far afield.
Thwaites was no coward, but he did not relish attacking the
great cunning beast single-handed. However, insubordination
must be crushed, at all costs. Besides, such a dangerous
animal might do incalculable harm. Better destroy it at once.
He could tell Trelone that the dog had gone mad and had to be
shot. He went into the house. Sirius guessed that he would
emerge with his gun. He therefore rushed to the house door
and crouched at one side of it. Thwaites stepped over the
threshold, looking round the yard. Sirius leapt at him, knocked
him over again, and seized the gun with his teeth. Both anta-
gonists rolled over and over. Thwaites struggled to his feet,
and tried to turn the muzzle of the gun against the dog's body.
One barrel went off harmlessly, then the other. Sirius let go
the gun and sprang away. Thwaites put his hand in his pocket
and brought out a couple of cartridges. Sirius leapt at him,
knocked him over again and seized his throat, gripping his
windpipe with the full power of his strong jaws. The flavour
of warm human blood and the sound of the man's stifled
gurgle filled him with an exultant, careless fury. In this
symbolic act he would kill not only Thwaites but the whole
tyrant race. Henceforth all beasts and birds should live
naturally, and the planet's natural order should never again be
disturbed by the machinations of this upstart species. These
thoughts flashed through his mind even as the couple floundered
and crashed about, gripping each other's throats.

Presently the man's struggles slackened, his grip weakened.
Then a change began to come over Sirius's mind. Fury gave
place to a more detached observation of the situation. After

all, this creature was only expressing the nature that the universe had bred in him. And so was the whole human race. Why this silly hate? The human stink suddenly reminded him of Plaxy's fragrance. The blood-taste nauseated him. The crushed windpipe between his teeth filled him with horror. He let go, moved away, and stood watching the feeble movements of his non-canine brother, whom he, Cain, had murdered.

Practical considerations presented themselves to him. The hand of man would now indeed be relentlessly turned against him. The hand of two thousand million human beings; all the race, save his own few friends. A panic of loneliness suddenly seized him. A solitary airman, flying over hostile territory, with nothing but enemies below and nothing but stars above, may sometimes feel desperately lonely; but that loneliness is nothing to the loneliness which now oppressed Sirius, with the whole human race against him, and his own species unable to comprehend him, and no pack anywhere to comfort him and accept his service.

He went over to the trough in the yard, drank, and licked his lips clean. Once more he stood watching Thwaites, who now lay still, with a torn and bloody neck. His own neck was stiff after Thwaites's desperate effort. Imagining the pain that his teeth must have inflicted, he cringed. He returned to the body and sniffed the neck. Already there was a very faint odour of death. No need, then, to risk his own life fetching a doctor to save this human being. Obeying a sudden freakish impulse, he fleetingly touched the forehead of his slaughtered brother with his tongue.

Distant footsteps! He took to his heels in sudden panic, leapt the yard gate and raced away for the fells. Lest they should come after him with bloodhounds, he used every fox-trick to mislead them. He doubled on his track, he took to streams, and so on. That night he slept under the bracken in a remote ghyll. Next day hunger forced him to go hunting. He managed to secure a rabbit, and took it to his lair, where he wolfed it. He spent the rest of the day hidden, and haunted by his crime; haunted, yet strangely exultant. Though it was indeed a crime, it was a positive act of self-assertion which had emancipated him for ever from the spell of the master race.

Henceforth he would fear no man simply as a man. Two more nights and the intervening day he spent in hiding. Then he set off to intercept Thomas, who was due at the farm in the afternoon. With great caution he worked his way back over the hills till he was looking down on the road to Thwaites's farm. He went to a point on the road where there was good cover and a hairpin bend. Here the car would have to slow down almost to walking pace. He hid himself in the undergrowth of a little wood, and waited. An occasional foot-passenger passed, and an occasional car. At last there was the unmistakable sound of Thomas's Morris Ten. Cautiously Sirius crept from his hiding, looking to see if any other human being was visible. There was no one. He stepped out into the road. Thomas stopped the car and got out with a cheery "Hello!" Sirius, with tucked-in tail, simply said, "I've killed Thwaites." Thomas exclaimed, "God!" then gaped at him in silence. The dog's keen ears heard distant footsteps, so they retired into the wood to discuss the situation. It was decided that Thomas should go up to the farm as though he knew nothing of the tragedy, while Sirius kept in hiding.

There is no need to record in detail how Thomas dealt with the problem. Naturally he did not tell the police that he had met Sirius. He strongly denied that his super-sheep-dogs were dangerous, and he produced evidence to that effect. He insisted that Thwaites must have treated Sirius very badly; and the man (it appeared) was known to be of a sadistic temper. Clearly he had attacked the animal with his gun, and had probably wounded it. In self-defence the dog had killed him. And where was the dog now? The valuable creature had probably died of wounds somewhere on the moors.

This much of the truth Thomas told Sirius, but not till long afterwards did the murderer learn the rest. Things had not in fact gone as well as Thomas had reported. The officers of the law remained suspicious, and ordered that if the dog was found it must be destroyed. Thomas therefore decided that in order to protect his unique canine masterpiece he must resort to trickery. After a suitable interval he would notify the authorities that the man-killing beast had at last found its way home, and that it had been duly destroyed. He would

sacrifice a certain large Alsatian super-sheep-dog, and palm
off his corpse as Sirius's.

It was not until late on the day of the inquest that Thomas
picked up Sirius at the hairpin bend. In spite of the black-out,
they drove home through the night, helped by a full moon.

CHAPTER XII

FARMER SIRIUS

IT was not till dawn on the following day that Thomas and
Sirius in the Morris Ten drove up the familiar Welsh lane,
and came to a stand in the yard of Garth. Elizabeth and
Plaxy were still asleep. When they woke, they were very surprised to find that man and dog had returned already. They
were surprised also at the wretched condition of Sirius. He
was filthy, his coat lacked its customary gloss, he was painfully
thin, and he was silent and dejected.

Plaxy, fresh from a busy and happy term at Cambridge, was
in the mood for a happy holiday. Moreover she was aware
that in recent meetings with Sirius she had somehow proved
inadequate, and she was anxious to make amends. She
therefore set about being "sweet" to Sirius. It was she who
gave him a thorough wash and carefully groomed his coat.
She also took a thorn out of one of his feet, and dressed a bad
cut in another. He surrendered himself to the firm and gentle
touch of her hands and the subtle odour that was for him her
most poignant feature. She pressed him to tell her all about his
doings in Cumberland, and he told her—everything but the
main thing. It was obvious that he was holding something back,
so she pressed him no further, though suspecting that he really
wanted to tell her. He did indeed long to confess to her. The
memory of the crime was a constant source of turmoil in his
mind. He had committed a murder. This was the stark fact
that had to be faced. It was useless to pretend that he had been
forced to kill Thwaites in self-defence, for he had hung on to

him much longer than was necessary to put him out of action. No, it was murder, and sooner or later Thomas's ruse would probably be found out. Even if Sirius remained uncaught he would have this thing hanging over him for ever; not just the fear of retribution, but the deadly remorse for the destruction of a creature who, though biologically alien to him, was none the less his fellow in the spirit. He longed for Plaxy's sympathy, but feared her horror. And anyhow, Thomas had insisted that no one should be told.

During that Christmas holiday Sirius and Plaxy spent many an hour talking about themselves and their friends; about art, particularly Sirius's music; about philosophy and religion, particularly his experiences with Geoffrey; about the war, for though both of them felt it to be utterly unreal and remote, and "not their fault anyhow," it could not be ignored. Several of Plaxy's friends were already in it.

But though at first they had much to say to one another, later they often fell into silence, and as time advanced these silences became longer and more frequent. He brooded over his prospects, she retired into her memories. She was beginning to yearn once more for human companionship. His nose told him that it was one of those phases when she was fully ripe for the love of her own kind. Her behaviour towards him alternated between exaggerated tenderness and aloofness. She seemed to want to maintain contact with him, but at these times the gulf between the human and the canine was generally too great. But not always. Sometimes the intensification of animal sex-feeling in the young human female linked up with her deep affection for the dog, so that she treated him with an altogether novel shyness, which somehow stimulated a similar sexually toned warmth of feeling in him. He would then, if she permitted, caress her with a new tenderness and ardour. But these passages were rare, and often they were followed on Plaxy's side by a frightened aloofness. It seemed to her, so she told me long afterwards, that in those strange, sweet moments she was taking the first step towards some very far-reaching alienation from her own kind. Yet while they lasted they seemed entirely innocent and indeed beautiful.

Once Sirius said to Plaxy, "The music of our two lives is a

duet of variations upon three themes. There is the difference between our biological natures, yours human and mine canine, and all the differences of experience that follow from that. Then there is the love that has grown up between us, alien as we are. It has gathered us together and made us one fundamentally, in spite of all our differences. It feeds on differences. And there is sex, which alternates between tearing us apart because of our biological remoteness and welding us together because of our love." They silently gazed at one another. He added, "There is a fourth theme in our music, or perhaps it is the unity of the other three. There is our journey along the way of the spirit, together and yet poles apart." Plaxy replied with sudden warmth, "Oh, my darling, I do, I do love you. We are never really poles apart, not in the spirit, I mean. But—oh, it's all strange and frightening. And you see, don't you, that I must be properly human. Besides— men can mean so much more to me than bitches can mean to you." "Of course," he answered. "You have your life and I have mine. And sometimes we meet, and sometimes clash. But always, yes, always, we are one in the spirit."

He wondered whether, if she knew about Thwaites, it would make any difference; and he realized that it wouldn't. She would be horrified, of course, but not revolted against him. Suddenly he realized that ever since the killing he had been anxiously condemning himself on behalf of Plaxy, and so nursing a sore resentment against her. But so deeply had he nursed it that he never till this moment recognized its existence. And now somehow he knew that she would not condemn him, and so the resentment became conscious and at the same time vanished.

Later in the vacation Plaxy busied herself with her studies. She was all behind-hand, she said. And when at last the day came for departure, she was as usual both sad and pleased. At the station she found an excuse to stray with Sirius to a less crowded stretch of the platform. "We have drifted apart again lately," she said, "but *whatever* happens I never forget that I am the human part of Sirius-Plaxy." He touched her hand and said, "We have a treasure in common, a bright gem of community."

During the vacation Sirius had been anxiously concerned with other things besides that treasure. He had been carrying on an urgent discussion about his future with Thomas and Elizabeth, with Plaxy as a disinterested critic. Sirius was determined not to go back to the subtly enervating life of Cambridge. The time had come, he said, when he really must strike out on his own. He was ready to agree that at least for a while he might be able to find self-expression through his skill with sheep, but he could do so only in a responsible position, not as a mere sheep-dog. What did Thomas propose to do about it?

In the end a bold plan was adopted. Owing to the scarcity of labour, Pugh, whose health was failing, had found great difficulty in carrying on his farm. Thomas decided to tell him the whole truth about Sirius's powers, and to propose that Sirius should join him not as a sheep-dog but as a prospective partner. Or rather, the Laboratory would legally be his partner, contributing capital to the farm. Elizabeth would be the Laboratory's resident representative, and would lend a hand with the work. Sirius, being only a dog, could sign no contract and hold no property. But he would in effect be in the partnership relation to Pugh, who would initiate him into the whole management of the farm, and the business of marketing sheep and wool. An important side-line would be the training of super-sheep-dogs for sale.

There were several long discussions with Pugh. This was perhaps an advantage, as it gave him an opportunity of learning to understand Sirius's speech with Thomas and Elizabeth present to help him. The old man was very ready to enter into the spirit of the game; but he was cautious, and he thought of many difficulties, each of which had to be patiently smoothed out. Mrs. Pugh regarded the arrangement with misgiving. She secretly feared that Satan, not God, was the worker of this miracle of the man-dog. That Thomas himself was responsible she never seriously supposed. The only other person who might have been concerned in the new arrangement was Pugh's daughter, but she was by now married and settled in Dolgelly.

It was not long before Sirius was established at Caer Blai in his new capacity. It was arranged that normally he should sleep at home at Garth, since he could cover the distance between the two houses in a few minutes; but at Caer Blai the room formerly occupied by the daughter of the house was allotted to him for emergencies. To the new quarters Thomas transferred the dog's accumulation of books on sheep and sheep-farming, also a spare writing glove and other writing materials. In addition Sirius kept at the farm several of the girths and panniers that had been made for him from time to time to enable him to carry things while keeping his mouth free. In early days the apparatus had to be fastened on him by human hands, but by now, owing to his increased "manual" skill and an ingenious fastener, he could saddle or unsaddle himself in a few seconds.

Pugh could not teach Sirius anything about the actual care of sheep. The dog had a closer practical experience of them, and a far more scientific knowledge. He was eager to improve the breed on the farm and to develop the pasture. But on the side of farm management he had everything to learn. Not only had he to understand prices and the whole book-keeping problem; there was also the small but important agricultural side of the farm. Before the war this had been entirely subordinate to sheep, producing only hay and roots and a very small amount of grain. But in war-time every possible acre had to be ploughed up to produce food, and by now Pugh had a good deal of land under oats, rye and potatoes. The handless Sirius could never do much on this side of the work, but he was determined to understand it and learn to direct it. The necessity of employing hired human labour raised the whole question of Sirius's contact with the outside world. Thomas, with his phobia of publicity, was very reluctant to let the countryside know just how developed a creature Sirius was, but clearly it would not be possible for him in his new life to masquerade as a dumb animal. However, said Thomas, let people discover the truth gradually. In this way it would be less of a shock to them. Pugh could begin by holding simple conversations with Sirius in public places. Gradually he could let it be realized that he respected the dog's judgment in all matters connected with sheep. In this manner Sirius would little by little become a congenial figure in the neighbourhood.

For some time Sirius was too busy learning his new responsi-
bilities to undertake the training of super-sheep-dogs. Old
Idwal and another of these animals, Mifanwy, a young bitch,
were on the farm already, and able to do far more intelligent
work than the brightest normal animal. Juno, who had been
one of the most intelligent of super-sheep-dogs, had developed
some obscure kind of brain trouble, so that Pugh had been
forced to destroy her.

After a while Sirius wrote to Thomas saying that he now
felt ready for the new venture, and Thomas sent him three
puppies of the right age for training. Sirius privately believed
that with sympathetic education by one of their own species
(though superior to them in intelligence) these animals could
be made into something far more capable than Idwal and
Mifanwy, or even Juno. He had also secret hopes that one of
them, or one of some future batch, might turn out to be a
creature of his own mental rank; but this, he had to admit, was
very unlikely, for presumably Thomas would have detected
any such animal long before it was old enough for training.
Many attempts had, as a matter of fact, been made to produce
another Sirius, but without success. Sirius himself seemed to
have been something of a fluke. The effort to repeat his type
had produced at best large-brained and highly intelligent
animals that were too frail to reach maturity, and more often
mental defectives of one sort or another. It seemed that, if the
cerebral hemispheres were increased beyond a certain size, the
discrepancy between them and the normal canine organization
was too great for reliable viability. Even in man, whose brain
and body had developed in step with one another for millions
of years, the large cerebrum seems to put a strain on the
system, and to be in fact something of a morbid growth,
leading all too often to mental disorder. In the case of the
dog, when it is suddenly given an enlarged brain, the stress is
far more serious.

Not only Sirius but Elizabeth also had to be trained for work
on the farm. Though normally she now spent more time in
Cambridge than in the country, it was arranged that for some
months she should live at Garth. She was now a middle-aged
but sturdy woman, and during the last war she had been a

land-girl. Pugh at first found it almost impossible to treat her otherwise than as a lady visitor, but the two of them gradually evolved a relationship which fitted his humour perfectly. She posed as the lazy and grumbling servant, he as the exacting master. He greatly enjoyed disparaging the results of all her labour, scolding her for idling, and threatening that he would report her to Sirius and have her sacked if she couldn't keep a civil tongue in her head. She, for her part, treated him with mock servility and affectionate insolence. It took Mrs. Pugh a long time to realize that the constant wrangling was all friendly. She was confirmed in her anxiety by the fact that Sirius, entering into the spirit of the game, sometimes acted the part of the faithful dog defending his beloved mistress against threatened attack. One day when Mrs. Pugh earnestly tried to curb her husband's tongue, Pugh shook a finger at her, winking at Elizabeth, and said, "Ah, but you don't know, my dear, how Mrs. Trelone and I behave together when you are not watching. Yes indeed, for all you know it is then we are the love-birds, isn't it, Mrs. Trelone?"

Both Sirius and Elizabeth were very busy during the Lent Term. Thomas contrived to spend several weeks in Wales to see how the venture was proceeding. On one occasion he brought two scientific friends to meet Sirius. On another, as Sirius was much interested in improving the local moorland pasture, dog and man went off for a couple of days to Aberystwyth to visit the Plant-Breeding Station. Sirius returned full of daring ideas to put before the sympathetic but cautious Pugh.

In a way this was probably the happiest time of Sirius's life, for at last he felt that he was using his super-canine powers adequately, and he had attained a degree of independence that he had never known before. The work was often worrying, since he was in many respects a novice, and he made many mistakes; but it was varied, concrete, and (as he put it) spiritually sound. There was little time to think deep thoughts, and less to write; but now that he was doing responsible work he did not feel the same urge for intellectual activity. And anyhow he promised himself that later, when he was more at home with the work, he would take up once more the threads of his former literary and musical activities.

His only recreation was music. In the evenings, with
Elizabeth yawning in an easy chair after the day of fresh air
and exercise, he would listen to broadcast concerts, or try
records on the radio-gram. Sometimes, when he was out on the
moors with his young pupils, he would sing his own songs,
some of which, the less humanized ones, had a strong emotional
appeal for the super-sheep-dogs.

Then there was the bright young bitch, Mifanwy. She was
an attractive creature, mainly collie but with a dash of setter.
She was slim as a leopard, and had a luxurious silken coat.
Sirius had intended to refrain from all sexual relations with his
underlings. Moreover he regarded Mifanwy as Idwal's pre-
serve. But Idwal was growing old. Merely a super-sheep-dog,
he was bound to sink far more rapidly into senescence than
Sirius, who was still in early maturity. When Mifanwy was
in heat she refused her former lover and did her best to seduce
Sirius. For a while he took no notice, but one day he indulged
in dalliance with this sweet sub-human though super-canine
charmer. Of course there was protest from Idwal; but the
heavier and biologically far younger dog could, if necessary,
easily have shown his senior that protest was futile. In fact,
however, Idwal was so overawed by, and faithful to, his canine
master, that his protest never developed beyond a conflict-
expressing whimper and an occasional rebellious growl.

In due season Mifanwy had a litter of five puppies. Their
heads, of course, were of normal size, but most of them bore
on their foreheads the large fawn patches which distinguished
Sirius, and his mother before him. In a few weeks the
Alsatian strain in them was obvious to all the world. It was
obvious too that if Sirius was not their father he must at least
be their grandfather. He was the original source of the
Alsatian characters which were now fairly common among the
dogs of the neighbourhood. There had been a time when the
local farmers had perversely hoped (without official encouragement) that in allowing the man-dog to have intercourse with
their bitches they would acquire super-canine puppies. Inevitably this hope was disappointed, though a dash of Alsatian
had proved a useful stiffening to the local sheep-dog strain.
Even when both parents were super-canine, the offspring were

of course normal. As for Sirius, he took no interest in his numerous moron progeny. His three sons and two daughters by Mifanwy were treated as mere chattels. One of each sex was promptly drowned. The other three were allowed to remain with their mother considerably longer than was usual, in fact until her super-canine but sub-human maternal feelings had waned sufficiently to make it possible to deprive her of her offspring without causing her distress. Sirius then sold his two remaining sons and his daughter.

Meanwhile super-canine puppies continued to arrive from Cambridge for Sirius to train. Mostly they were turned into super-sheep-dogs, but owing to the war a new profession seemed to open up for Thomas's bright animals.

The need for war economy was seriously interfering with the work of the Laboratory. Thomas foresaw the time when the whole organization would have to close down or turn over to some kind of war research. It was at this time, in the spring of 1940, that the war changed from its "phony" to its violent phase. The collapse of Holland, Belgium and finally France made the British feel that they really had to fight for their lives. Thomas had always regarded the war as a gigantic irrelevance. It was beneath the notice of minds that were given wholly to the advancement of science. But at last he was forced to recognize that this gigantic irrelevance must not be ignored or it would destroy the very possibility of science. He began to puzzle over two problems. How far, if at all, could his present work be made useful for winning the war? If it was quite useless, what kind of war-work could the Laboratory undertake? He saw that his super-sheep-dogs, if they could be produced in large enough numbers, might have an important function in war. The Government was already training normal dogs for running messages in the battle area, and clearly the super-sheep-dog mentality would be far more useful. He therefore set about the task of discovering a simplified technique for the mass-production of these animals. He also told Sirius to give some of his brightest pupils special training in running messages.

The time came when Thomas was ready to display three of his animals to the brass-hats, and after much importuning he secured an interview with a high military authority. The performance of the animals was brilliant. Thomas was assured that the War Office would undoubtedly make use of his super-canine messengers. He then waited impatiently for many weeks, wrote many respectful letters, and was repeatedly assured that the necessary machiery was now in action for adopting his suggestion. But somehow nothing happened. Every official whom he interviewed was at least sympathetic, and often eager to take any amount of trouble to help the great scientist. Yet nothing resulted. The vast and venerable institution remained unresponsive. Meanwhile the whole energy of the Laboratory had been turned over to the mass-production of "missing-link" dogs for war. The more interesting but less useful task of producing creatures of the calibre of Sirius had been abandoned; and Thomas's dearest dream, the stimulation of a human foetus to super-normal brain growth, now faded into mere fantasy.

Sirius, no less than Thomas, now realized that the war had to be won, otherwise all that was best in the tyrant species would be destroyed. But he lived in the depth of the country, and he was wholly absorbed in his new work; which, moreover, seemed to him a piece of worthy national, or rather human, service. Consequently he did not realize the war emotionally as fully as Thomas. Moreover, though one side of his nature was wholly identified with this glorious human species, another side was secretly and irrationally gratified by the tyrant's plight. Intellectually he knew that his future depended on the future of Britain, but emotionally he was as detached from the struggle as, at a later stage, the threatened millions of India were to be emotionally aloof from the menace of Japan.

When Plaxy came home, she found the Caer Blai atmosphere rather unreal. Of course she could not help being impressed by Sirius's success. He really did seem to have come into his own, even from the point of view of war. But she was rather shocked at his aloofness from the agony of the human race, and perhaps also a little jealous of his new-found peace of mind. For she herself was painfully torn between revulsion from the whole crazy disgusting mess and the urge to play her part in the desperate crisis of her species. In Cambridge she always made a point of maintaining her accustomed detachment, for so many of her friends seemed to her obsessed by the war; but in Wales she found herself warning Sirius that he was living in a fool's paradise, and that at any moment all familiar and precious things might be swept away in a tide of German invasion. She herself, she said, was feeling uncomfortable about her own work, a teaching post which she was to take up at the end of the summer. Perhaps she ought to do something more directly useful.

Sirius was impressed by all this talk, but emotionally he remained as unenthusiastic as ever. Perhaps he ought to go and be an Army messenger dog. (Anyhow he was training messenger dogs.) But to hell with the whole war! He had found his job, for the present, producing wool and food for the dominant species; which was probably destroying itself, anyhow. And good riddance, too! Good riddance? No, he didn't really mean that. But damn it, anyhow it wasn't his fault, and man was not his responsibility.

At this time Plaxy had become very much concerned with politics. For a short spell she had been a member of the Communist Party, but she had resigned, "because, though they are energetic and devoted, they're also intolerably cocksure and unfair." Nevertheless she remained very much under the influence of Marxism, though she was hard put to it to find room in Marxism for her faith in "the spirit," which was playing an ever deeper part in her life. "The spirit," she said, "must be the highest of all dialectical levels, the supreme synthesis." While she was at home she talked much to Sirius about "equality of opportunity," "the class war," "the dictatorship of the proletariat," and so on. And she insisted that if Communism was not, after all, the whole truth, then nothing short of a great *new* idea, based on Communism, could win the war and found a tolerable social order. Sirius had always been sympathetic with the desire for revolutionary social change. His spell in the East End had shown him how necessary it was. He had heartily agreed with the plea for common ownership of the means of production, and for creative social planning. But now that he had property to look after he found himself, much to his own surprise, looking at the whole matter from a different angle. "That's all quite true," he would say, "but I'm a bit anxious about your new order. Are you going to merge all the farms into great collective farms? It all smells a bit dangerous. It's too theoretical. And what about eccentric creative enterprises like Thomas's? And what on earth would become of oddities like me, if I ever existed at all? The point is, *who* is to do the social planning? It's all very well to say the people will do it, but God save us from the people. Anyhow they can't *really* do it at all. Some minority will do it, either mere demagogues or bosses. Somehow we have to get the *wide-awake* people to do it. It's always the wide-awake people who do everything worth while, really. The rest are just sheep." "But surely," said Plaxy, "it's *ordinary* people that all the planning is *for;* and so its the ordinary people that must settle the aims of all the planning, and control it. The wide-awakes are servants of the community. The sheep-dogs serve the sheep." "Rot," said Sirius, "sheer tripe! The dogs serve a master, who *uses* the sheep, and the dogs." Plaxy protested, "But the people, if they are a free people, have no master but themselves. The people as a whole are the master." "No, no!" cried Sirius. "You might as well say the sheep as a whole are the master. I, at any rate, acknowledge only one master, not forty-five million two-legged sheep, or two thousand million, but simply and absolutely the spirit." The answer came promptly, "But who is to say what the spirit demands? Who is to interpret the spirit?" "Why, the spirit itself, of course," he replied, "working in the minds of its servants, its sheep-dogs, the wide-awake people." "But, Sirius, dear, dangerous, ridiculous darling, that's the way straight to Fascism. There's a leader who *knows*, and the rest do what they're told. And there's a Party of faithful sheep-dogs who make them do it." Sirius protested, "But a Fascist Party is *not* made up of wide-awake people. Its members don't really know at all what the spirit is. They don't know the smell of it. They can't hear its voice. All they can ever be, even at their best is just sheep-dogs run amok, wild sheep-dogs, wolves under a wolf leader." "But, Sirius, my own, don't you see, that's just what they would say about *us*. Who is to judge between us?" He had his answer ready. "Who judged

between Christ and the High Priest? Not the people. They
said 'Crucify him.' The real judge was Christ's master, the
spirit, speaking in Christ's own mind; *and* in the High Priest's,
if only he would listen. The point is, if you serve the spirit you
can't serve any other master. But what the spirit demands
always is love and intelligence and strong creative action in its
service, love of the sheep as individuals to be made the most of,
not *merely* as mutton or as coral insects in a lovely coral
pattern, but as individual vessels of the spirit. *That* spirit—
love, intelligence and creating—is precisely what 'the spirit'
is." Plaxy's reply was merely ribald. "The Reverend Sirius
preached one of his most profound and helpful sermons."

They were sitting together on the lawn at Garth, and he
playfully attacked her, pushing her over and making for her
throat. Accustomed from childhood to such battles, she
gripped his ears and tugged hard. Before his teeth had softly
seized her, or his tongue had begun its tickling caresses, he
squealed for mercy. They smiled into each other's eyes.
"Sadistic little bitch!" he said. "Sweet cruel bitch!" With
one hand she seized his lower jaw and pressed it backwards
and downwards into his neck. The sierras of ivory closed
gently on the back of her hand. Dog and girl struggled playfully for a while, till she let go, exhausted. Wiping her hand
on his coat, she protested, "Slobberry old thing!" They lay
quietly on the grass.

Suddenly Plaxy said, "I expect you have great fun with
Mifawny, don't you?" He heard a faint tension in her voice.
There was a pause before he answered, "She's lovely. And
though she's so deadly stupid, she really has the rudiments of
a soul." Plaxy pulled a piece of grass and chewed it, looking
at the distant Rhinogs. "*I* have a lover, too," she said. "He
wants me to marry him, but that would be so binding. He has
just joined the R.A.F. He wants me to have babies, lots of
them, as quickly as possible. But it's too soon. I'm much too
young to pledge myself for ever to anyone." There was a long
pause. Then Sirius asked, "Does he know about me?"
"No." "Will he make any difference to—us?" Promptly she
answered, "*I* don't *feel* any different. But perhaps I don't
really care enough about him. I love him terribly as a human

animal, just as you love Mifawny, I suppose, as a canine
animal. And I love him very much as a friend too. But I don't
know whether that's enough for marriage. And it must be
marriage, for the children's sake, because they need a permanent father. They ought to grow up in the community of their
parents." Another long pause came between them. She threw
him a quick sidelong glance. He was staring at her, his head
very slightly tilted to one side, his brows puckered, like any
puzzled terrier. "Well," he said at last, "marry him, and have
your litter, if you must. And of course you must. But all this
is much more serious than bitches. Oh, Plaxy, fundamentally
it's you and I that are married, for ever. Will he spoil that?
Will he put up with it?" She pulled nervously at the turf, and
said, "I know, I know we're somehow married in the spirit.
But if that makes me ever unable to love a man whole-heartedly
enough to want to be his wife and have babies with him, oh,
I'll *hate* the hold you have on me." Before he could reply she
looked squarely at him and continued, "I didn't mean that.
I *can't* hate the hold you have on me. But—oh, God, what a
mess!" Tears were in her eyes. He stretched forward to touch
her hand, but thought better of it. Then he said, "If I am
spoiling your life, it would have been better if Thomas had
never made me." She put a hand on his shoulder, and said,
"If you had never been you, then I should never have been I,
and there would have been no difficult, lovely 'us.' And even
if I do hate you sometimes, I love you much more, always.
Even while I am hating you, I know (and the best of me knows
gladly) that I am not just Plaxy but the human part of Sirius-
Plaxy." He answered quickly, "But to be that properly you
must be as much Plaxy as possible, and so you must somehow
live your human life fully. Oh, yes, I understand. Being
human, and a girl, and in England, and middle class, you can't
merely have lovers and an illegitimate litter. You must have a
husband." To himself he added, "And I, perhaps, must
sometimes kill your kind." But the memory of Thwaites
murdered suddenly came upon him, and revolted him with its
contrast to the present happy situation. It was as though,
running on the moor in bright weather, he had suddenly been
swallowed by a bog. And somehow it seemed that only Plaxy

could pull him out. On a sudden impulse he told her the whole story.

CHAPTER XIII

THE EFFECTS OF WAR

BY the autumn of 1940 Sirius was well established at Caer Blai, was planning great improvements for the pasture, the breed and the arable land, and was known in the neighbourhood as "Pugh's man-dog." Precisely what his mental stature was, no one could decide. Pugh, by telling the whole truth about him, had put them off the scent. It was known that the man-dog had a marvellous facility with sheep, and was managing them on the latest scientific principles. But all this was vaguely thought to be less a matter of intelligence than of a sort of super-instinct mysteriously implanted in him by science. It was known too that he could understand a good deal of speech, and was actually able to use words himself to those who had the key to his queer pronunciation. He was learning a bit of Welsh; and the fact that his Welsh was so rudimentary, and that this was the language which alone was familiar in the district, disguised from everyone his true linguistic gifts and his fully human mentality.

Even so, had it not been war-time, the newspapers would certainly have publicized him, and with far more success than befell the stunt of the talking mongoose at an earlier date.

Sirius made himself thoroughly popular with most of the surrounding farmers and villagers, but there were a few who stubbornly regarded him with suspicion. Devout chapel-goers affirmed that the man-dog's real master was not Pugh but Satan, and that Pugh had sold his soul to the Devil to help him out of the labour-shortage. Some of the sexually obsessed, aware of the great affection that held between the man-dog and the scientist's younger daughter, whispered that it was Thomas, in the first instance, who had sold his soul, in order to gain scientific fame, and that Satan, incarnate in the dog,

habitually gratified himself in perverse sexual intercourse with
Thomas's daughter. And she, they said, for all her charm, was
little better than a witch. Anyone could see that there was
something queer and inhuman about her. Rumours of a
different type were spread by the cruder sort of patriots. They
declared that Thomas was in the pay of the Nazis, who had
found in his man-dog the ideal kind of spy. It was no accident
that the animal was established in the neighbourhood of a big
artillery camp.

Most people were too sensible to take these rumours
seriously. Pugh was popular, and so was Sirius; for he was
certainly a genius with sheep, and he lent distinction to the
district. Thomas, though an Englishman, had won a place in
local esteem; and his daughter, in spite of her new-fangled
ways, was an attractive girl. Not till the pressure of war had
been much prolonged, driving simple folk to look for scape-
goats, was public opinion to become hostile.

When the great air attacks on London began, Elizabeth
received a long letter from Geoffrey describing conditions in
his parish, and urging her to take in some of his refugee children, and plant out others in suitable homes in her district.
Geoffrey was one of those who believed in personal responsibility. He suspected all Government organization; consequently he was anxious to avoid as far as possible merely
handing over his charges to the official evacuation authorities.

Geoffrey's account of the devastation, heroism, muddle,
callousness, and human kindness in the great blitzes had a deep
effect on Sirius. He remembered vividly the smell of Geoffrey's
home, and of the bare little church and all the stuffy houses that
he had visited. And these olfactory images called up in his
mind a rich picture of human beings struggling against a
hostile environment and their own inadequacy. He remembered many of the people whom Geoffrey reported as casualties, and many of the children for whom hospitality was
required. He had a generous impulse to rush off to London
at once with his panniers filled with first-aid equipment. But
it was a foolish impulse. He would only be in the way. Besides,
it was one thing to enjoy a generous impulse and quite another
to put it in action. He suspected that he would be a thorough

coward in an air raid; and anyhow, fundamentally he felt aloof from the whole war. If the human race was fool enough to torture itself in this crazy manner, what had *he* to do with it? Nevertheless he could not help being deeply moved by Geoffrey's story, and by affection for Geoffrey himself. The plight of London became even more vivid to him and to the local population when, by one of those flukes which seem common in war, a single bomb, dropped at random by a stray raider, fell neatly on a lonely cottage in the neighbourhood, killing or wounding all its occupants.

Elizabeth undertook to take three London children into her house, and Mrs. Pugh, with much misgiving, agreed to accommodate two more. Sirius gave up his room at Caer Blai. Most of the local wives had already either taken on evacuees from bitzed towns in the north-west, or had refused to do so; but Elizabeth, after paying many calls, was able to tell Geoffrey that she had accommodation for fifteen more children and two mothers. It so happened that the neighbourhood had been rather lucky so far with its little immigrants. Though there had been a good deal of grumbling on the part of some hostesses, on the whole the scheme had worked. But the twenty little Londoners were a different kettle of fish. They were smelly, lousy, unruly little brats, and it was said in the district that no decent housewife would have had them across her doorstep if she had known what they were like. They made horrid messes in the house, broke the furniture, ruined the garden, lied, stole, bit one another and their hostesses, tormented the cat, and used dreadful language.

Some of the hostesses had the wit to realize that these children were simply the product of circumstances. It was shocking, they said, that society should allow its more unfortunate members to grow up in such degradation. The less imaginative housewives, however, indulged in orgies of self-righteous indignation against the children themselves and their parents. Some took the line that the immigrants were English, and that was what the English were like. As for Elizabeth, her popularity suffered somewhat. She alone was responsible for this recent affliction. It was remembered in some quarters not only that she was English, but that her husband had sold his soul to the Devil. Matters were made worse by the fact that her own evacuees turned out quite well. She was one of those who had a natural gift for treating children as human persons and expecting to be treated decently in return. There were troubles enough at first. But in a few weeks the little girl and her two small brothers were proudly helping with the house and the garden.

One day Elizabeth had news from Geoffrey that his church had been destroyed, but that he was continuing to devote his whole time to the care of his parishioners. He was elated that after long agitation he and others had secured great improvements in the public shelters in the district. A few days later she received a letter in an unknown hand saying that her cousin had been killed.

The news of Geoffrey's death seemed to bring the war strangely near to Sirius. For the first time someone whom he knew and loved had vanished. This somehow put the whole thing into a new perspective. It should not have done so. He thought he had imagined the personal impact of war pretty well, but evidently he had not. Geoffrey had simply ceased to be, like a match flame when it is blown out. So simple, and yet somehow so incredible! For in a queer way Geoffrey now seemed more real than before, and nearer to him. For days he caught himself quietly talking to Geoffrey and getting perfectly good answers from him in his own mind. Queer! Just a trick of imagination, no doubt. But somehow he couldn't really in his heart believe that Geoffrey had simply been snuffed out. Or rather, part of him believed it confidently and another part just couldn't. He had a fantastic dream. Geoffrey sought out Thwaites in Hell, and found him with Sirius's soul in his pocket. Somehow Geoffrey brought Thwaites up to Heaven, and his reward was the freeing of Sirius.

The war was soon to come even nearer to Sirius. In May Thomas took him by car to visit a farm near Shap, where several super-sheep-dogs were being successfully used to do practically the whole routine work on the sheep. The route back to North Wales passed through Liverpool. There had been a good deal of raiding on Merseyside from time to time, and Thomas judged it wise to be well across the river before dark. Unfortunately they were late in starting, and did not arrive in Liverpool till dusk. Somewhere in the outskirts of the town they developed engine trouble, and by the time an overworked garage hand had put matters right it was dark. They set out once more, but were much delayed by the condition of the town. There had been a bad raid on the previous night, and the streets had not yet been properly cleared. The result was that, before they could reach the entrance of the famous tunnel under the Mersey, a raid began. It was not far to the tunnel, so Thomas decided to hurry on. Sirius was terrified. Probably the noise was even more trying to his sensitive ears than to the duller human organ. Anyhow he had always been a coward, save in the wolf-mood. The moaning of planes, the prodigious smack and racket of anti-aircraft guns, the tearing rush of bombs (like a raucous and vastly amplified whisper, he thought), followed by such a crash as he had not believed possible, and then the clatter of falling masonry, the roaring and crackling of fires, the scurrying of human feet, the screams of casualties demanding help as the car passed a wrecked shelter, all this had a shattering effect on his morale. Sitting there in the back of the car he had nothing to do but be terrified. Then there were the smells, the stinging smells of gases from explosives, the dusty smell of shattered masonry, the pungent smell of burning woodwork, and occasionally the stench of mangled human bodies.

It seemed madness to go on any farther, so Thomas drew the car into the side of the road, and they dashed for the nearest shelter. The blast from a bomb pushed the side of a house across the street at them. Thomas was pinned under it; Sirius, though bruised and cut, was free. The lower part of Thomas's body was covered with masonry. With great difficulty and in great pain he gasped out, "Save yourself. By the tunnel. Down the street. Then to Wales. Save yourself, for my sake. Please go, please!" Sirius tried frantically to shift the debris with his paws and teeth, but could not. "I'll get help," he said. "No, save yourself," Thomas gasped. "I'm —done—anyhow. Good luck." But Sirius hurried off, and presently was tugging at a man's coat, and whimpering. It was obvious that he wanted help for someone, so a party came back with him. But when they reached the place where Thomas had been, they found only a fresh crater. The men returned to their former task, leaving Sirius blankly gazing. He sniffed about for a long while, whimpering miserably. Then his terror, which had been blotted out by action, welled up again. But his head was clear. He must find the tunnel entrance, which Thomas had said was quite near. He hurried along by the light of fires reflected from the clouds. At one point the road was completely blocked by fallen masonry, and he had to clamber over it. At last he reached the tunnel and managed to sneak in unobserved. He cantered along the footpath; and though a stream of cars was travelling towards Birkenhead, making a terrifying noise in the confined space of the tunnel, no one took much notice of him. At the Birkenhead entrance he made a dash for liberty, and found himself once more in the threatening racket of war and under the fire-lit sky. But the bombs were falling mostly on the Liverpool side of the Mersey.

Sirius gave me a very full account of his long trek from Birkenhead to Trawsfynydd, but there is no need to report it here in detail. Tired and mentally shattered, he made his way westward through the town and out across the Wirral towards Thurstastone Common. As he cantered through the night his mind kept reverting to the complete disappearance of Thomas, the being who had made him, whom he had at first adored with uncritical canine devotion, and more recently had strongly criticized, while always retaining a deep affection for him, and a deep respect for his powers. Intellectually he had little doubt that Thomas had simply ceased to exist; yet, as with Geoffrey's death, he could not really believe it. Lobbing along a stretch of road, he found himself arguing with Thomas on the subject. The dead man insisted that there was now nothing anywhere in the universe which could reasonably be called Thomas Trelone, no mind continuous with that mind's thoughts, desires, feelings. "Well, you ought to know," said Sirius; and then came to a sudden halt, wondering if he was going mad.

From Thurstastone he travelled along the shore of the Dee

Estuary and over the salt marshes to Queensferry, then by road
and field and moorland, always in a south-westerly direction.
Often he wondered how much he was guided by the sub-human
mammal's proverbial "homing faculty," how far by vague
memory of Thomas's maps. The long stretches of road he
found very tiring. The motor traffic was a constant worry,
for the drivers gave him little consideration. He imagined the
tyrant species as a composite creature made up of man and
machine. How he hated its harsh voice and brutal ways!
Yet only yesterday he himself, sitting in Thomas's open tourer,
had exulted in the speed and the wind as they streamed across
the Lancashire plain. His present plight made him realize
more clearly than ever how contemptuous and heartless men
were towards "dumb animals" that did not happen to be their
own pets.

Whenever he passed through a populous area he was careful
to attract as little attention as possible. He slowed down and
strayed about the road, sniffing at lamp-posts, like any local
dog. When anyone made inquisitive or friendly advances,
which was fairly often, for he was a striking animal, he replied
with a nonchalant tail-wag, but never stopped. After crossing
the Clwydian Range and the wide Vale of Clwyd, he made his
way up into ample moors, and went badly astray in mist; but
at last he dropped down into lower country near Pentrevoelas,
and soon he was heading for the high wild hills of Migneint.
Toiling up a steep grassy spur he entered heavy cloud, and it
began to rain. Tired as he was, and with a painful task
awaiting him, he exulted in the cold wet wind, the scents of
the bog and turf and sheep. Once he caught the unmistakable
odour of fox, that rare, intoxicating smell of the most illusive
quarry. God! How the qualities of sensation seemed to hint
at exquisite hidden things, always to be pursued, never found.
Even sight could do it. The driving mist, the half-seen rocks,
appearing and vanishing, and all the little grass-plumes
jewelled with mist-drops, how they stabbed him with sweet
familiarity and with a never-comprehended lure! No doubt it
was all electrons and wave-trains and the tickling of nerve-
endings, but oh how sweet and mysterious and frightening
with uncomprehended truth! Somehow the beauty of it all

was intensified to the point of agony by the horrors that he had
so recently witnessed.

On and on he climbed, surprised at the height. Then suddenly the mist cleared for a moment, and he found himself
almost at the top of a considerable mountain, which he soon
identified as Carnedd Filast. Long ago, before he had taken
to sheep, he used to hunt on these moors from Garth, but it
was not often that he came quite so far afield.

Now that he was once more on the high hills, a change of
mood came over him. Why should he go back to the tyrant
species at all? Why give himself the pain of telling Elizabeth
that her husband would not return? Why not live wild on the
moor, free, spurning all mankind, feeding on rabbits and perhaps an occasional sheep, till at last man did him to death?
Why not? He had lived wild for a time after killing Thwaites,
but that had been spoilt by conscience. This time it would
be different. It was clear by now that life had little to offer him.
True, he had found a niche of sorts, but only by man's aid and
tolerance. And it was a cramping niche. He could not extend
his powers thoroughly. Strangely, on this occasion, it was the
thought not of Thomas but of his sheep unshepherded that
turned his attention from these gloomy meditations.

The mist now closed down heavily on the mountains, and
it was already twilight; but he had taken his bearings, and was
able to grope his way down towards a high boggy valley, and
then up round a shoulder of Arenig Fach. Soon he was on
little Carnedd Iago, then stumbling down in darkness towards
the road, which he crossed near the head of Cwm Prysor.
Leaving the wild moorland valley on his left, he came into
home pastures. Now, even in darkness, every crag, every
hummock, every pool, almost every tussock of heather or grass
was familiar, and redolent with associations. Here he had
found a dead sheep and half-born lamb. Here he had sat with
Thomas, eating sandwiches on one of those long walks that
would never be repeated. Here he had killed a hare. But
though every step was familiar, increasing darkness and the
heavy mist greatly delayed him. It was almost midnight when
he reached Garth. I calculate that, since leaving Thurstastone
Common in the early morning, he must have covered altogether,

including all his lengthy aberrations from the direct route, well over eighty miles. Much of the journey was on hard roads or through difficult, hedged agricultural country.

At the door of the darkened house he gave his special summoning bark. Elizabeth promptly let him into the blinding light and the familiar smells of home. Before he had said a word, she had closed the door, knelt down, and put her arms round him, saying "Thank God one of you is safe." "Only me," he said. She gave one small moan, and clung to him in silence. Held in a rather awkward position, tired out after the strain of the last few days, and oppressed by the indoor atmosphere, he suddenly went deadly faint, and wilted in her arms. She laid his head low on the floor and went to fetch some brandy. But in a moment he recovered, staggered on to his feet, dutifully but feebly wiped them on the door-mat, and walked unsteadily into the sitting-room. Then he realized that his under surface was covered with the wet black mud of the bog. When Elizabeth returned, he was standing with trembling legs and hanging head, wondering what to do. "Lie down, precious," she said. "The mess is nothing." Presently she had him lapping up sweet tea, and then eating bread and milk.

CHAPTER XIV

TAN-Y-VOEL

THOMAS'S death affected the female members of the Trelone family very deeply. The two boys were away at the war, but Tamsy and Plaxy both came home to spend a week or so with their mother. Sirius at a later date told me that Tamsy was superficially more distressed than Plaxy. She wept a good deal, and by her too demonstrative sympathy she increased rather than assuaged the emotional strain that inevitably fell upon Elizabeth. Plaxy, on the other hand, was strangely cold and awkward. With a pale face, and an almost sullen expression, she occupied herself mainly with housework, leaving her mother and sister to dwell upon the past. One day

Tamsy unearthed from Thomas's chest of drawers a dilapidated
handkerchief-case wihch Plaxy as a child had made and given
to her father on his birthday. With swimming eyes Tamsy
brought this relic to her sister, obviously expecting it to be a
stimulus to sweet sorrow. Plaxy turned away, muttering, "Oh,
for God's sake, don't!" Then, unaccountably, and with a look
almost of fury, she rushed at Sirius and gave him so brusque
a hug that he wondered whether it was meant as a caress or as
the opening of a wrestling bout. I mention this incident
because it suggests that Plaxy's relations with her father were
in fact rather complex and emotional.

As for Sirius himself, his very real grief, he told me, was
mingled with a new deep sense of independence. His canine
nature lamented the loss of his master, and he was haunted
by memories of Thomas's affectionate guidance; yet his
human intelligence now breathed more freely. At last he was
his own master, not literally perhaps, but emotionally. At last
he would be master of his fate and captain of his soul. Sometimes the thought frightened him; for he had grown up in
complete emotional dependence on Thomas's ultimate
authority over him. Even when he stood out for his own will,
he did so always in the hope of persuading Thomas to agree
with him, never with any depth of intention to resist the will
of his revered creator. And so, now that Thomas was gone,
his creature was torn between anxious self-distrust and a
strange new decisiveness.

But though Sirius was now emotionally freed from Thomas,
he was destined to be for a while bound more closely than ever
to his foster-mother.

Though Thomas's death was a heavy blow to Elizabeth, she
would not let it crush her. She carried on with her normal life,
looking after the three little evacuees, digging and planting in
the garden, helping Sirius with the sheep; for Pugh had grown
very rheumatic and found the outlying pastures almost
inaccessible. Plaxy had offered to give up teaching and settle
down at home, but Elizabeth would not hear of it. "The child
must live her own life," she said.

Inevitably Elizabeth became more and more devoted to
Sirius, who was the supreme achievement of Thomas's creative

power, and also her own adopted child. Indeed Sirius now seemed more to her than her own children, who were independent, and in no further need of her help. But Sirius constantly needed her more than ever. Once when she found him struggling to repair a wire fence with his teeth, he had cried out, "Oh for hands! At night I dream of hands." She answered, "My hands belong to you till I die." Between the dog and the middle-aged woman a very close, affectionate, but not entirely happy relationship developed. Elizabeth had always maintained towards her chidren a friendly detachment towards which they had readily responded. Sirius also she had formerly treated in the same way. But now, her devotion to her husband combined with maternal hunger to fix her attention obsessively upon Sirius. Helping him became her constant passion. Now that Pugh was partially incapacitated, and skilled labour was so hard to obtain, her help was valuable. But Sirius came to find it rather tiresome. She was *too* anxious to help, and *too* full of suggestions, which he tended to reject if he could find any plausible excuse for doing so. It was strange and tragic, and entirely unexpected, that a woman formerly so quiet-hearted and so unpossessive should in middle age have become so clinging. I cannot account for the change. It is easy to point to influences in her life making for neurosis, but why should they have taken effect so late, and so extravagantly as they were destined to do? How frail a thing is the human spirit, even at its best!

Elizabeth showed an unwelcome inclination to take part in the actual management of the farm, and particularly all contacts with the outside world. Sirius strongly disliked this, not only because she had insufficient experience and sometimes made bad mistakes, but also because he was anxious to accustom the local population to dealing with him direct, and it was his ambition to play an active part in the common life of the district. Already he had earned respect. Not only the local papers but the great national dailies had referred to "the brilliant man-dog of North Wales." Only the paper shortage and the over-mastering interest of warfare had prevented them from using him for a stunt. Consequently he had been able to make himself known in the neighbourhood by personal contact without attracting too much attention from the rest of the country. Intellectuals of one sort or another did visit him now and then with introductions from the Laboratory; and these visits he greatly enjoyed, because they enabled him to keep in touch with movements of contemporary cultural life. He never gave up his intention of playing a part in that life as soon as the farm had been fully developed and regularized.

To return to Elizabeth. Perhaps out of loyalty to Thomas, who had always been extravagantly fearful of publicity, she did her utmost to keep Sirius from the public eye, and indeed from all social contacts. When at last she sent away her three little evacuee children in order to devote all her time to the farm, Sirius was torn between satisfaction at the prospect of having more help and fear of increased interference; and between affection and an exasperation which kindness forbade him to express. Why was it that one who had always been so tactful and detached in her relations had suddenly turned so difficult? He put it down to overwork and the emotional strain of losing her husband. No doubt advancing age had also something to do with it. Only when one or other of her own children was at home did she return almost to her normal self. Then Sirius would feel with relief that he was no longer the apple of her eye, and would be able to devote himself to his own affairs without having to consider her.

It was in the autumn of 1941 that Elizabeth fell ill. Her heart was tired, but Dr. Huw Williams told her that there was nothing seriously wrong with it. She had merely overstrained it, and must take things easy for a few weeks. Sirius saw the doctor to his car, and asked him whether he had told the truth or merely said what would comfort the patient. After Sirius had repeated the question several times, the doctor understood, and assured him that he had spoken the truth, and emphasized the need for a long rest. In a week Elizabeth refused to stay in bed any longer, and insisted on taking up light jobs on the farm. This led to another collapse, and the whole cycle was repeated several times in spite of Sirius's strong protest. It was obvious that Elizabeth would work herself to death. She seemed to be impelled by some obscure passion for self-expression through self-destruction in service of Sirius. The perplexed dog could not keep a constant watch over her unless he gave up his work entirely. In despair he wrote to Tamsy, but she had just had her second baby; she could find no one to look after her family and free her to nurse her mother. Sirius and Mrs. Pugh took turns with the invalid; but when at last Elizabeth was taken more seriously ill, and the doctor's optimism had given way to exasperation and despair, it was suggested to Elizabeth that she had better have a real rest in a nursing home. She rejected the idea with scorn. Very reluctantly Sirius now summoned Plaxy.

For several weeks Sirius and Plaxy and Mrs. Pugh kept a close watch on Elizabeth. The common task drew the girl and the dog closer to one another than they had ever been before. They were often together, but seldom alone together. This frequent compresence and infrequent intimacy generated in each a great longing for unrestrained talk, and an increasing sensibility towards each other's slightest changes of mood. Both, of course, were mainly and anxiously concerned with the patient. Some exasperation was inevitable, but was tempered and indeed almost wholly silenced by the strong affection which both had felt for her since their infancy. Both were put to strain by the necessity of sacrificing their own urgent activities, perhaps for a very long time. Each knew that the other was strained, and the two were drawn closer by that knowledge.

Under Plaxy's firm and loving treatment Elizabeth made good progress; but as her health improved she became increasingly restless. One day she insisted on dressing and going downstairs. It so happened that on the table there was an unopened newspaper. She picked it up and opened it. "BRITISH CRUISER SUNK," said the main headline. It was the ship on which Maurice was serving. Owing to the fact that the Germans were the first to announce the sinking, the Admiralty had been forced to break their rule and publish the information *before* the next of kin had been told of the casualties. The shock of the news, and the suspense that followed it, killed Elizabeth before word came through that her son was among the survivors.

Plaxy, though "scarcely human," though cat-like and fay,

was human enough to have deep feelings for her mother, who
had always shown special affection for her youngest child,
and yet had built up with her an even freer, happier relationship than with the elder children; for she had learnt by her own
past mistakes with them. Elizabeth's death therefore hit Plaxy
hard. Sirius too was greatly distressed, on his own account,
and still more on hers. For himself, he was again strangely
perplexed by this business of death. The dead Elizabeth kept
talking to him. And it was not the Elizabeth that had just died,
the over-strained and difficult Elizabeth; it was Elizabeth as
she was in her prime. Again and again, with variations, she
made or seemed to make a very intelligent contribution to his
thoughts. She said, "Don't puzzle your old head about it so!
Minds like ours just aren't clever enough to understand, and
whichever way you decide you're sure to be wrong. Don't
believe I still exist, for that would be false to your intellect;
but don't refuse the *feeling* of my presence in the universe, for
that would be blind."

Shared grief and common responsibility tended to bring
Plaxy and Sirius into an ever closer intimacy. They now sank
exhausted into mutual dependence. And there was much work
to do together. With the aid of the family solicitor and a
representative of the Laboratory, they had to wind up the
Trelone affairs. Obviously the house must be sold. But the
decision to surrender the home in which they had been brought
up together was momentous both to girl and dog, for it meant
severing the remaining tangible link between them. They spent
many hours of many days sorting out the contents of the house.
All the furniture had to go, save the few pieces that Tamsy
wanted for her own house, and the fewer that were to be given
to Sirius, who must now be re-established at Caer Blai. Books,
crockery, kitchen utensils, clothes, all the multifarious possessions of the dead parents, had to be sorted out. The property
of the absent children must be separated from the rest, and
packed up and dispatched. Plaxy's own and Sirius's own
things must be collected and sorted. A great bonfire of sheer
rubbish was made every morning, and carefully extinguished
at night, because of the black-out. Photographs of the parents
themselves, of *their* parents and relatives, of the four children

and Sirius at all ages, of super-sheep-dogs, of holiday expeditions, of Sirius at work with sheep, all had to be looked at by dog and girl together, squatting on the floor of the dismantled sitting-room. All had to be talked over, laughed over, sighed over, and finally assigned either to the rubbish pile or to the collection of things too good to destroy.

When the labour was over, when the furniture was all gone, when there was nothing in the house but a few packing cases not yet dispatched and the few crocks and scraps which the two had been using for their meals; when the floors were bare board and the house was the mere shell of a home, Plaxy prepared a final meal for the two of them. It was lunch. She was to leave by train early in the afternoon, and he was to begin at once to catch up with arrears of work at the farm. They sat together on the floor of the empty sitting-room, and ate almost in silence. They had as a matter of course settled down in the spot by the fireplace where they had so often sat together during the past two decades. The old soft hearth-rug had gone. They sat on Plaxy's mackintosh, spread on the floor boards. She leaned against a packing case instead of the vanished couch. The solemn little picnic was soon finished. Sirius had licked out the last drop of his last bowl of tea. Plaxy had stubbed her cigarette-end in her saucer. Both sat silent.

Suddenly Plaxy said, "I have been thinking hard," And he, "So it seems, oh wise woman." "I've been thinking about us," she continued. "Mother was useful on the farm, wasn't she?" He agreed, and wondered how they would manage without her. "The new land girl," he added, "is not a patch on the last. She tries to keep her hands soft." "Suppose," said Plaxy, looking hard at her toe, "well—would you like it if I stayed to help you?" Sirius was licking a cut on his paw. He stopped to say, "Wouldn't I just! But that's impossible." He went on licking. "Well," said Plaxy, "why *shouldn't* I, if I want to? And I have decided that I do want to, very much. I *don't* want to go, I want to stay, if you'll let me." He stopped licking, and looked up at her. "You *can't* stay. It's all arranged. And you don't *really* want to stay. But it's nice of you to think you do." "But, Sirius, sweet, I do really want to, not for always, but for the present. I have thought it all out, right here. We'll rent Tan-y-Voel." This was the labourer's cottage on Pugh's land, where later I was to discover them. "It'll be fine," she cried brightly; then with sudden shyness, for he was gazing at her sadly, she added, "Or *wouldn't* you like it?" He reached out and nuzzled into her neck. "You needn't ask," he said, "but you have a life of your own to lead. You can't give it all up for a dog." "But," she answered, "I am sick of teaching, or rather trying to. I suppose I'm not really interested enough in the little brats. Perhaps I'm too interested in *me*. Anyhow, I want to live." "Then what about Robert," he said, "and being a mother, and all that?" She looked away and was silent for a while, then sighed. "He's a dear. But— oh, I don't know. Anyhow, we have agreed that I must be myself, and being myself just now means staying with you."

In the end she had her way. They went straight off to tell the Pughs of the change, and announce that they intended to seize the empty cottage at once. Pugh was of course overjoyed, and with innocent mirth he remarked, "I congratulate you, Mr. Sirius, on your bride." Plaxy coloured, and did not respond well to this sally; so that Pugh had to smooth matters over by saying, "Just an old farmer's joke, Miss Plaxy. No offence, indeed." Mrs. Pugh scolded him, "For shame, Llewelyn! You are a horrid old man, and you have a nasty mind like a bubbling black bog." They all laughed.

Before the lorry came to transport the last load from Garth, Plaxy had opened one of the cases and taken out some bedding, towels and so on. She dumped the remaining crocks and pans into the one empty case. Together they made a list of essential furniture which must be fetched back from the store and sent to Tan-y-Voel. When the furniture removers returned, they were mildly annoyed at the change and the confusion, but Plaxy used all her charm, and they duly delivered the goods at the cottage.

Even a two-roomed cottage takes some settling into, and Plaxy spent most of the following day arranging their new life. She brushed out the two rooms, scrubbed the stone floors, cleaned the grate, improvised black-out curtains for the little windows, and bought such stores as were possible in war-time. In the evening Sirius returned from his work to find a smiling

home and a smiling though rather exhausted Plaxy. The table
was laid for her supper, and on the carpet beside her chair was
Sirius's customary "table-cloth" and bowl. Sirius had two
distinct styles of feeding. In the wild he fed wild, on rabbits
and hares and so on; in the house he was given porridge, soup,
bread-and-milk, bones, crusts of bread, cake and a good deal
of tea. At one time it had been very difficult to buy enough to
feed him adequately, because of the rationing system; but
Thomas had pulled wires and secured a special ration for him
as a valuable experimental animal.

After the meal, when Plaxy had washed up, they sat together
on the couch that had been rescued from the old home. They
had been gay, but now a sadness settled on them. Sirius said,
"This is not real. It is a very lovely dream. Presently I shall
wake up." And she, "Perhaps it will not last long, but it is
real while it lasts. And there is a rightness in it. It had to be,
to make us one in spirit for ever, whatever else may come. We
shall be happy, never fear." He kissed her cheek.

They were both tired after the day's work, and very soon they
were yawning. Plaxy lit a candle and put out the lamp. In the
next room her familiar bed was awaiting her, and on the floor
was Sirius's old sleeping basket, a vast pan of wicker containing
a circular mattress. Strange! They had been brought up
together, child and puppy, sharing the same room; and even
when they were grown up she had been thoroughly used to
undressing before him without any self-consciousness; yet
now, unexpectedly, she was shy.

At this point I cannot resist pausing to ask the reader a
question. Does not Plaxy's momentous decision to give up
her career and live with Sirius need some explanation? Here
was a young woman of outstanding charm, with many admirers,
and one of them her accepted lover. She had taken up a teaching
post which she filled with distinction, and in which she was
finding a good opening for self-expression. Suddenly she gave
up her work and practically broke off relations with her lover
in order to join her life with the strange being who was her
father's most brilliant creation. Does it not seem probable
that the underlying motive of this decision was the identification
of Sirius with her father? Plaxy herself, now my wife, scorns

this explanation, holding that it does not do justice to the power of Sirius's own personality over her. Well, there is my theory, for what it is worth.

On the morning after the occupation of Tan-y-Voel, Plaxy began her apprenticeship on the farm. She cleaned out a pigsty, harnessed the horse, loaded muck into the cart and unloaded it on the manure heap. She also helped Sirius to attend to a sick sheep on the moor. Towards the end of the day she put in some hard work on the wilderness that was meant to be the cottage garden. In such style, with variations, the days passed. Her face took on the healthy glow that delighted me when in due season I discovered her. With mingled distress and pride she watched her hands go blistered, grime-ingrained, scratched, cut and hard. Mrs. Pugh taught her to milk. Pugh himself taught her to broadcast a field with oats, while the instrument which she insisted on calling the "sowing machine" was out of order. Always there were countless nameless jobs to do about the farm. Her main function, she said, was to save Sirius's teeth, which were beginning to wear down with too much gripping of wood and iron. So far as possible he confined his attention to the sheep and the super-sheep-dogs, but there was no end to the number of small unexpected tasks which really called for hands but could most easily be disposed of at once by his own clumsy jaws. On the farm premises he was always, in spite of his painfully acquired skill with those unsuitable instruments, too pitifully handless. But on the moors he was in his element. Plaxy greatly enjoyed the expeditions into the hills with Sirius and his canine pupils. Bounding through the bracken, he was a storm-tossed but seaworthy boat. Trotting around, giving orders to his pupils, he was a general and his charger all in one. When a sheep broke away and had to be retrieved, he would streak after it, belly to earth, like a torpedo.

In this new life there was almost no leisure, no time for reading, music, writing. Contact with the world beyond the hills was at a minimum. Expeditions to sheep sales were rare excitements. On these occasions both Sirius and Plaxy would accompany Pugh, she as Pugh's unofficial land-girl. The bustle, the babble of Welsh voices, the clamour of sheep, the

variety of human and canine types, the social atmosphere of
the pubs, and of course the young men's unconcealed admiration of this bright and humorously self-important, this forthcoming but rather queer land-girl (not in uniform)—all this
Plaxy vastly enjoyed as a change from the seclusion of the farm.

Apart from these infrequent excursions, social intercourse
was to be had only on expeditions to the village, and on visits
to neighbouring farms to borrow or lend tools, or simply for
friendly intercourse. Often Plaxy would tidy herself up and
revert as far as possible to the gay young lady; and it was with
deep peace of mind that she walked through the fields with the
great sinewy beast at her side. With a careless, queenly self-
confidence she accepted the inevitable admiration of the young
farmers and shepherds, and sensed their puzzlement over her
indefinable oddity.

After she had been with Sirius for several months, however,
something happened which spoiled these social occasions for
her. She was made to realize that, though she was so popular
with many of the local people, there were some who were
outraged by her living alone with the man-dog. Increasingly
it was made difficult for her to be unselfconscious with Sirius
in public. And her observed shyness with him fomented the
salacious rumours.

The trouble began with a visit from a local nonconformist
minister. This earnest young man took it upon himself to save
Plaxy from damnation. He was simple enough to be impressed
by the notion that Sirius was inspired by Satan, and he listened
to the rumours of perverse relations between the dog and the
girl. As the cottage lay within his sphere of responsibility, he
felt it his duty to intervene. He timed his visit well. Plaxy had
returned from the farm to prepare supper, and Sirius was still
at work. Plaxy foresaw a late meal, but she treated the
Reverend Mr. Owen Lloyd-Thomas with friendly ease. Indeed
she made a point of being sweet to him, knowing that his good
opinion counted. After beating about the bush for some time,
he suddenly said, "Miss Trelone, it is my difficult duty as a
minister of the Lord to speak to you on a very delicate matter.
It is believed by simple people in the neighbourhood that your
dog, or Mr. Pugh's dog, is not merely an extraordinary animal

but a spirit clothed in a dog's flesh. And simple people, you know, sometimes go nearer to the truth than clever people. In spite of all the wonders of science, it may really be *less false* to say that the dog is possessed by a spirit than that it is just the work of man's scientific skill. And if it is indeed possessed, then perhaps the spirit in the dog is of God, but perhaps it is of Satan. By their fruits ye shall know them." He fell silent, cast a self-conscious glance at Plaxy, and fell to twisting the brim of his soft black hat. At last he continued, "It is felt by the neighbours, Miss Trelone, that for you to live alone with the animal is unseemly. It is believed that Satan has already snared you through the man-dog into sin. I do not know what the truth is. But I believe you are in danger. And as a minister I offer you advice. Change your way of living, even if only because it is an offence to the neighbours."

According to the reverend young man's reading of womanly nature, Plaxy should have blushed, either with innocent modesty or with guilty shame. If indeed she was guilty, then she might be expected either to confess with tears of penitence or to deny with self-righteous and unconvincing indignation. Her actual behaviour disconcerted him. For some time she just sat looking at him; then she rose and silently moved off into the minute larder. She came back with some potatoes, and sat down to peel them, saying, "Excuse me, won't you, I must get the supper ready. We can talk while I do this. You see, I love Sirius. And to leave him alone now would be unkind. And it would hurt our love, because it would be a running away. Mr. Lloyd-Thomas, your religion is love. You must surely see that I can't leave him."

At that moment Sirius appeared in the doorway. He stood with his nostrils moving, to catch the smell of the visitor. Plaxy stretched out her arm to welcome him to her, and said. "Mr. Lloyd-Thomas thinks we ought not to live together, because you may be Satan dressed up as a dog, and perhaps you have taught me to live in sin." She laughed. This was not a very tactful beginning, but tact had never been Plaxy's strong suit. It is possible that if she had not made this remark their whole future would have been different. Lloyd-Thomas flushed, and said, "It is not good to jest about sin. I do not know whether you have done this thing, but I know now that your spirit is frivolous." Sirius moved over to her, and she laid a hand on his back. He was still analysing the visitor's smell. She felt the hair on his back rise against her hand. A very faint growl made her fear lest he should go wild. He advanced half a pace towards the cleric, but she clasped him round the neck with both arms. "Sirius!" she cried, "don't be silly!" Lloyd-Thomas rose with careful dignity, saying, "This is not a good time for us to talk. Think over what I have said." In the garden he turned, and saw through the open door Plaxy still holding Sirius. Girl and dog were staring at him. She bowed her head to the dog's head, and laid her cheek to it.

When he had gone, Sirius said to Plaxy, "He smells as if he were in love with you. He smells a decent sort, really; but probably he would sooner see you dead than living in sin with me; just as McBane, I suspect, would rather see me dead than fail to squeeze every drop of information out of my body and mind. Morality and truth! The two most relentless divinities! I'm afraid we're for it with Lloyd-Thomas sooner or later."

Lloyd-Thomas's sermons began to have obvious references to Plaxy and Sirius. He prayed for those who had been snared into unnatural vice. Some of his congregation were very receptive to the new minatory trend of his services. Little by little, among those who had no personal contact with Plaxy, there grew up a considerable movement of censure and indignation; and also anxiety, for would not the Lord punish the whole neighbourhood for harbouring the wicked couple? Fresh rumours seemed to sprout every day. Someone claimed that he had seen Plaxy swimming naked in a lonely llyn with the man-dog. This harmless story developed into unpublishable accounts of dalliance on the turf while they were basking in the sun before the bathe. A boy also reported that one Sunday he had peered through the hedge at Tan-y-Voel and seen Plaxy lying naked on the grass ("black as a nigger, she was, with the sun"), while the dog licked her from head to foot. The patriots and spy-hunters were also roused. It was affirmed that Sirius's panniers contained a radio-set with which he signalled to enemy planes.

Sirius's friends ridiculed these stories, or indignantly reprimanded those who spread them. Plaxy was still able to do her shopping in an atmosphere of friendly attentiveness. There were, however, a few unpleasant incidents. A village girl who worked for Mrs. Pugh on the farm was forbidden by her mother ever to enter Tan-y-Voel; and after a while she ceased to come to Caer Blai at all. Sometimes, when Plaxy entered a shop, conversation between shopkeeper and customers would suddenly cease. Some young hooligans, apparently in the hope of collecting evidence for scandal, haunted the spur of the moor overlooking the cottage. One evening, just before black-out time, a bold lad crept up to the window and peered into the lamp-lit room. Sirius with ferocious clamour chased him out of the garden and half-way to the main road.

These little incidents were of no great moment in themselves, but they were significant of a spreading movement of hostility. Plaxy began to be reluctant to go to the village. Both she and Sirius grew suspicious of callers. And between them there developed a rather tense emotional relationship, which alternated between reserve and tenderness.

Hitherto they had lived very happily. Their days were spent in hard work on the farm or away on the moors, often in co-operation upon the same task. Plaxy found a good deal to do in the cottage itself, cleaning and cooking, and there was always work in the little vegetable garden. The evenings they sometimes spent with the Pughs or at one or other of the neighbouring farms, where music often formed the medium of social intercourse. The musical Welsh were at first hostile to Sirius's own unconventional creations, but his singing of human music won their applause. And in a few houses the more sensitive were becoming interested in his distinctively canine modes. But under the influence of scandal these social occasions were reduced. Far more often Plaxy and Sirius spent their evenings at home upon household chores, or singing in private the strange duets and solos that Sirius still occasionally conceived. Sometimes they would spend their evening with books. Sirius still took a deep delight in listening to prose and poetry read aloud by a good human voice. Often he would persuade Plaxy to read to him. And not infrequently he would suggest subtle modifications of tone or emphasis; for though his own

reading was inevitably grotesque, his sensitive ear had detected
many emotional cadences and changes of timbre, which human
beings were apt to overlook until their attention was drawn
to them.

As Plaxy and Sirius became more aware of the hostility and
suspicion round about them, their relationship began to change.
It became more passionate and less happy. Isolation, combined with contempt for the critics, drew girl and dog into
closer intimacy, in fact into a manner of life which some readers
may more easily condemn than understand. Plaxy herself, in
spite of her fundamental joy in her love for Sirius, was increasingly troubled by a fear that she might irrevocably be losing
touch with her own species, even that in this strange symbiosis
with an alien creature she might be losing her very humanity
itself. Sometimes, so she tells me, she would look at her own
face in the little square mirror over the dressing-table, and feel
a bewildering sense that it was not *her* face at all, but the face
of the tyrant species that she had outraged. Then she would
find herself in the same breath hating her unalterably human
physiognomy and yet being half surprised and wholly thankful
that it had not suffered a canine change.

This fear of ceasing to be human occasionally induced in her
a dumb antagonism towards Sirius, which sprang not from any
real sense of sin or even of indecorousness, for she was convinced that her behaviour was a fitting symbol of their deep
spiritual union. No, the source of her infrequent fits of gloom
was simply her consciousness of alienation from the world of
normal human beings. The call of her kind was still strong in
her, and she was tormented by her outlawry. The solemn
taboos of humanity still dominated her through her unconscious nature, though consciously she had long since declared
her independence of them. Once she said to Sirius, "I must
indeed have become a bitch in a girl's body, and so humanity
has turned against me." "No, no!" he answered. "You are
always fully human, but just because you are also more than
merely human, and I am more than merely canine, just because
we are both in essence intelligent and sensitive beings, we can
rise far above our differences, to reach across the gulf that
separates us, and be together in this exquisite union of oppo-

sites." Thus, in the rather naïvely formal diction that he was apt to use when he was speaking most earnestly, he tried to console her. In his mind there was no conflict over their intimacy. His love of her combined a dog's devotion with human parity in comradeship, and blended the wolf's over-mastering hunger with the respect of spirit for spirit.

At a later date both Plaxy and Sirius told me much about their life together at this time; but though after our marriage she urged me to publish all the facts for the light they throw on Sirius, consideration for her feelings and respect for the conventions of contemporary society force me to be reticent.

It was at such times that she would write those tortured letters to me, and by all sorts of devices contrived to have them posted far from home, lest I should track her down. For while she longed increasingly for human intimacy and human love, while she yearned to take up once more the threads of her life as a normal English girl, she clung with passion to the strange life and the strange love that fate had given her. It was clear from her letters that in the same breath she longed for me to take her away, and yet also dreaded the disruption of her life with Sirius.

CHAPTER XV

STRANGE TRIANGLE

I HAVE already told how I found Plaxy with Sirius at Tan-y-Voel, and how clear it was to me that any attempt to persude her to leave him would have alienated her from me. It was not till some days after our first meeting, and after many talks with Plaxy, that I realized how intimate her relations with the dog had become. The discovery was a shock to me, but I took pains not to betray my revulsion; for Plaxy, finding me sympathetic, soon poured out in a flood of confession the whole story of her emotional relations with Sirius. When she had many times dwelt upon this theme I found myself putting aside the conventional feelings of the outraged lover. I could not but realize that the passion which united these two dissimilar creatures was deep and generous. But this made me all the more fearful lest I should never win my strange darling back again. And I was deeply convinced that for her own sake, no less than for mine, she must in the end be won back to human ways.

During the few remaining days of my leave I spent much time at Tan-y-Voel, sometimes with Plaxy alone, sometimes with the two of them. Sirius was busy all day, but Plaxy allowed herself a good deal of time off duty to be with me. We used to work together in the garden. Indoors I helped her to clean and cook, and so on. I also constructed a number of labour-saving gadgets for her. I have always been fairly apt with my hands, and I thoroughly enjoyed putting up shelves and curtain rods, and improving the arrangements for washing up. Sirius's sleeping-basket needed repairing, but it seemed better not to put this right until much later, when I had established friendly relations with him. While I was occupied with all these little manual tasks we would talk, sometimes seriously, sometimes with the old familiar banter. Sometimes I even ventured to tease her about her "canine husband"; but on one of these occasions (she was washing up and I was drying) she broke into tears. After that I was more tactful.

It was my fixed intention, of course, to wean Plaxy from her present life, though not to tear her from Sirius. I made no suggestion that she should come away with me. Indeed it was part of my plan to persuade her and Sirius that I fully accepted the continuance of their intimacy and of their present régime. My improvements in the house were calculated to strengthen this impression. They also accidentally served another purpose. They allowed me to take a rather mean advantage over Sirius, who could not himself help in this way. I could see that my handiness galled him; and, seeing it, I was ashamed of hurting him. Yet whenever an opportunity offered I failed to resist the temptation of triumphing over him and delighting my darling. After all, I told myself, all is fair in love and war. But I was ashamed; the more so because Sirius with inhuman generosity encouraged me to help Plaxy whenever possible. Perhaps it was in the long run a good thing that I indulged myself in this manner, for Sirius's magnanimity forced me to realize quickly how fine a spirit he was, and compelled me to treat him with warm respect, not merely for being loved by Plaxy, but for his own sake.

Relations with Sirius were at first very awkward, and I feared at one time that our presence in the same house would prove intolerable to both of us. He made no attempt to get rid of me. He treated me with friendly politeness. But I could see that he hated to leave Plaxy with me. Obviously he feared that she might at any moment vanish out of his life. One source of strain between us was that I had at first very great difficulty in understanding his speech. Though in the end I learned to follow his uncouth English fairly easily, during that first visit to Wales I was often entirely at a loss, even when he spoke word by word and with many repetitions. In these circumstances it was almost impossible for us to come to terms at all. However, before we parted I succeeded at least in dispelling the initial chill by showing him that I had no intention of acting as the jealous rival, and that I did not condemn Plaxy for her relations with him. I went so far as to assure him that I did not want to come between them. To this he replied with a little speech which I laboriously made out to be, "But you *do* want to come between us. I don't blame you. You want her to live with you, always. And obviously she *must* live with you, or some man. I cannot give her all that she needs. This life is only temporary for her. As soon as she wants to, she must go." There was dignity and sanity in this statement, and I felt rebuked for my lack of candour.

By judicious wangling I was able to secure an extension of leave, so that I could spend some ten days with Plaxy and Sirius, conscientiously returning to my hotel every night. Sirius suggested that I should sleep at the cottage, but I pointed out that if I did there would be an added scandal. It seemed strangely tantalizing to me, who had been, and in a manner still was, Plaxy's acknowledged lover, to kiss her good night at the garden gate while Sirius tactfully remained indoors. A revulsion little short of horror (which I was at pains to dissemble) would sometimes seize me at the thought of leaving her with the non-human being whom she strangely loved. On one of these occasions I must have somehow infected her with my own distress, for she suddenly clung to me with passion. A surge of joy and hunger swept over me, and I lost my presence of mind so far as to say, "Darling, come away with me. This life is all wrong for you." But she disengaged herself, "No, dear Robert, you don't understand. Humanly I do love you very much, but—how can I say it?—super-humanly, in the spirit, but therefore in the flesh also, I love my other dear, my strange darling. And for him there can never possibly be anyone but me." I protested, "But he can't give you what you really need. He said so, himself." "Of course not," she answered, "he can't give me what as a girl I need most. But I am not just a girl. I am different from all other girls. I am Plaxy. And Plaxy is half of Sirius-Plaxy, needing the other half. And the other half needs me." She paused, but before I had thought of an answer she said, "I must go. He may be thinking I shall never come back." She kissed me hastily and hurried to the cottage door.

The next day was Sunday, which the Welsh keep with dreadful strictness. No work could be done on the farm, beyond feeding the beasts, so Sirius was free. I went round to Tan-y-Voel after breakfast and found Plaxy working in the garden, alone and rather self-conscious. Sirius, she said, had gone off for the day, and would not be back till after sunset. I was surprised, and in answer to my questions she explained, "The wild mood is on him, he says. It takes him and then leaves him. He has gone over the Rhinogs by the Roman Steps to a farm near Dyffryn to his crazy-making Gwen, a beautiful super-sheep-dog bitch. She should be ripe for him just now." I showed signs of disgust and sympathy; but she promptly said, "I don't mind. I did mind once, before I understood. But now it seems quite natural and right. Besides——" I pressed her to continue, but she went on digging in silence. I forcibly stopped the digging. She looked me in the eyes, laughing, and said nothing. I kissed her warm sunned cheek.

There was human love-making in the cottage that day, and a great deal of talk. But though my darling responded to my caresses with ardour, I knew that she was all the while withholding her inmost self. Sometimes I found myself imagining with horror how a beast had awkwardly mauled the sweet human form that I now so fittingly embraced. Sometimes, on the other hand, it seemed to me that, after all, the lithe creature in my arms, though humanly, divinely shaped, was inwardly not human at all but some exquisite fawn-like beast, or perhaps a fox or dainty cat transformed temporarily into the likeness of a woman. Even the human form was not quite human; so spare and supple and delicately muscular was it that she did indeed seem more fawn than girl. Once she said, "Oh lovely, lovely to be human again, even for a little while! How we fit, my dear!" But when I urged, "This, Plaxy darling, is what you are meant for," she answered: "This is what my body was meant for, but in spirit I cannot ever be wholly yours." How I hated the brute Sirius in that moment! And she, sensing my hate, burst into tears, and struggled in my arms like a captive animal till she had freed herself. But the quarrel was soon made up. We spent the rest of that day as lovers do, wandering on the hill, sitting about in the garden, preparing and eating meals.

When the sun was low in the west I prepared to leave her, but she said, "Wait for Sirius. I do so want you to be friends." Not till late in the evening, when we were sitting talking in the little kitchen, did we hear the garden gate. Presently Sirius opened the door and stood blinking in the lamp-light, his nostrils taking the scent of us. She held out both arms towards him, and when he reached her she drew his great head to her cheek. "Be friends, you two," she said, taking my hand. Sirius looked at me steadily for a moment, and I smiled. He slowly waved his tail.

During my last few days I saw more of the dog than I had done before. We no longer avoided one another; and by now I could understand his speech rather better. One morning, while Plaxy was helping Mrs. Pugh in the dairy, I went out with Sirius and his pupils to the high pastures. It was wonderful to watch him controlling these bright but sub-human creatures with barks and singing cries that were to me quite unintelligible. It was wonderful, too, to see them at his bidding capture a particular sheep and hold it down on the ground while their master examined its feet or mouth, sometimes treating it from the panniers, which, by the way, were carried by one of the pupils. Between whiles we talked of Plaxy and of her future, and of the war, and of the prospects of the human species. Conversation was difficult, because he had so often to repeat himself, but gradually we established a genuine friendship. On the way home he said, "Come often to see us while Plaxy is still here. It is good for Plaxy. And it is good for me too to have your friendship. Some day, perhaps, it will be my turn to visit you two, if you will have me." I felt a sudden warmth towards him, and I said, "If she and I have ever a home, it must certainly be your home too."

CHAPTER XVI

PLAXY CONSCRIPTED

DURING the next few months I spent frequent week-ends at Tan-y-Voel. The more I saw of Sirius, the more I was drawn towards him. Always, of course, there was a latent but an acknowledged conflict over Plaxy. All three of us, however, were determined to work out a tolerable relationship, and between Sirius and me the strain was eased by a genuine mutual affection. Sometimes, of course, the latent conflict became overt, and only by heroic tact and restraint on one side or the other could friendliness be maintained. But little by little the identical spirit in each of us, as Sirius himself said, triumphed over the diversity of our natures and our private interests. Had I not actually experienced this close-knit triple relationship I should not have believed it possible. Nor should I, perhaps, have been able to sustain my part in it, had not my love for Plaxy been from the onset unpossessive; owing to the fact that I myself, like Sirius in his canine style, had sometimes loved elsewhere.

The three of us were drawn more closely together by the hostility of a small but active section of the local people. The Rev. Owen Lloyd-Thomas had on several occasions issued veiled warnings from his pulpit. A few other ministers, realizing, perhaps subconsciously, that the theme of the "unnatural vice" of a girl and dog was likely to increase their congregations, could not resist the temptation to use it for that end. The result was that a small but increasing number of persons who were in one way or another emotionally frustrated and in need of an object for persecution were using Plaxy and Sirius for the same sort of purpose as the Nazis had used the Jews. The neighbours were mostly far too friendly to be accessible to this disease of self-righteous hate; but farther afield, in fact throughout North Wales, rumours were spreading both about the vice and the supposed treasonable activities of the couple in the lonely cottage in Merioneth. Plaxy received anonymous letters which caused her much distress. Messages for "Satan's Hound" were pinned on the door at night, including several threats that unless he released the spell-bound girl he would be shot. Pugh's sheep were sometimes found maimed. One was slaughtered and laid at the cottage door. Obscene drawings of a girl and dog were scrawled on blank walls. A local paper published a leading article calling the population to action. A battle occurred on the moors between the canine inhabitants of Caer Blai and a number of youths and dogs who had come out to do Sirius to death. Fortunately they had no firearms, and they were routed.

Meanwhile events of another type were threatening to change the fortunes of all three of us. I was expecting to be sent abroad very soon. The prospect caused Plaxy to treat me with increased tenderness. And if Sirius's grief was feigned, the imitation was very convincing. But worse than the prospect of my departure was the official order that Plaxy herself must take up some form of approved national service. We had hoped that she might be allowed to remain in peace as a farm worker, but her position was anomalous. The authorities could not see why a girl with a university training, living alone with a dog in the depths of the country, should be let off merely because she voluntarily helped on a neighbouring farm. The officials, however, were at first friendly, and anxious to interpret the regulations in a human manner. But just when it seemed most probable that Plaxy would be allowed to remain with Sirius, there was a marked and unaccountable change of tone. I suspect that some local enemy of Sirius had been telling tales of the scandalous and reputedly treasonous actions of the strange couple. Anyhow, whatever the cause, Plaxy was told that her appeal was rejected. Pugh put in a strong plea for her retention, but it was pointed out that he could easily find a land-girl to take her place. She could then be used for national service more suited to her capacity. Pugh offered to take on Plaxy herself as a land-girl, paying her the official wage. This was too obviously a put-up job. Authority became increasingly suspicious and uncompromising. Plaxy must either join one of the military organizations for women or take a temporary post in the civil service. She chose the latter, hoping to get herself attached to one of the great government offices evacuated into Lancashire or North Wales.

Plaxy was greatly distressed at the prospect of leaving. "This is my life," she said to Sirius. " *You* are my life, for the present, anyhow. The war matters terribly, I know; but I can't *feel* that it matters. It *feels* an irrelevance. At least, I can't feel that it makes any difference to the war whether I stay or go. Surely I'm doing more useful work here, really, even for the war. It's as though the hand of man were turning more and more against us. And oh, my dear, my sweet, what will you do without me to brush you and wash you and take thorns out of your feet, to say nothing of helping you with the sheep?" "I shall manage," he said. "And you, though part of you hates to go, another part will be glad of it, wanting to be entirely human again. And you will be freed from all this silly persecution." She replied, "Oh, yes, part of me wants to go. But that part of me isn't really *me*. The real I, the whole real Plaxy, desperately wants to carry on. The bit of me that wants to go is just a dream self. The only consolation is that perhaps when I am gone the persecutors will leave you alone."

At last the day came for Plaxy to go. Sirius would henceforth live with the Pughs, but Tan-y-Voel was to be kept ready to receive them whenever Plaxy had her leave. On the last morning Sirius did his best to help her with her final preparations, his tail (when he could remember it) kept bravely up. Before the village car was due to take her to the station she made tea for the two of them. They sat together on the hearth-rug, drinking it almost in silence. "How glad I am," she said, "that I decided as I did on that last morning at Garth!" "And I," he answered, "if it has not drawn you away too far from your kind." They heard the taxi hoot as it turned out of the main road. It roared up the hill in bottom gear. Plaxy sighed deeply and said, "My species has come to take me from you." Then with sudden passion she clung to him and buried her face in the stubborn mane on his neck. Twisting himself round in her embrace, he snuggled to her breast. "Whatever happens now," he said, "we have had these months together. nothing can destroy that."

The taxi stopped at the garden gate and hooted again. They kissed. Then she stood up, tossed back her hair, seized some luggage and met the taxi-man at the door. Seated in the car, she leaned out of the window to touch Sirius, saying only "Good-bye, good luck!" It had been arranged that this should be their parting. He would not go with her to the station.

CHAPTER XVII

OUTLAW

PLAXY had hoped to be stationed in North Wales, but she was sent to a much more remote part of the country, and would only be able to visit Sirius for a fortnight in the year. Meanwhile he was having a difficult time. Pugh had engaged an extra land-girl, Mary Griffith, to take Plaxy's place. She had not been long on the farm before she began to be frightened of Sirius. She could not reconcile herself to the fact that the dog could talk and was in authority over her. Presently she began to hear of the scandal connected with him. She was terrified, and fascinated. Badly equipped by nature as a charmer of the male of her own species, she had never suffered the flattery of persecution. Though her moral sense was outraged by the possibility that the great brute would make love to her, something in her whispered, "Better a dog for a lover than no lover at all." Spell-bound, she awaited pursuit.

Sirius gave no sign. She did her best to understand his speech, hoping that his instructions might include endearments. Sirius's conduct remained coldly correct. She herself began to make clumsy attempts to entice him. His failure to give any sign that he had ever noticed these signals roused a perverse hunger in her, and the thought that even a dog rejected her was too repugnant to be admitted to her consciousness. She protected herself against it by illusions that, as a matter of fact, it was he that had made unseemly advances, and she that had refused. She began to invent incidents, and allowed them to be transformed in her mind from fiction to false memory. She recounted her stories to her acquaintances in the village, and began to gain a welcome notoriety. Once, when she had vainly done her utmost to excite Sirius, she stayed out in the fields for half the night. Next day she declared that the animal had driven her with snarls and bites to the lonely cottage to rape her. Rents in her clothes and marks on her arm were said to be due to his teeth.

This improbable story was welcomed by Sirius's enemies. They did not trouble to inquire why the girl did not complain to the Land Army authorities and get herself transferred to another post. They merely redoubled their activities against Sirius. A deputation called on Pugh to persuade him to destroy the lascivious brute. Pugh laughed at their stories and dismissed them with a quip. "You might as well ask me to destroy the nose on my face because you don't like the way it dribbles. No! It's worse than that, because my poor old nose does dribble, but the man-dog does none of the foul things you say he does. And if you try to do any harm to him, I'll put the police on you. If you hurt him there'll be gaol for you, and thousands of pounds damages to pay to the great Laboratory at Cambridge." He sacked the Griffith girl, but found to his horror that no substitute was to be had. Rumour had been busy, and no girl would risk her reputation by working at Caer Blai.

Sirius's enemies were not to be intimidated. Whenever he went to the village, a stone was sure to be thrown at him, and when he whisked round to spot the culprit no one looked guilty. Once, indeed, he did detect the assailant, a young labourer. Sirius approached him threateningly, but immediately a swarm of dogs and men set on him. Fortunately two of his friends, the local doctor and the village policeman, were able to quell the brawl.

Meanwhile Pugh and his wife were sharing the unpopularity of Sirius. Cows and sheep were damaged, crops trampled. The police force had been so depleted by the war that the miscreants were seldom caught.

Matters were brought to a head by a serious incident. This I recount on the evidence of Pugh, who had the story from Sirius himself. The man-dog was out on the hills with one of his canine pupils. Suddenly a shot was fired, and Sirius's companion leapt into the air, then staggered about yelping. The charge, no doubt, was meant for Sirius; it winged the other dog. Sirius at once turned wolf. Getting wind of the man, he charged in his direction. The second barrel of the shotgun was fired, but the assailant had lost his nerve; he missed again, and then he dropped his gun and ran to some steep rocks. Before he could climb out of reach, Sirius had him by the ankle. There followed a tug of war, with the human leg as rope. Sirius had not secured a good grip, and presently his teeth slipped on the ankle bone, coming away with a good deal of flesh. The dog rolled backwards down the slope, and the man, though in great pain, clambered out of reach. Sirius's rage was now somewhat cooled. He wisely sought out the shot-gun and sank it in a bog. His companion had vanished. Sirius overtook him limping homewards.

When the wounded man, whose name was Owen Parry, had dragged himself back to the village, he told a story of gratuitous attack by the man-dog. He said he had found Sirius squatting on a hillside overlooking the camp, counting ammunition cases that were being unloaded from lorries. When the brute saw him it attacked. The more gullible villagers believed the whole story. They urged Parry to prosecute Pugh for damages, and to tell the military of the canine spy. Parry, of course, took no action.

Some weeks later Plaxy received a telegram from Pugh saying "S.O.S. Sirius wild." As she had a good record with her superiors she was able to secure a spell of "compassionate leave." A couple of days after Pugh had telegraphed she arrived at Caer Blai, tired and anxious.

Pugh told her a distressing story. After the incident with Parry a change seemed to come over Sirius. He carried on his work as usual, but after work hours he avoided all human contacts, retiring to the moors, and often staying out all night. He turned morose and touchy towards all human beings except the Pughs. Then one day he told Pugh he had decided to leave the farm so that the flock and the crops should be safe from violence. "He was very gentle in his speaking," said the farmer, "but there was a look of the wild beast in his eye. His coat was out of condition, not all glossy as it used to be when you were here to look after him, Miss Plaxy, dear. And there was a little wound on his belly, festering with the mud that was always being splashed on it. I was frightened for him. He made his wildness so gentle for us that my eyes dribbled like my nose. I said he must stay, and not be beaten by a bunch of dirty-tongued hooligans. Together we would teach them. But he would not stay. When I asked him what he would do if he left, he looked very strange. It gave me the creeps, yes indeed, Miss Plaxy. As though it was a wild beast I was speaking to, with no sense and no human kindness. Then he seemed to make an effort, for he licked my hand ever so gently. But when I put my other hand on his head he jumped like a shot thing, and stood away from me, looking at me with his head cocked over, as though he was torn between friendliness and fear, and didn't know what to do. His tail was miserable under his belly. 'Bran,' I said, 'Sirius, my old friend! Don't go off till I have fetched Miss Plaxy.' Then he wagged his old tail under his belly, and he cried softly. But when I put out a hand to him he sprang away again, and then he ran off up the lane. When he was beside Tan-y-Voel he stopped for a moment, but soon he lolloped away up the moel."

After Sirius's disappearance several days passed without incident in the neighbourhood. No one saw anything of the fugitive. Pugh was so busy with farm work, and trying to find help to replace Sirius, that he could not make up his mind whether or not to tell Plaxy of the dog's disappearance. Then one day he came upon Sirius outside Tany-y-Voel and hailed

him, but in vain. At this stage Pugh telegraphed to Plaxy.
Then a farmer in the Ffestiniog district found one of his sheep
killed and partly eaten. Nearer home a dog that had been one
of Sirius's opponents in the battle was found dead with its
throat torn. The police then organized a party of armed men
and dogs to search the moors for the dangerous beast. The
party, said Pugh, had just returned. They had drawn the whole
district round the slaughtered sheep, arguing that Sirius would
return to the carcass to feed, but they had seen nothing of him.
To-morrow a larger party would search the whole moorland
area between Ffestiniog, Bala and Dolgelly.

While Pugh was telling the story Plaxy listened in silence.
"She stared at me," he afterwards said, "as if she was a
frightened hare, and me a stoat." When Pugh had finished she
insisted that she must sleep at Tan-y-Voel. "In the morning,"
she said, "I will go out and look for him. I *know* I shall find
him." Mrs. Pugh urged her to stay at Caer Blai, but she shook
her head, moving towards the door. Then she checked, and
said piteously, "But if I bring him home they will take him
from me. Oh, what am I to do?" The Pughs could give no
helpful answer.

Plaxy groped her way over to Tan-y-Voel in the dark, lit
the kitchen fire, and changed into her old working clothes.
She made herself tea, ate a large number of biscuits, and stoked
up the fire, so that there might be smoke visible in the morning.
Then she went out again into the dark. She made her way over
the moors by a familiar route, until after several hours she
reached the place where long ago she had found Sirius with the
dead pony. The eastern sky was already light. She called his
name, or chanted it with the accustomed lilt that she had used
ever since childhood. Again and again she called, but there
was no answer; nothing but the sad bleating of a sheep and the
far-off rippling pipe of a curlew. She wandered about till the
sun rose from behind Arenig Fawr. Then she searched carefully round the bog where the pony had lain, until at last she
found a large dog's footprint. Bending down she scrutinized it
eagerly, and others. One of them, the print of a left hind paw,
gave her what she wanted. The mark of the outer toe was very
slightly irregular, recording a little wound that Sirius had

received when he was a puppy. Plaxy surprised herself by
weeping. After standing for a while mopping her eyes, she
unbuttoned her coat and dragged out from her waist a corner
of the old blue and white check shirt, well known to Sirius.
With her clasp knife, often used in the past for paring the hooves
of sheep, she cut the hem, and tore out a little square of
the material. This she laid beside the footmark. Sirius's
monochrome vision would miss the colour, but he might pick
up the bold pattern from afar, and when he came near he
would recognize it. Moreover, since the shirt had been next
her body, it would hold the smell of her for a long time.
He would know that she had seen the footprints and would
return.

Then she wandered about the moor again for some time,
frequently using a little monocular field-glass that I had
recently given her for use with the sheep. (In the choice of a
gift I had perhaps unconsciously emphasized the pleasure of
human eyesight, which was so much more precise than any
dog's.) At last fatigue and hunger forced her to return to
Tan-y-Voel. There she made herself tea, ate the rest of the
biscuits, changed into smarter clothes and went straight into the
village. People stared at her. Some greeted her warmly for old
time's sake. Others looked away. Most of the hostile ones
were sufficiently impressed by her elegant appearance to treat
her with respect, but a bunch of lads shouted at her in Welsh,
and laughed.

She went to the police station, where the search party was
already collecting. Her old friend the village constable took
her into a private room and listened with distress to her earnest
appeal for mercy. "I shall find him," she said, "and take him
away from Wales. His madness won't last." The constable
shook his head, and said, "If *they* find him they'll kill him.
They want blood." "But it would be murder," she cried.
"He's not just an animal." "No, he's far more than an animal,
Miss Plaxy, I know; but in the eyes of the law that's just what
he is, an animal. And the law says that dangerous animals
must be destroyed. I have done my best to delay matters, but
I can't do more." In desperation Plaxy said, "Tell them he's
worth thousands of pounds and must be taken alive. 'Phone

the Laboratory at Cambridge, and they will confirm this and put it in writing." He fetched the inspector, who had come over from H.Q. to take charge of the search. After some discussion the inspector allowed Plaxy to call up the Laboratory. She summoned McBane and told him, incidentally, to come with his car as soon as possible to take Sirius away if she could recover him. The inspector then spoke to McBane and was sufficiently impressed to alter his plans. The search party would do their utmost to bring the animal back alive. With some reluctance he even agreed that the search should be called off for a day to give Miss Trelone a chance to capture her dog undisturbed.

When she left the police station she was almost light-hearted. And though she was shocked by the cold reception given her at the grocer's, where she laid in a store of food, the baker was kindly and hopeful, and the warm-hearted lame tobacconist, whose meagre stock was sold out, produced a packet of cigarettes from his own pocket and thrust it upon her, "because you will need them, Miss Plaxy, and for old time's sake." She toiled up the lane to Tan-y-Voel, with a reeling head, made herself a good meal, changed into working clothes, called to tell the Pughs how things stood, and went straight out on to the moor. All morning she searched in vain. Then after eating her lunch she lay down in the sun, and sleep overcame her. Some hours later she woke, sprang to her feet, and renewed her search. At the pony-bog the bit of shirt remained as she had left it. She hurried away in the afternoon light to explore a remoter region, and in particular a certain rocky cleft in the wildest part of the moor, which in the past they had sometimes used as a lair. Near this she found a dog's excrement, not recently dropped; but there was no other sign. Once more she left a piece of her shirt as a token. Then with weary limbs and a heavy heart she groped her way back in the dusk, and arrived in pitch darkness at the pony-pool. At a loss to know what to do next, she finally decided to wait there till dawn. She found a sheltered spot among the rocks and heather overlooking the bog, and made herself as comfortable as possible. In spite of the cold, she fell asleep. Not till the sun had risen did she wake, chilled and aching. Once more there was no sign of Sirius. After some desultory searching and calling she set off for home.

At the cottage she made herself breakfast, changed her clothes, attended to her haggard face, and returned to the police station. There she learned with horror that on the previous day a man had been killed and partly eaten. It had happened on the eastern shoulder of Filast, far beyond Arenig. He was a local sheep-farmer. Hearing that Sirius had been seen in the neighbourhood, he announced that he would hunt the brute down and destroy it, no matter what its value to the godless scientists. He went out with an old army rifle and a dog. In the evening the dog returned in great distress without his master. A search party had found the man's body, and near it the rifle, with an empty magazine.

After this incident the police determined to bring about the destruction of Sirius as quickly as possible. Parties of Home Guards were being sent out to comb all the moorland areas of North Wales.

In great distress Plaxy hurried away to the moors again. At the pony-bog the bit of shirt was missing, and there were fresh canine footprints; but whether they were Sirius's or not she could not determine. She put down another bit of shirt, then set off towards the lair, searching every hillside and valley with her field-glass. Once she saw on the distant skyline two men with rifles on their shoulders, but there was no other sign of the searchers. It was a bright day, with the wind in the north-west; no day at all for avoiding detection. But the moors were vast, and the searchers few.

As she was approaching the lair, she saw Sirius, his tail between his legs, his head low, like a tired horse. She was coming up wind, and behind him, so that he was unconscious of her presence till she called his name. He leapt at the sound, and whisked round, facing her, with a growl. In his mouth was the bit of shirt. She advanced, repeating his name. Seeing her, he stood still with his head cocked over and his brows puckered; but when she was within a few paces he backed, growling, away from her. At a loss, she stood still, with outstretched hand, saying, "Sirius, dear darling, it's Plaxy." His tail under his belly trembled with recognition and love, but his

teeth were still bared. He whimpered with the stress of conflict in his bewildered mind. Every time she advanced, he
backed and growled. After Plaxy had tried many times to win
his confidence, her spirit broke. She covered her face with her
hands and threw herself on the ground sobbing. The sight of
her impotent distress evidently worked the miracle which her
advances had frustrated; for Sirius crept foward, crying with
the strife of fear and love, till at last he reached out and kissed
the back of her neck. The intimate smell of her body woke his
mind to full clarity. While she continued to lie still, fearing
that any movement might scare him away, he nuzzled under
her face. She turned over and let his warm tongue caress her
cheeks and lips. Though his breath was foul as a wild beast's
and the thought of his recent human killing revolted her, she
made no resistance. At last he spoke. "Plaxy! Plaxy! Plaxy!"
He nosed into the open neck of her shirt. Then she dared to
put her arms round him.

"Come to the lair," she said. "We must hide till after dark,
then we'll go down to Tan-y-Voel and wait till McBane comes
with his car to take us away. I told him to hurry."

The lair was as good a retreat as they could expect. At the
foot of the cliff was a tangle of heather and broken rocks. A
huge slab had split from the side of the cliff and moved away,
leaving a gap. This formed the lair. Its floor was below the
surrounding wreckage and heather clumps. The buttress above
was inaccessible, so no one could look down on them. Inside
lay the remains of the heather which Plaxy herself had gathered
to form a couch long ago. She now added a fresh supply. They
nestled close together, and little by little, by talk about their
common past, she weaned his mind away from madness. For
some hours they remained talking with increasing ease and
happiness. Plaxy often spoke about their future, but whenever
she led his attention forward a dark cloud seemed to settle on
his mind. Once she said, "We will leave this district and start a
flock somewhere in Scotland, as soon as we can find a place."
He answered, "There is no place for me in man's world, and
there is no other world for me. There is no place for me anywhere in the universe." She answered quickly, "But wherever
I am there is always a place for you. I'm your home, your

footing in the world. And I'm—your wife, your dear constant bitch." He caressed her hand, and said, "In the last few days, whenever I was not raging mad against your whole species, I was longing for you; but you—must not be tied to me. And anyhow you cannot make a world for me. Of course, any world that I could live in must have you in it for its loveliest scent, drawing me along the trail; but you can't make a whole world for me. Indeed, it's not *possible* for me to have a world at all, because my own nature doesn't make sense. The spirit in me needs the world of men, and the wolf in me needs the wild. I could only be at home in a sort of Alice-in-Wonderland world, where I could have my cake and eat it."

A distant voice set both their hearts racing. She clung to him, and they waited in silence, thankful for the deep shadow of the lair, for it was already almost sunset. They heard quite near at hand the scrape of a nailed boot on rock. Sirius began to move in her arms, and growl. "Idiot! Be quiet," she whispered. She tried to hold his mouth shut with one hand while she desperately gripped him with the other. Footsteps moved past the entrance of the lair, then faded into the distance. After some minutes she could hold on no longer. Cautiously she let go, saying, "Now, for God's sake keep quiet."

For a long time they sat together waiting and occasionally talking. Twilight was now far advanced, and Plaxy began to feel that the worst of their ordeal was over. "Soon it will be dark enough to go home," she said, "home to Tan-y-Voel, my dog, and a great big meal. I'm hungry as hell. Are you?" He said nothing for a moment; then, "Yesterday I ate part of a man." He must have felt her shudder. "Oh," he said, "I was savage. And I shall be again, unless you hold me tight with your love." She hugged him, and a surge of joy made her softly laugh. Her imagination leapt forward to the time when they would be safely on the way to Cambridge.

Presently she rose, and went cautiously out to look round. The sunset colour had almost gone. There was no sign of the enemy. She moved round a projecting rock, and still there seemed to be no danger. After straying about for a few moments, searching the landscape, she felt the need to relieve herself. She crouched down in the heather, and sang softly the

little tune which since childhood had been associated in both
their minds with this homely operation. He should have
responded with one or other of the appropriate antistrophes,
but he was silent. She repeated her phrase several times,
but there was no answer. Suddenly alarmed, she hurried round
the intervening rock and saw Sirius standing outside the lair
sniffing the wind. His tail was erect, his back bristling. At that
moment another dog came into sight, and Sirius, rousing the
echoes with his uproar, charged the intruder, who turned tail,
with Sirius on his heels. Both dogs vanished round the shoulder of the hill. There was a savage sound of dog-fight, then
human voices, and a shot, followed by a canine scream. Plaxy
stood fixed in horror. After a moment's silence a man's voice
cried, "Blast! I've hit the wrong one. The devil's got away."
Two more shots were fired. Another voice said, "No bloody
good. Too dark." Plaxy from behind a rock peered at the
men. They strode over to inspect the dead dog; then moved
off down the valley. When they were out of sight, she wandered about looking for Sirius. After a while she returned to
the lair, hoping to find him there. It was still empty. Anxiously
she strayed about in the dark, sometimes softly calling his name.
For hours she wandered. Some time in the middle of the night
she heard the sirens wailing far off in the villages. Searchlights
fingered the clouds. After a while the wavering drone of a
plane passed overhead towards the north-east; then another,
and many others. There was distant firing, and one larger
thud. Dead tired, Plaxy still strayed farther and farther over
the dark moor, sometimes calling.

At last, almost at her feet she heard a little sound. She
stepped aside and found him stretched out on the grass. The
end of his tail beat feebly on the ground for greeting. She knelt
beside him. Passing her hand along his body, she found that
his flank was wet and sticky. One of the Home Guards' last
shots had taken effect, though in the failing light he had seen
only that the dog had not been immediately stopped. The
badly damaged animal had staggered off towards the mountains, but shock and loss of blood had at last brought him
down. With the first-aid outfit that she had carried on all her
searches she put a pad on the wound and contrived to pass a

bandage round his body to hold it, though he trembled with
the added pain. Then she said, "I must go and get help and a
stretcher." He protested, with feeble earnestness; and when she
rose to go, he cried piteously for her to come down to him
again. In despair she sank beside him, and lay down to put her
face to his cheek. "But, my darling," she said, "we *must* get
you home before daylight, else they'll find you." He feebly
cried again, and seemed to say, "Dying—stay—Plaxy—dear."
Presently he said "Dying—is very—cold." She took off her
coat and laid it over him, then tried to lie closer to him to
warm him. He said something which she guessed to be,
"I don't fit you. Robert does." Stabbed with love and compassion, she said, "But dearest darling, our spirits fit." His
last words were "Plaxy-Sirius—worth while." Some minutes
later she saw his mouth fall open a little, revealing the white
teeth in the faint light of dawn. His tongue slipped out. She
buried her face in the strong fur of his neck, silently weeping.

For a long while she lay, till discomfort forced her to move.
Then a shuddering sigh heaved her body, a sigh of bitter grief,
but also of exhaustion; of love and compassion, but also of
relief. Presently she realized that she was deadly cold and
shivering. She sat up and rubbed her bare arms. Gently she
took away the coat from dead Sirius, and put it on herself once
more. The act seemed callous, and she wept again; then
stooped once more to give the great head a kiss. For a while
she sat by Sirius with a hand in the side pocket of her coat. She
found that her fingers had closed upon the little field-glass that
I had given her. Even this seemed a disloyalty to the dead; but
she reminded herself that Sirius had accepted me.

Presently the sirens sounded, far down in the villages, steady,
sad and thankful. A sheep called mournfully. Very far away
a dog barked. Behind Arenig Fawr the dawn was already like
the glow of a great fire. "What must I do now?" she wondered.
She remembered how, a few hours earlier, with happiness too
soon in her heart, she had sung for him to answer, but in vain.
The memory overpowered her with a sense of the gulf that now
divided them. He that had been so near seemed now as remote
as their common mammalian ancestor. Not again would he
sing to her.

But now at last she thought of a fitting thing to do. She
would sing his requiem. Returning to her dead darling, she
stood erect beside him, facing the dawn. Then in as firm and
full a voice as she could muster, she began singing a strange
thing that he himself had made for her in his most individual
style. The wordless phrases symbolized for her the canine and
the human that had vied in him all his life long. The hounds'
baying blended with human voices. There was a warm and
brilliant theme which he said was Plaxy, and a perplexed one
which was himself. It began in playfulness and zest, but
developed in a tragic vein against which she had often protested.
Now, looking down on him she realized that his tragedy was
inevitable. And under the power of his music she saw that
Sirius, in spite of his uniqueness, epitomized in his whole life
and in his death something universal, something that is common to all awakening spirits on earth, and in the farthest
galaxies. For the music's darkness was lit up by a brilliance
which Sirius had called "colour," the glory that he himself, he
said, had never seen. But this, surely, was the glory that no
spirits, canine or human, had ever clearly seen, the light that
never was on land or sea, and yet is glimpsed by the quickened
mind everywhere.

As she sang, red dawn filled the eastern sky, and soon the
sun's bright finger set fire to Sirius.